NO MORE TEARS

The heat was becoming unbearable as he carried his mother back through the kitchen and out the flaming doorway. Once outside, he tried to draw deep breaths of fresh air into his aching lungs as he laid her body on the cool ground, then quickly stamped out the flames that were chewing at the edges of the blanket. Without hesitation, back into the burning house he charged. Grabbing his father's body by the boots, he dragged the heavy man out the door and onto the porch, barely seconds before he heard the sound of roof timbers crashing to the floor inside.

Anxious to get away from the scorching heat, he pulled his father to the edge of the porch until his boots reached the ground, then grabbed his wrists and pulled him upright. Franklin Chapel was a big man, but his thirteen-year-old son pulled his body over on his shoulder and picked him up, carrying him away from the burning house to lay him gently on the ground beside his wife. Then the boy sat down beside his parents and cried.

It was the last time he would ever cry.

DEATH IS THE HUNTER

Charles G. West

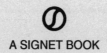

A SIGNET BOOK

SIGNET
Published by New American Library, a division of
Penguin Group (USA) Inc., 375 Hudson Street,
New York, New York 10014, USA
Penguin Group (Canada), 90 Eglinton Avenue East, Suite 700, Toronto,
Ontario M4P 2Y3, Canada (a division of Pearson Penguin Canada Inc.)
Penguin Books Ltd., 80 Strand, London WC2R 0RL, England
Penguin Ireland, 25 St. Stephen's Green, Dublin 2,
Ireland (a division of Penguin Books Ltd.)
Penguin Group (Australia), 250 Camberwell Road, Camberwell, Victoria 3124,
Australia (a division of Pearson Australia Group Pty. Ltd.)
Penguin Books India Pvt. Ltd., 11 Community Centre, Panchsheel Park,
New Delhi - 110 017, India
Penguin Group (NZ), 67 Apollo Drive, Rosedale, Auckland 0632,
New Zealand (a division of Pearson New Zealand Ltd.)
Penguin Books (South Africa) (Pty.) Ltd., 24 Sturdee Avenue,
Rosebank, Johannesburg 2196, South Africa

Penguin Books Ltd., Registered Offices:
80 Strand, London WC2R 0RL, England

First published by Signet, an imprint of New American Library,
a division of Penguin Group (USA) Inc.

First Printing, February 2012
10 9 8 7 6 5 4 3 2 1

For Ronda
. . . and in loving memory of my sister, Marcia

Chapter 1

"Little Bit" Morgan pulled his gray gelding to a halt at the top of a gentle rise, took off his hat, and waved it in the air to signal the six riders following a short distance behind. "There's a farmhouse up ahead," he said when they caught up to him. He put his hat back on, carefully cocking it just so. The black wide-brim hat with a silver chain around the flat crown was his pride and joy.

"Good," Webb Jarrett said to Bevo Rooks, who was riding beside him on the dusty Texas trail. "We'll stop and get some of this grit outta our throats."

"These horses is plum wore out," Bevo said. "If we don't rest 'em pretty soon, we'll be walkin' to Injun Territory." The horses had been ridden hard in the gang's race to beat a sheriff's posse to the Red River. At nine o'clock that morning they had held up the new bank in the little town of Sherman, leaving a teller dead, shot down when he attempted to run out the back door. It appeared that they had successfully lost the posse, but even if it persisted in trying to get on their trail, they were confident that a posse of Sherman citizens would be reluctant to stay after them once they were across the river in Oklahoma Territory. Once there, they wouldn't worry about any Texas Rangers coming to look for them.

They caught up to Morgan, who was referred to as Little Bit. This was partly due to his short stature but more so because of a short fuse when his temper was riled. Little Bit said, "Looks like a nice little nest somebody's built right next to the river. Might be we could stop and visit a spell. That looks like a smokehouse behind the house. This time of year there oughta be some hams hangin' up in there. That'd be all right. Wouldn't it, Webb?"

Webb Jarrett grinned. "It'd sure be to my taste right now. I swear, robbin' banks makes a man hungry." He paused to look the place over while the rest of his men pulled up beside him to have a look as well. "A right smart little farm that feller's got for himself." Off the corner of the house, opposite the smokehouse, was a modest-sized barn that looked to accommodate maybe two horses or mules. The house had a nice front porch, which indicated that the woman of the house had a say in the decisions. "Yes, sir," he continued, "a right smart little farm. I expect we wouldn't be polite if we was to ride on by without stoppin' to visit." His comment brought forth the malicious grins he expected. "Let's ride on in and pay our respects. Jake, you ride on back to that hill yonder and keep your eyes peeled. I think we most likely lost that posse, but you hightail it back here if you catch sight of 'em—give us enough time to slip across the river."

"Hell, Webb," Jake complained. "Why me? Why can't somebody else do it? Besides, we ain't seen hide nor hair of 'em in the last hour."

"'Cause you're the one that shot that teller, and most likely stirred up the folks there into comin' after us," Webb said. "I'll send somebody to spell you. You ain't gonna miss much."

Franklin Chapel walked out of his barn in time to see the six riders descending the low ridge that bordered the river on the south side. He paused and shielded his eyes with his hand as he tried to see who they might be. His first impulse was to go back in the barn and dig into the corn bin for the .44 Colt hidden there, but there had been no trouble from Indians or outlaws on this stretch of the river for quite a long time, so he decided he was being too cautious. It wouldn't be a very neighborly reception to meet a group of visitors with a gun in his hand. Still, he studied the riders intently as they approached, obviously not planning to bypass his house. When they reached the end of the corral where the cow was penned, Franklin called over his shoulder toward the house, "Ruth, there's company comin'." Not waiting to see if she had heard him or not, he walked forward to meet the strangers. "Afternoon," he said in greeting.

"Afternoon, sir," Webb returned politely. "We're a company of Texas Rangers on the trail of some bank robbers. Wonder if you'd mind if we watered and rested out horses here for a short spell."

Franklin replied, "Why, no, I wouldn't mind. You're

welcome to rest here, and I expect my wife could rustle you fellows up somethin' to eat as well." He was relieved to hear they were rangers, for he had decided they were a rough-looking group of men. Even though this area along the river had been trouble free, with the Civil War having just ended, there were a lot of outlaw gangs roaming the northeastern part of Texas. "You fellows step down, and I'll tell my wife to get somethin' goin' on the stove."

"That's mighty neighborly of you, friend," Jarrett said. "Me and the boys have been ridin' hard for a few hours, and that's a fact."

"Well, there's good water at the well, there, and if you want to take the saddles off, you can turn your horses in with the cow. I'll go in and get Ruth started." He paused to consider the six rough men before making a suggestion: "I expect it'd be best for you fellows to come on up on the front porch when you're ready."

"We're much obliged," Jarrett said. He waited until Franklin disappeared through the kitchen door, then turned to remark, "Did you hear that, boys? He's gonna go in and get Ruth started. She's gonna fix us rangers a big meal."

After the horses were watered and turned out with the cow in the corral, the outlaws strolled over to the front porch. Webb took one of the two rockers there and Bevo took the other, while the rest of the gang sat down on the edge of the porch to await their supper. Franklin Chapel returned to make conversation with his guests while they waited for Ruth to fry some bacon and boil some beans that she had planned to cook later for supper. "You fellows say you're chasin' bank robbers?" Franklin asked.

"That's right," Little Bit answered. "We're chasin' some dangerous outlaws."

"Where'd they rob a bank?" Franklin asked.

"Down in Sherman," Webb replied. "It's a new bank. First Bank of Sherman, I think was the name of it."

"Did they get away with much?"

Bevo grunted and said, "Not as much as they thought they was gonna get."

"You said they robbed it this mornin'," Franklin said. "You fellows got on to 'em pretty quick. I never knew there was a ranger station anywhere near Sherman."

Webb smiled patiently. "There's a new ranger headquarters just a few miles south of Sherman, so it didn't take long to get on their trail." He glanced at Bevo in the rocker beside him and winked.

"That's right," Bevo said. "We were in the saddle almost as soon as the bank robbers." His comment drew a chuckle from the other three sitting on the edge of the porch.

The response caused Franklin to become a little nervous; he was unable to see the humor in Bevo's remark. Word of a new ranger station as close as a day's ride from his farm would ordinarily have spread rapidly throughout the small community of farmers just across the river from the Indian Nations—and he had heard nothing at all, not even a rumor. "Well, I reckon it's lucky you boys were that handy." Feeling a bit uncomfortable then, he was glad when the door opened and his wife came out on the porch, carrying a huge pot of coffee, fresh off the stove, and an armload of cups. *Best to get them fed and back in the saddle,* he thought.

"I'm Ruth Chapel," his wife announced as all six outlaws scrambled to grab a cup from her. "You gentlemen caught me without much food prepared, but in a few minutes I can at least feed you some bacon and beans. I'm sorry I don't have time to bake any bread." Ignoring the fact that every eye was locked upon her, she went along the line, filling each cup. "How about you, Franklin? Do you want coffee?"

"I reckon not," he replied. His discomfort was gradually becoming more intense, and he wondered if he had made a mistake in not fetching his .44 when he first had the notion. When Ruth had filled each cup, he stated, "I'll go in and give you a hand." Then he followed her into the house.

"Ol' Franklin looked like he all of a sudden got sick in the stomach," Little Bit remarked. "You reckon he's startin' to smell a skunk?"

"Don't make a whole lotta difference if he did," Bevo said. "There ain't a helluva lot he can do about it, is there?" He took a gulp of the hot coffee and smacked his lips in appreciation. "That wife of his ain't a bad looker. How old a woman you reckon she is?" he asked Webb.

"Hell, I don't know," Webb answered. "Old enough, but not too old, I reckon." Bevo's question sparked an enthusiastic interest in the rest of the men.

"I swear, Bevo," Little Bit taunted. "You ain't been married but about a year, and you're already eyeballin' women older'n you are."

Bevo grunted stoically. "I got married," he said. "I didn't go blind."

Little Bit chuckled. "I bet you don't tell Pearl Mae that. She's damn near as big as you, and she looks like she might be a little tougher."

"One of these days that mouth of yours is gonna open a door you ain't wanna go through," Bevo warned.

"Is that a fact?" Little Bit replied. "I ain't worried about openin' no door. My style is to kick the damn door down and kick whoever's ass is on the other side." His taunting grin invited Bevo to take the next step, while his hand dropped to rest on the skinning knife he wore.

"You two just simmer down," Webb ordered, "before they come back."

The incident advanced no further because the door opened just then and Ruth informed them that their food was ready. "You can come on in the kitchen and get your plates," she said. "The food's on the table, such as it is. You can help yourselves." She stood aside as the rough crew filed inside, each one eyeing her openly. She sent a worried glance her husband's way as he stood near the pantry door. He had held a hurried conversation with her in the short time they were alone in the kitchen, and she was in agreement that there was something awry in the manner of these self-professed Texas Rangers. As a precaution, he had loaded his shotgun and stood it up just inside the pantry door. She hoped with all her heart that there would be no occasion for him to use it. She didn't fear just for her and her husband's safety. Their son, John, was

somewhere down the river hunting and had been gone
since early morning. She was in a quandary over
whether she wished he would show up, or whether she
should pray that he didn't. John was only thirteen, but
he seemed older than his years and was unacquainted
with fear in any form. If these men were evil, as she
now suspected, he would not hesitate to attack them
with no thought of the consequences.

Ruth and Franklin stood back and watched while
the six men attacked the pot of beans and the plate
laden with fresh meat. Like a pack of hungry wolves
around the carcass of a cow, they set upon the modest
fare until there was nothing left. One of them, a tall,
lanky beanpole of a man named Earl, set his empty
plate on the table and wondered aloud, "You reckon
we oughta saved some for Jake?"

"We might have at that," Webb replied. "Tell you the
truth, I plum forgot about him."

"There's another one of you?" Ruth asked.

"Yeah, there's one more," Webb said, "but he don't
need nothin' to eat." He looked at Earl then and said, "I
reckon you oughta go on back there and tell him to
come on."

"Ain't he gonna be hot when he finds out we been
settin' around the table eatin'?" Little Bit remarked,
amused by the prospect. "I can't wait to see his face."
His remarks drew a round of chuckles from them all.

Growing more fearful by the minute, Ruth made a
subtle attempt to verify their claim that they were
rangers. "You know," she said, "I don't believe I've ever
seen a Texas Ranger badge."

Bevo Rooks cocked a wary eye in her direction.

"Looks like any other badge," he said. "Nothin' fancy about it."

"May I see yours?" She said it before she gave herself time to reconsider.

"My what?" he responded with an impish grin, causing Little Bit to snicker.

"Your badge," she said, flushing with embarrassment.

"We don't always wear our badges," Webb interjected, "so the outlaws don't run off when they see us comin'."

"Oh," she responded fearfully. She knew then that her suspicions had been confirmed. As she met her husband's worried gaze, it was obvious that he had reached the same conclusion. Her foremost hope now was that they would leave, since they had been fed and their horses watered and rested. Seeing Franklin inching his way closer to the pantry door, she frowned at him, trying to discourage him from making any suicidal attempts for the shotgun. He paused with his hand almost touching the doorknob.

"Well, I reckon you fellows are anxious to get on your way," Franklin said. "I'll help you saddle up." He walked to the kitchen door and opened it. None of the men made a move toward it.

"Why, we ain't in no hurry a'tall," Bevo said, leering at Ruth. "Are we, boys? We got time to get better acquainted. Now, me, I been wonderin' how an ugly son of a bitch like ol' Franklin got himself a spunky-lookin' woman like you. Hell, I'm as handsome as he is. My wife says I'm like a bull in season when I get to goin' good. If you ask me real polite-like, I'll be glad to show you." He cocked his head to sneer at her husband.

"Ol' Franklin won't mind, will you, Franklin?" Bevo's friends stood there grinning, enjoying the show and anticipating their participation to come.

"All right, fellows," Franklin spoke up, "this has gone far enough. We welcomed you and fed you. Now I'm tellin' you it's time you got on your horses and left." He looked at Ruth and said, "You go on back in the parlor till they've gone."

She hurried toward the door, but was not quick enough to evade the lecherous grasp of Bevo Rooks. She uttered a frightened squeal when he grabbed her arm. It seemed to please him. "Sounds like a rabbit when a hawk catches him," he said with a chuckle. "Let's me and you go in the bedroom. You got a few gray hairs on ya, but I bet you can still buck, can't ya, honey?" He started pulling her toward one of the two bedroom doors.

It was too much for Franklin to endure. "Get your filthy hands off her!" he roared, and ran to the pantry, where he managed to get to his shotgun. But that was as far as he got before Webb Jarrett calmly shot him down. Horrified, Ruth cried out once more before her legs collapsed beneath her and she fainted.

Young John Chapel was beginning to regret not taking one of the horses when he left the house early that morning. He had always hunted on foot, even when going after a deer or antelope. He could cover a lot of ground in a short time, and keep it up for hours, trotting at a pace faster than walking but slower than running. Strong for his age, he didn't mind packing his kill back home on his shoulders after he had gutted it and cut away the parts he couldn't use. But on this morning, he could have used one of the horses to pack meat back to the house, because he had a clear shot at two deer. Consequently, he took only the one shot that brought the young doe down. The second doe had frozen still for only a few seconds, but that would have been enough time for John to eject the shell and reload the single-shot rifle. The shot was from a distance of at least two hundred yards. The rifle, his father's Remington Rolling Block, was accurate at longer range, using a large-caliber cartridge that would bring down a buffalo, had there been any left in the territory.

Hunting was the only respite from the hard work on his father's farm, and since he was an accomplished hunter at the age of thirteen, it provided welcome variation from the pork they raised. His father never openly expressed it, but John knew he appreciated that his son showed the ability to do a man's work without complaining. There was no reason to complain as far as John could see. He wasted no thoughts on whether work was hard or whether he was enjoying his life. Life was what it was, and he faced it without a great deal of thought about his life being harder than the lives of other boys his age. He didn't know any boys his age. His mother had almost died when she gave birth to him, and she had never been able to become pregnant again. So their one son had not gone to school or played with other children because of the remoteness of their homestead. His mother had insisted upon teaching him to read and write, although he had never seen any practical use for that ability. He was accustomed to living in a lonely world, but he didn't really know he was lonely. He had never known anything else, so hard work and serious thought were what he perceived as normal. Forced to become the man of the house for the three years his father served with Wells' Texas Cavalry Battalion, there was no choice other than to become far advanced of his actual age. He had stood up to the challenge, however, and when his father returned after being wounded in action near Fort Gibson in Indian Territory, he found a seriously mature son of eleven doing a man's work every day. Now, two years after his father's return, the two of them had worked hard enough to expand the small remote farm to something more productive.

Ready to start back home in order to feed the stock and do his other chores, he hefted the carcass up and settled it upon his shoulders. Then, with his rifle in one hand, he set out toward the hills that stood between him and home. He was grateful for the cool fall weather, for it would have been a long hot walk back to the house otherwise. He and his father had butchered three hogs and hung them in the smokehouse, but there was still room for his deer. There would be plenty of meat for the winter. These were the thoughts running through his mind when he first caught sight of the smoke. At once alarmed, he quickened his walk, for the smoke was in the direction of his home. With at least two miles remaining before he reached the farm, he broke into a trot, still with his deer across his shoulders.

He labored on. His breathing grew more and more strained as he refused to lessen his pace. A wide column of smoke climbed high over the hills that hid the house from him, but he knew from the sheer volume of it that either the house or the barn was on fire. He shrugged the deer carcass off his shoulders and began to run. Already short of breath from walking with the heavy load, he now panted and gasped for air as he pushed up to the top of the hill. The sight that awaited him caused him to drop to his knees. Below him, in the tiny valley, he saw the inferno that once was the house and barn. Both were ablaze, engulfed in flames that were rapidly eating up the walls of the structures.

He was stunned only for a moment before he forced himself to act. "Ma!" The word was involuntarily forced from his lips as he got to his feet and ran down the hill. There was no sign of his mother or father outside the house, and no horses to be seen. "Ma! Pa!" he shouted as he neared the burning buildings, but there was no answer. The only noise to be heard was the roaring fire as it consumed his home; all else in the valley was deathly silent. With no way of knowing if his parents were inside the house, he became frantic to force his way through the flames to find out.

Near the well, he found a blanket. There were blood-stains on one side of it, but he didn't take the time to wonder about them. As fast as he could move, he drew a bucket of water from the well and soaked the blanket in it. Then he draped the wet blanket over his head and shoulders and ran around the house, looking for a place to enter. He quickly decided that the kitchen door was his only possible access. The door was already burned off and hanging by one hinge, so he kicked it aside and plunged through the narrow hole in the flames. As soon as he was inside the raging hell, he felt the stinging hot air in his lungs, and on his face and hands. He knew he would soon be unable to breathe at all as he frantically looked around him at what was once the kitchen. A dark form on the floor by the pantry door caught his eye through the smoke-filled room. He rushed to the body. It was his father, his shirt soaked with blood from the bullet hole in his chest. The realization of what had happened struck him like a blow from an axe, and he roared out in agony. Knowing that he didn't have much time, he left his father's body to look for his mother. Staggering from the heavy smoke that threatened to fill his lungs, he pushed into the short hallway and kicked the bedroom door open to discover his mother's battered naked body lying on the bed. The flames had already caught the edges of the sheets and blanket, and plumes of white smoke swirled in the air over her head. In a fit of uncontrollable rage, he wrapped the blanket around her and lifted her from the bed. The heat was becoming unbearable as he carried his mother back through the kitchen and out the flaming doorway. Once outside, he tried to draw deep breaths of fresh air into his aching lungs as he laid her body on the cool ground, then quickly stamped out the flames that were chewing at the edges of the blanket. Without hesitation, back into the burning house he charged. Grabbing his father's body by the boots, he dragged the heavy man out the door and onto the porch, barely seconds before he heard the sound of roof timbers crashing to the floor inside.

Anxious to get away from the scorching heat, he pulled his father to the edge of the porch until his boots reached the ground, then grabbed his wrists and pulled him upright. Franklin Chapel was a big man, but his thirteen-year-old son pulled his body over on his shoulder and picked him up, carrying him away from the burning house to lay him gently on the ground beside his wife. Then the boy sat down beside his parents and cried.

It was the last time he would ever cry.

Chapter 2

He wasn't sure how long he sat there beside the bodies of the two people who made up his entire family, but he didn't stir until shadows began to spread across the little valley. He got up then to take care of his parents. It was a grim task, but he knew he must bury them, and then he would search for the people who had performed this murderous act. His first thought had been that the horror he had come home to was the work of a stray band of Indians. But since his parents had not been scalped, and there were no other signs of an Indian raid, he changed his mind. His life had but one purpose now, and that was to avenge the deaths of his parents. The only tool not totally destroyed by the fire in the barn was a shovel that had been left propped against the middle rail of the corral. *Pa would have striped my behind for forgetting to put this in the tack room*, he told himself, then shook his head sadly at the thought. His pa had always been a stickler for putting the tools away. It didn't matter anymore. There was no one left in the world to tell him what to do, or what not to do.

With eyes dry of tears, he draped his blanket over the top rail of the corral to let it dry close to the still-burning structure. Then he walked up a little knoll west of the barn to a spot beneath the cottonwoods. There he began digging the final resting place for his parents, overlooking the small farm they had planned to grow into a working ranch. It would take him several hours before he was ready to lay them together in the deep grave. Darkness had set in fully by the time he had finished digging the grave as deep as he wanted, and he sat down to rest. But the whole yard around the house and barn was brightly illuminated by the two burning buildings. He sat there for a long time while the still-hungry flames destroyed all that had ever been real in his life, and he thought about what he must do now. His gaze fixed upon the two bodies lying at the edge of the firelit yard. From where he sat at the top of the knoll, they looked small and insignificant; yet they were all the family he had ever known, and it was up to him to seek vengeance for their deaths.

After a while, he got to his feet and descended the knoll. Hefting his father's body up on his shoulder again, he climbed back up to the grave and dropped it as gently as he could manage under the strain. When he went back for his mother, he was very careful to make sure the scorched blanket was wrapped tightly around her before he picked her up in his arms and carried her to lie beside her husband. Then came the hardest part of the burial, and he hesitated before shoveling dirt over his mother and father, committing them to the ground forever. He dropped down in the grave and pulled his father's jacket off, then used it to cover both of their faces. Only then could he bring himself to shovel dirt over them.

Once the burial was finished, he turned his attention immediately to the task he had set for himself. There would be little to salvage from the house or barn, if anything at all. After the flames died down to some degree around midnight, he tried to determine whether the intruders had taken the horses. A search of a wide circle of the area resulted in no sign of either horse, and he had to conclude that they had been stolen. If not, then maybe he could find them in the morning. He would need a horse for what he had to do, but he would have to wait for daylight anyway in order to track his parents' murderers. The one building left untouched by the fire was the smokehouse, so he pulled a partially burned piece of doorjamb from the edge of the house and, using it as a torch, looked inside the smokehouse to see if food had been stolen as well. There was one ham left hanging there, all the others having been taken. Evidently the raiders had no room for more, and he knew there was more than one in the murderous raid because his father could never have been overcome by one man—even if surprised. John would use the ham for his food supply when he went after the outlaws in the morning. Although he had eaten nothing since that morning, he had no appetite now, and there was nothing left for him to do but try to sleep. So he lay down on the ground, warmed by the still-burning house.

Sleep did not come easily, but weariness finally called him to slumber in the hours before dawn. He was awakened by the first rays of sunlight that skipped off the muddy water of the Red River, and he was up at once. Looking around to take stock of the remains of his home in the light of day, he saw that the buildings were still smoking, but the flames had died out except for small flickering flames here and there. He went first to the barn to see if there was anything left to salvage, only to discover the first major setback. The aroma of roasted horse flesh struck his nostrils even as he approached the charred timbers. With the help of a rail taken from the corral, he was able to shove enough of the timbers aside to get a glimpse of a carcass lying amid the carnage, but there was only one. They had evidently taken one of the horses to pack all they had stolen. Rather than set the other one free, they shot it. The discovery stopped him for only a moment, but it was in no way enough to cause him discouragement; it merely called for a change in method. He paused to think about it.

Since he was old enough to shoot a gun, he had always hunted on foot, and over the years, he had walked or trotted hundreds of miles, sometimes bearing considerable loads. On his feet, he wore Indian-style moccasins that he had made himself, much to his father's amusement. He would stalk these murderers on foot. There would be problems; however, none would be insurmountable. He could not carry an entire ham, so he would slice off what he could pack in his parfleche and then kill what he needed after the ham ran out.

Seeing that the lower half of the back wall of the barn had been partially spared by the fire, he realized that, luck being with him, there might be something to be salvaged. Using the corral rail again to pry fallen timbers aside, he managed to make his way inside the wall, where he found the corn bin still intact. Scooping out several handfuls of the burned corn on the top, he dug down in the kernels of shelled corn to find the .44 handgun and cartridge belt his father had hidden there. It was wrapped in a cloth sack, and while still warm, it appeared to be unharmed. To be sure, he loaded the cylinder and fired a round. Satisfied, he strapped the weapon on, feeling that now he was sufficiently armed with pistol and rifle.

His stomach reminded him then that he had not eaten for some time. As his father liked to tell him, "If you've got work to do, you need to give your body some fuel." And he had work to do. So he returned to the smokehouse and cut some more strips from the one remaining ham. It was a simple matter to find a fire to roast it over. There were many to choose from. After he had satisfied his hunger, he began a serious scout of the house and barnyard. To him, tracking came as a natural ability, and it didn't take long for him to form a picture of what had taken place before and after the massacre. He found where the raiders had ridden into the farm from the south, and where they had departed to cross the river into the Nations. In further confirmation of his previous assumption, the tracks he found were all from shod horses, so they were not Indian ponies. And when he followed them down to the river, he decided there were as many as seven, maybe even eight horses. He could not be sure how many riders there were, for he had no way of knowing if there were packhorses. Standing on the bank of the river, he took a quick inventory of his possibles—weapons with what ammunition there was; his parfleche with food, flint, and steel; his blanket; his skinning knife—everything he needed to hunt, no matter his quarry. Satisfied, he took one long look back at the place he had known as home, then waded into the river and headed into Oklahoma and the Nations.

Leaving the river, his clothes wet from the waist down, John started out at a comfortable trot, a pace he could maintain for half a dozen miles before dropping back to a fast walk. The tracks he followed led almost straight north until reaching the Boggy River. At that point, they veered a little more to the west, following the river. *Maybe they're heading to Atoka,* he thought. He had never been to the town in the Choctaw Nation, but his father had told him where it was, and that it was probably forty or forty-five miles from their home on the Red River. The boy had often crossed over the river to hunt in the Indian country, but he had never gone more than five or six miles north of the Red River.

By the time the sun was high overhead, he came to a fork in the river where Clear Boggy Creek and Muddy Boggy Creek came together to form the single river he had been following. From the remains of a small fire and some horse droppings, he was able to determine that the men he trailed had stopped there to water their horses. The droppings were plentiful and fairly fresh, and there were signs that they had camped there for the night. Apparently they were in no hurry.

Probably feeling safe now that they're in Indian Territory, he thought. He was a fair judge of distance, and by his estimation, they could not have been more than twenty-five miles from Atoka. When they had left this camp, they had followed Muddy Boggy, which told him they were definitely on their way to that town. He picked up his pace again, hoping he could catch up to them before they reached it, because it would be difficult for him to stalk them in town.

Jogging along at a steady trot, he followed their obvious trail beside the Muddy Boggy, his trained eye scanning the thick growth of trees and bushes that bordered the creek in case they might have doubled back to make sure they weren't being followed. Never stopping to eat, and taking only a few moments to drink, he figured he was getting fairly close to Atoka when he spotted some farm buildings in the distance. His first thought upon seeing them was that he was going to be too late to catch up with the men he pursued before they reached town. Striding hurriedly down across a narrow ravine, he suddenly caught sight of some horses among the cottonwoods next to the creek. Dropping at once to his belly, he strained to see beyond the trees, but he could see only the horses, so he backed away from the rim of the ravine and followed it to the creek where he could take advantage of the cover of trees and brush. Once there, he worked his way along the bank to a point where he had a better view of the bluffs up ahead. It was them, all right. He was almost sure of it. But what if he was wrong and the tracks he had been trailing had gone on by this place, and this was a different bunch? If he could be one

hundred percent sure, his first impulse would be to
bring his father's Remington Rolling Block rifle to bear
on the best target and blow a hole in him. As if willing
to accommodate him, one of the men walked toward
him, then stopped to relieve his bladder, presenting
the boy with a clear shot. He was a big man and a
tempting target. John raised his rifle and set his sights
on the big man's chest, but he couldn't risk shooting an
innocent man. He lowered the rifle, deciding it best to
wait and watch for a while until they moved out, or
made camp. Then he could determine if the tracks he
followed did in fact belong to them.

"You tellin' me you think you oughta be the one callin'
the shots now?" Webb Jarrett asked, his voice soft but
deadly.

"Ah, hell no, Webb," Earl replied at once. "You're the
boss. I was just wonderin' why we need to bother with
this farm, why we don't just go on into town. Hell, we've
got money to spend from that bank job, and there's
women in that town."

"There might be women in that farmhouse," Webb
said, the threat gone from his tone. "And you won't
have to give them no money."

"Just like that last place," Little Bit said. "That ol' gal
had a lotta miles on 'er, but she was in fine shape. Didn't
you enjoy your turn with her?"

"I didn't get no turn with her—Jake neither. You
sent me to get him, but, by the time we got back, the
rest of you had already had your fun and set the damn
house on fire."

"It wouldn't been no pleasure for you, anyway,"

Little Bit said. "She was already dead by the time you got back." His comment brought a laugh from the others.

Seeing Earl's sour expression, Webb said, "So we'll let you and Jake go first this time. Even if there ain't nothin' worth droppin' your britches for, I could use another home-cooked meal, somethin' besides beans and side meat this time." He didn't mention how much his twisted mind had enjoyed the killing as much as he did ravaging the woman.

"Like I said," Earl conceded, "you're the boss."

"Glad you realize that," Webb replied, and untied his horse's reins from a bush. "Now, let's ride on in before it gets dark, so we can take a good look around." Then he called to Bevo Rooks, who had walked to the edge of the trees to watch the farmhouse. "You see anythin' we need to worry about?"

"Nary a thing," Bevo called back. "Looks to me like there's one man—he's in the barn right now—and a couple of young'uns runnin' around in the yard. Can't say who's in the house."

"Don't sound like much to worry about," Webb said. "We'll go in and see if they've got anythin' worth takin', but if we do, we can't leave no witnesses. This place is too close to town." That said, he stepped up in the saddle and led them out of the woods.

Sixteen-year-old Samuel Watts came up on the back porch carrying a load of firewood for the kitchen stove. He dumped it in a box built for the purpose just outside the kitchen door. "That oughta be enough to last you for a while," he said as he walked in the door.

"Supper's about ready," his mother said. "Go on out to the barn and tell your daddy it's time to wash up. And tell Stanley and Kay to get in here and wash their hands."

"Yes'um," Samuel replied dutifully, then turned to leave, pausing briefly to eye the food already on the table.

"Go on, Son," Louise told him, "before everything gets cold." She then turned to her daughter. "Honey, check on those biscuits. They oughta be getting done by now."

"I think they're done," Bonny replied. "They're starting to brown up just right." At fourteen, Bonny was almost as good a cook as her mother, which was a source of great pride for Louise.

Samuel was halfway across the yard to the barn when he saw the group of riders on the road by the cornfield. He paused to watch them until they turned in at the path that led to the house. He hurried to the barn door then and called to his father. "Pa, there's a bunch of riders comin'—seven of 'em." He stood there by the door, waiting for his father. "They're a pretty rough-lookin' bunch. Wonder what they want."

"Well, we'll have to see, won't we?" Leonard Watts said when he came out to stand by his son. There were many outlaws flocking to Indian Territory since the end of the war, but because he and his family were close to Atoka, they seldom saw any. This was one reason he had taken over the abandoned farm when he mustered out of the Texas Battalion at Boggy Station. His was a prime piece of land on Muddy Boggy Creek, and the original owner, a Choctaw, had abandoned it when he felt ill-suited to farming.

Remembering his mother's instructions, Samuel called to his younger brother and sister, who were playing a game of hopscotch in the yard. "Kay, Mama said supper's ready. You two get on in the house and wash your hands." The two youngsters heard, but they had spotted the group of riders approaching the house, so they remained to see who was calling.

"This place looks a helluva lot more prosperous than that last place," Little Bit remarked as the riders passed along the cornfield. "It might be worth lookin' around at that." He reached over and nudged Earl. "I don't know about you and Jake," he teased. "That feller looks pretty old to have a wife as young as that last one." He threw his head back and laughed. "But I reckon when you're in heat, it don't make a helluva lot of difference."

"Shut up, Little Bit," Webb ordered, "before they hear your big mouth."

Little Bit's assessment of Leonard Watts' farm was accurate. It was a prosperous operation. A patient man, Watts had developed a mutual respect between his family and the Choctaw people, and he was well-thought-of by the Indians. Atoka was to be a thriving little town on the railroad, so he was able to get anything he needed in exchange for his crops. *Samuel was right*, Leonard thought. *They are a rowdy-looking lot.* He and his son walked forward to meet the men approaching them. "Good evenin'," he called out to them. "What can I do for you?"

"Good evenin'," Webb Jarrett returned. "We thought you might not mind if we watered our horses here." He nodded toward the horse trough by the barn.

"You're welcome to," Leonard replied. While he was a patient man, he was not a stupid man, and the logical question came to his mind. *You just came from the creek. Why did you not water your horses there?* "Are you fellows headin' to Atoka?" he asked.

Before Webb could answer, Little Bit spoke up, thinking to use the same ruse as before. "Yeah, we're Texas Rangers chasin' after some bank robbers."

Leonard didn't respond for a second or two while he took a critical look at the seven men. "Texas Rangers?" He responded then. "You know you're in Oklahoma Territory, I reckon."

"Why, sure," Webb replied quickly before Little Bit could respond with something equally as ignorant as his first statement. "We're workin' with the marshal's office over in Fort Smith. You see, these fellers we're chasin' robbed a bank in Texas."

There was enough to cast suspicion in Leonard's mind. He hadn't a clue as to what the men were up to, but he felt certain they were up to no good, and his immediate concern was to make sure his family was safe. To deepen his fears, the strangers casually moved to partially surround him and Samuel. "Well," he said, "you and your men can water your horses at the trough. I know you're probably anxious to get after those bank robbers." The situation was worsened at that moment by the appearance of Bonny on the front porch.

Surprised to see the group of riders in the yard, she nevertheless delivered the message her mother sent her to convey. "Daddy, Mama said to come eat supper." All heads turned when she called out.

"Hellooo," Bevo Rooks drew out, muttering low in appreciation of the young girl's obvious charms.

"Did she say supper was ready?" Webb asked with a wicked grin. "I bet you was just fixin' to invite us to share it." He had a pretty good idea that the main form of resistance to his gang was standing right in front of him in the persons of Leonard and his son—and they were unarmed. These were odds he found appealing. With six pairs of eyes leering at the young girl on the porch, Webb told Leonard, "I expect we'll be takin' supper with you."

"And anythin' else we fancy," Bevo finished for him.

"Before you go gettin' any ideas, Bevo," Earl blurted, "just remember me and Jake get to take a turn before any of the rest of you."

"Quit your bellyachin', Earl," Bevo came back. "You'll get your turn. Look at ol' Tom over there. He didn't get no turn, either, and he ain't said a word about it."

"I reckon Tom ain't got the needs me and Jake's got," Earl replied.

Hearing the bickering between the men, Leonard was struck by the horrible knowledge that his worst fears had indeed become reality, and that his position was hopeless. With great effort to remain calm, he told Samuel, "Go on in the house, Son, and tell your ma we've got company." He thought he might be able to stall the men long enough for Samuel to get the shotgun kept in the bedroom and defend Louise and the children. Equally alarmed as his father by then, Samuel understood and turned to leave. He had not taken more than two steps before he was stopped.

"You just stay right here with us, boy," Webb ordered, and nodded to Jake, who pulled his horse around to block the boy's path.

Leonard knew he was helpless to stop the menacing gang leering down at him from doing what evil they intended, but still he tried. "You've got no cause to harm my family," he pleaded. "I'll give you food and water, and feed for your horses, and you can be on your way."

"What's your daughter's name?" Little Bit asked, ignoring Leonard's plea. When Leonard just shook his head in answer, Little Bit said, "I bet it's Sugar Bottom. Whaddaya think, Earl?"

"Yeah," the dull-witted Earl replied excitedly, "Sugar Bottom!"

Leonard's brain was threatening to black out from the horror that had descended upon his peaceful home. Staring in wide-eyed terror at the leering Earl, who was literally salivating in anticipation of an assault upon his daughter, he was suddenly stunned by the impact of the slug that hit Earl's chest, knocking him from the saddle. The solid report of the high-powered rifle was heard an instant later. For a few moments everyone—outlaws, father, and son—was frozen in shock, unable to understand what had happened. That first shot was followed almost immediately by a second that ripped a wide hole in Jake's midsection. In the chaos that followed, everyone scampered for some protection. Leonard and Samuel ran to the house, while the five remaining outlaws galloped for the barn. All but one of them reached safety, as one more shot found the middle of Jack Frye's back, knocking him from the saddle.

In the house, Leonard grabbed his shotgun and tossed a revolver he kept in a drawer to Samuel. Next, he herded Louise and the terrified children ahead of him to the large pantry off the kitchen, as he would have had it been a tornado that struck his farm. Only this time, he sat before his family with his shotgun aimed at the door and waited. "You be ready, Son," he said to Samuel. "Anybody jerks that door open, you shoot." He wasn't sure what was happening. Three of the men who had threatened to do his family harm were dead—by whom, he didn't know. He wasn't sure if he should be thankful for that, or if something more terrible had descended upon his family. All he could do was sit and wait, and pray they would all be spared.

While those in the house prayed, the four survivors of Webb Jarrett's gang cursed the sudden turn of events. "They got three of us quicker'n a cat can catch a nap," Little Bit said, the usual flippant manner replaced by one of nervous concern.

"Them shots came from that cornfield," Bevo said. "Couldn'ta come from anywhere else." He stood at the hinge side of the barn door, peering through the gap between the door and jamb.

"How many you reckon there are?" Little Bit asked, standing back in the middle of the barn holding the horses.

"How the hell do I know?" Webb snapped. "Who the hell are they is what I wanna know. Ain't likely that damn posse outta Sherman coulda caught up with us."

"Well, somebody's caught up with us," Bevo said, "and they got some sharpshooters with 'em." He paused for a moment to strain his eyes in an effort to pick up some movement in the cornfield. "Maybe it's a marshal's posse."

"How'd they get onto us so quick?" Little Bit asked.

"I don't know," Bevo answered. "'Cause we laid around that camp too long last night, I expect. I knew we shoulda got off our behinds and got goin'. But I'll tell you one thing—I ain't plannin' to hang around here to find out who the hell they are. I got a young wife back in Texas that ain't even broke in good yet, and I ain't ready to make her a widow. I don't see but one way outta here, and that's through that back door yonder. I don't know how many of them there are, but I ain't gonna wait to let 'em send somebody around behind us—if they ain't already."

"Bevo's right," Webb said. "They might be workin' around behind this barn already. I say we make a run for it, every man for hisself. Might be best if we split up, so they can't follow all of us. I'm thinkin' 'bout headin' for Cheyenne Canyon in the Cherokee Outlet. We can meet up there if we all make it. At least that's where I'll be."

"What about them horses out front?" Little Bit asked. Three horses with empty saddles were standing near the horse trough and the stolen packhorse off to one side.

"You wanna go out front and get 'em, you go right ahead," Webb said. "And good luck to ya."

"I was just thinkin' about them three shares of that bank money in the saddlebags," Little Bit lamented.

"You think about it all you want," Bevo informed

him. "I'm gettin' outta here right now." He didn't wait to see who was going to follow.

Young John Chapel loaded another cartridge into the chamber of his Remington rifle and changed his position among the corn rows for the second time since firing his first shot. There had been no hesitation before taking the shot, for he was certain the riders were the same seven he had tracked from the Red River. When they had left the trees by the creek, he made sure it was the same trail he had been following to that point. Three of his parents' murderers had been dealt with, but nothing short of the entire seven would satisfy the boy's need for justice.

Moving closer to the edge of the field, he was now studying the house and yard, trying to decide where he could slip out of the field and approach the barn without being seen. His best bet, he concluded, was to run across the rows to a point where the house stood between the field and the barn, so he hesitated no longer. When he was opposite the rear of the house, he left the cover of the cornfield and moved to a position at the end of the back porch in time to see the back door of the barn open. He laid the rifle across the corner of the porch and waited. In a moment, a head appeared and looked around cautiously. A second later, a man led a horse out of the barn, followed immediately by his three partners. It was the first opportunity for John to get a good look at the men he stalked, and he hesitated to fire until he had seared the images of their faces into his brain. He waited a moment too long, for they mounted and sped off quicker than he anticipated, limiting him to only one shot before they disappeared into the trees behind the barn. They were moving too fast, however, and he missed, leaving him with four men to settle with. He ran out in the yard toward the barn in hopes of getting a chance for another shot, but the trees were too dense and they were gone.

Still huddled inside the pantry, Leonard Watts and his frightened family were jolted by the sudden discharge of the Remington right outside the back door. Fearful that the shooter was about to enter his house, Leonard raised his shotgun to his shoulder and prepared to fire. But no one came to the pantry door. In fact, everything was quiet outside. Still, he waited until the tension became unbearable and he had to see what had happened. "I'm goin' out," he announced finally.

"I'm goin' with you," Samuel said.

"Best the rest of you stay hid," Leonard told his wife. Then he opened the pantry door a crack and peered through to the kitchen. There was no one there, so he eased out, his shotgun cocked and ready to fire, with Samuel right behind him. "They might be in the house," he whispered, and started tiptoeing toward the front room.

"Pa, wait," Samuel whispered. Leonard turned to find his son peering out the kitchen window. "Look— standing in the yard."

Leonard hurried to the window. There, standing in the middle of the yard, was a solitary figure, a boy by all appearances, holding a rifle. He was gazing out toward the trees behind the barn, and seemed to show no interest in the house behind him. "Well, for pity's sake . . . ,"

Leonard started, but never finished, astonished by what he saw. "Who in the world is that?" he exclaimed. "Have you ever seen him before?"

"No, sir," Samuel replied. "There must be somebody else with him." He left the window then and hurried through the rest of the house, peering out the windows in every room. He was back in a minute. "There's no sign of anyone else outside."

Anxious to find out who and what was responsible for the brief shoot-out at his home, Leonard walked to the back door and went out on the porch. Hearing the door open, John Chapel turned to face him. Even though Leonard held his shotgun ready to pull the trigger, he was relieved when John made no motion toward raising the rifle. For a long moment they stood looking at each other, not knowing what to say. Leonard shifted his gaze to notice the bodies lying in his barnyard, then back to the solemn face of the boy. When it became obvious that the boy was not going to offer any explanation for the shooting, Leonard asked, "Who are you?"

"Chapel," was the simple answer.

"You ain't by yourself, are you? Where's the rest of you?"

"There ain't nobody else," John answered.

Still finding that hard to believe, Leonard pressed the stoic young stranger for information. "Are you from around here?" When John shook his head, Leonard remembered then the deadly circumstances he was facing moments before the first shot startled them all. "Who were those men? I reckon I owe you thanks for showin' up when you did, young fellow. We were in a rough spot with those fellows. How did you know they were comin' here?"

"I didn't. I tracked 'em here," John replied. It had not occurred to him that he might have come to the aid of another potential victim of the gang of murderers. It had not been his intent to save Leonard and his family. His only purpose was to kill those who had taken his mother and father from him. He didn't care about anything beyond that. In fact, in the middle of the cornfield, he was too far away to determine what was being said between this man and the outlaws. And now he was interested only in the fact that the remaining four outlaws were getting away, and he was anxious to get back on their trail. "I've gotta go now," he said.

"Wait! Wait a minute," Leonard insisted. "Who are those men, and why are you trackin' them? You can at least tell us that before you run off."

Reluctantly, John told a brief story of the reason he was tracking them. "They killed my ma and pa, the same as they were likely plannin' to do to you folks. I've been trackin' 'em from the Red River, and I need to get goin' now, else I might lose 'em for good."

Leonard and his son still found it hard to believe what had happened. Looking around again at the bodies of three men, and the horses standing idly about the barnyard, he hardly knew what to say. "You're only a boy. It's dangerous for you to go after men like that," he finally said. "You need to go to the law and let them go after these men. If you want, I'll go into town to the sheriff with you, and you can tell him what's happened."

"I don't need no sheriff," John answered simply, his voice devoid of emotion. The fact that he was only a boy had never entered his mind. He looked around him then at the outlaws' horses. "When they killed my folks, they stole one of our horses—that one over yonder"—he pointed toward the one horse without a saddle—"and they shot the other one. So I'm takin' my horse and one of theirs." Ending the conversation, he turned and went to examine the horses, leaving Leonard and Samuel to stand gaping in disbelief. He didn't spend much time inspecting the mounts, immediately narrowing his pick between a buckskin and a gray, and finally picking the buckskin because of the lever action Henry rifle in the saddle sling. Looking at his father's horse then, loaded with the hams stolen from the smokehouse, he led the buckskin over next to it. He untied all the hams but one and left them on the ground, seemingly oblivious to the man and his son staring at him in stark disbelief. He then tied the lead line to the saddle of the buckskin. With not so much as a glance in their direction, he climbed up in the saddle, gave the horse his heels, and went off through the trees at a lope. "Those are good smoked hams back yonder," he called over his shoulder.

Leonard and Samuel stood astonished, watching him until he disappeared. "Thanks," Leonard remembered to call out after him when he was well out of hearing. "If that don't beat all I've ever seen . . . ," he murmured.

They turned to look at each other in wonder, then looked about their yard again at the bodies that had to be dealt with. "Looks like we got us two new horses,"

Samuel said, unaware of the extra bonus of bank money in each of the saddlebags. "I guess I oughta go into town and tell the sheriff what happened," he said.

"I expect so," his father said. "We certainly have to go get him before we do anything about those dead men, but there's no hurry. They aren't goin' anywhere. We'll carry them into the barn, so your mother and the young ones won't have to see them. Let's get the saddles off those horses and put 'em in the corral. I don't know if the sheriff's gonna wanna take charge of them, himself, but maybe, if they ain't out where he can see 'em, he might not think about 'em. We'll pick up those hams and hang 'em in the smokehouse. I don't see any reason the sheriff oughta even know about the hams. You go catch those horses. I'll go tell your mother she can come out now."

Chapter 3

The tracks of the four galloping horses were easy enough to follow, allowing the boy, who was being careful not to ask too much of his new horse, to hold the buckskin to a steady pace. Judging by the tracks he followed, it would not be much farther before their horses were going to have to rest. Far from panic or anxiety, he maintained a sense of patient determination, knowing that no matter how long or how far, he would follow the trail to an inevitable end—and he had the rest of his life to do it.

Just before dark, he came upon the place where their horses had given out. The tracks told him that the horses had stood at the edge of a small stream for some time. The boot prints of their riders were liberally in evidence as well, telling him that the outlaws had dismounted and were leading the tired mounts when they left the stream, still following Muddy Boggy Creek. They could not be that far ahead of him now. Thinking

it best to give the buckskin a brief rest, even though the
horse had shown no signs of tiring, he dismounted
and let it drink. While he waited, he drew the Henry
from the saddle scabbard to examine his new weapon.
It was the first one he had ever seen, but his father had
told him about the repeating rifle some of the Union
soldiers carried. Some of the Confederates said, "You
could load on Sunday and shoot all week." A heavy
rifle, it held a full magazine of .44 cartridges. It would
greatly increase his firepower.

He slipped the rifle back into the scabbard and
looked to see what was in the saddlebags. There were
various items of a personal nature—a razor, which he
had no use for as yet; a flint and steel, which he already
carried in his parfleche; some extra socks and a shirt.
In the second saddlebag, he found something he had
not anticipated. Wrapped in a paper sack, there were a
sizable bundle of money and a handful of gold coins,
as well as two boxes of .44 cartridges for the Henry.
Instantly, he had become a man of means. The discovery eliminated the concern that had begun to worry
him—how he was going to buy cartridges for his Remington rifle. Now he was armed with a Henry. Nodding his head in grim satisfaction, he put everything
back in the saddlebags and climbed in the saddle again
after adjusting the stirrups to fit his legs.

Shortly before it became too dark to follow the tracks,
he came to a spot where the outlaws split up. Two of
their number continued on along the creek, and two
veered off to the west. John paused to decide which
two to follow. With no thoughts of giving up on any of
them, he pulled his knife and cut a chunk out of the

trunk of a tree, marking the spot where he could pick up the second trail when he was done with the other two. He pushed on until darkness made the tracks impossible to see, stopping then to consider the possibilities. The two men he followed had continued to follow the creek. His father had told him that Muddy Boggy Creek would lead straight to Atoka. He wondered now if the outlaws were going to Atoka. It made little sense to him that two outlaws would intentionally head to a town that might have a sheriff, and the man at the farm he had just left said there was a sheriff there. He also remembered hearing his father talk about the blatant disregard for the law in Indian Territory, especially since the war. If he guessed wrong, and rode on to Atoka, it might mean he would lose their trail altogether. It didn't take him long to decide. He wasn't content to wait out the night to be certain, so he cut a chunk of bark from another tree trunk to mark that place, then continued up the creek to Atoka.

"You reckon we shoulda headed west with Bevo and Tom?" Little Bit asked when the dimly lit buildings of Atoka came into view. "He mighta been right about there being a sheriff here."

"I don't care if there *is* a sheriff," Webb replied. "I'm gettin' tired of runnin' from a posse we ain't even got a look at. Hell, we don't even know if that was a posse that hit us back there. Anyway, if we ain't seen them, then maybe they ain't seen us close enough to get a good look at us. We'll just be two strangers passin' through. They'll play hell tryin' to arrest me. I'll tell you that right now. I want some hot supper and a drink of whiskey."

"Where you gonna find a drink of whiskey in Injun Territory?" Little Bit asked.

"There's always somebody who's got some whiskey for sale. A few questions and a little money will loosen a lot of tongues."

"I hope you're right," Little Bit said, "but right now I'm lookin' for somethin' to eat. I hope there's a dining room there." He thought about it for a moment before commenting, "I don't reckon we'll see ol' Bevo and Tom again. Do you?"

"I don't much care one way or the other," Webb replied. "Let's find us someplace to get somethin' to eat."

They were in luck. Most of the little town was buttoning up for the night, but one building at the end of Court Street proclaimed itself to be a hotel, and it appeared to be the one busy place on the short street. They headed straight for it.

A full moon had found its way over the dark creek bank by the time John reached Atoka. He pulled up to look over the collection of buildings huddled in the moonlight. Like the two men he pursued, he was drawn to the one place that seemed to be alive, so he guided his horses toward the hotel. There were several horses tied at the hitching rail. The two that attracted his attention were tied slightly apart from the others and showed obvious signs of having been ridden long and hard. Satisfied that these were the ones he had been following, he led his horses around to the side of the building and tied them to the porch rail. With the same emotionless determination he had employed to execute the prior three outlaws, he drew the Henry rifle from his saddle and cranked a cartridge into the chamber. Then he walked unhurriedly to the door, where he stood just inside and scanned the half-filled dining room, his intense gaze skipping from table to table as he studied the patrons seated there. A few diners, seated near the front door, turned to stare at the strange, solemn-looking boy standing there holding a Henry rifle, the muzzle pointing to the floor. Ed Mullins, who managed the hotel's dining room, left the cleaning rag on the table he was in the process of clearing, and walked over to the door. "If you're coming in to eat, son, I think you'd best leave that rifle by the door here."

John made no immediate reply, for at that moment his gaze settled upon two men seated at a back-corner table. Both were rough-looking men. One was a big man, the other smaller. What had snared John's attention was the black wide-brim hat with the belt of silver around the crown.

"Did you hear me, son?" Ed insisted. "I said you'd best leave that rifle by the door."

"Yes, sir," John replied respectfully. "I heard you, but I'm gonna need it for a minute. I ain't stayin'."

There was no time for Ed to stop the blatant execution that took place before his eyes in the next few seconds. Horrified, he could only stand paralyzed while the boy whipped the Henry up waist-high and pulled the trigger, knocking the larger man at the back table over in his chair. In a flash, the boy cranked another cartridge into the chamber and slammed Little Bit in the side before he could get untangled from his chair.

The sudden explosion of the Henry rifle in the confined dining room sent the other patrons scrambling to the floor seeking cover. In the confusion of the moment, John turned and walked purposefully out the front door, leaving Ed Mullins standing in shock. Outside in the moonlight, he walked around the corner of the porch, climbed in the saddle, and headed back toward the Muddy Boggy while behind him several unnerved diners ran to find the sheriff. The executioner would be long gone before the lawman was able to be found. There were two more murderers to deal with.

The lone rider, leading a packhorse, was soon beyond the sound of the excited voices he had left in the little town. He didn't stop to make camp until he had returned to the tree beside the creek with the mark in its trunk. Planning to start west from there as soon as it was light enough to find the tracks, he built a fire and fashioned a spit from the limb of a bush to cook some of his ham. He thought of his mother and father before he went to sleep, as he had on nights before. *That's all but two of them,* he thought, *but I'll get them. I promise.*

Morning found him up and ready to saddle the buckskin as soon as the first rays of light filtered through the oaks on the east side of the creek. Looking up at the sky, he realized he had probably slept longer than he had intended, for the sky was overcast with heavy dark clouds. In contrast to the clear moonlit sky of the previous night, it promised to be a day of rain, so he hurried to find the place where the two outlaws had departed from the creek and headed west. When he found the tracks, he followed them until he was satisfied they were holding to a constant direction. Then he looked out toward the horizon for as far as he could see in that direction to fix it in his mind in case the clouds overhead decided to deliver their apparent promise. Starting out at a lope, he guided on a distant hill, pausing only occasionally to verify that the tracks were still with him.

By what he estimated to be about noon, the rain started, a gentle sprinkle at first, but it increased in strength until he was soon riding in a light rain that gave no sign of slackening. Still, it was not enough to erase the tracks he followed. He untied the rain slicker rolled up behind J.F.'s saddle—those were the initials carved into the stock of the Henry rifle he had become heir to—and pushed on through the rain. He was reluctant to stop while he could still read sign; nevertheless, after another hour, he pulled his horses up in a thick grove of oaks at the foot of a grass-covered hill to rest them. It occurred to him then that he was hungry, so he built a small fire up close under the branches of a tree where there was some protection from the rain. He would let the horses rest only a short time while he ate more of the ham, for neither horse was carrying much of a load. As a wiry thirteen-year-old, he didn't weigh that much when added to the weight of the saddle and rifle, and the packhorse had very little to carry in addition to the ham.

While he sat up against the trunk of the tree, chewing on the salty ham, watching his two horses graze, he took a moment to consider how far he had come in a few days' time. The cold fact that he, at his age, had killed five men did not weigh heavily on his single-track mind. There was no question in his thoughts as to the morality of his actions, no more so than if he had gone out to eliminate a pack of rabid wolves. Neither was he impressed with his ability to accomplish what he had against seven hardened murderers. He felt no sense of pride in what he had done—only the onus to finish the job he had promised he would do.

Back in the saddle again, he continued on toward the hills in the distance while the rain continued at a steady rate, interrupted occasionally by heavier showers. It was after one of these showers that he had difficulty finding the tracks that verified he was still on the trail. Still, there were a few places where the grass was thin enough to reveal some traces of hoofprints. Late in the afternoon, he reached what he figured had to be Clear Boggy Creek. Crossing over, he scouted up and down the creek for about fifty yards in both directions, but there were no tracks to be found. Disappointed, but not discouraged, he spent the rest of the day until nightfall scouting up and down both sides of the creek. There was no trail for him to follow, and finally discouragement crept into his mind with the stark realization that he had lost the two surviving killers. Even then, he would not accept it, and he cursed the rain that continued to fall, but vowed to search again in the morning. Forced by darkness to make his camp, he unsaddled the buckskin, unloaded his packhorse, and resigned himself to a wet night.

Morning brought another gray day, but without the rain of the day before. He spent a portion of the early hours searching for some sign that would put him back on the trail, but there was nothing. With no better option, he decided to push on in the direction the trail had run since he had first left the Muddy Boggy, and would hope for luck to guide him. He reasoned that the men he chased must have had some destination in mind, for they had never veered from a straight western course. After a full day's ride, he came upon a road that led to a small gathering of huts, and he paused to decide if he should follow it, or if it would be better to avoid the town, if that was what it turned out to be.

While he was still making up his mind, he saw a man and woman coming up the road. They were on foot, but they were leading a horse with packsaddles. The boy decided to wait for them in hopes that they might have seen the men he searched for. As they approached him, he could see they were Indians—Chickasaw, he assumed, since he should have surely left the Choctaw Nation by this time. They seemed wary of him at first but continued toward him, surprised somewhat when they realized he was a boy. "Howdy," John greeted them.

"Howdy," the man replied, even more puzzled when he observed the obviously heavily armed young man.

"I'm lookin' for two white men that mighta come along here, maybe last night or this mornin'," John said, then asked, "You understand English?"

The man exchanged a quick glance with his wife, then nodded. "I speak it," he said. "I don't see no white man around here. You the only one."

John was disappointed but not surprised. "What is that down the road?" he asked, pointing toward the cluster of shacks some distance away. "Is that a town?"

"That Tishomingo," the man replied. "No white man there."

John knew then that he had lost the two remaining killers of his parents, and maybe for good. In all likelihood, the outlaws had turned back toward Texas, following the Clear Boggy. He didn't know where to turn at this point, in the middle of the Chickasaw Nation without a hint of a clue as to where he should go from there. The thought stung his mind when he was forced to acknowledge defeat in the complete vengeance he so desperately needed. But he was realistic enough to know that, with no trail to follow, it would take a miracle to find the two outlaws. He glanced then at the puzzled expressions on the faces of the Indian couple as they watched him agonizing over his dilemma. "Much obliged," he said, and gave the buckskin a nudge.

He continued on in his original direction, trying to decide what to do. One thing he was certain of was that he had no desire to return to his father's farm on the Red River, but there was no other place he wanted to go, either. Unable to make a decision, he continued to ride west until it struck him that he had no thoughts toward any future. *I reckon I'll just take one day at a time,* he decided, *and see where I end up.* That seemed as good a plan as any, so he urged his horse to a comfortable lope and took the easiest course ahead of him, planning to put a little distance between him and the village of Tishomingo before camping for the night. He found a good spot just before dusk.

The following day was little different from the day before. Each time he approached a village, he altered his course a little to the north to pass it by while still generally traveling west. He could think of no reason why he wanted to visit a village. The farther away from people, the better, he figured. With no destination in mind, he just continued riding, trusting that he would eventually come to a place that looked right to him. Another day and another night found him gazing at a line of tree-covered mountains in the distance, so he rode toward them, thinking that maybe it was time to consider finding a more permanent camp. The nights were already getting chilly, with winter coming on before much longer, and there would be more shelter in the mountains. The only clothes he had after his home had been burned to the ground were those on his back, and his one blanket was all he had for warmth. He had no experience in making clothes from animal hides, but he knew how to hunt and skin, and he had made the moccasins on his feet, so he was confident that he would sew himself a coat of some fashion. Feeling his first enthusiasm for anything since having to admit his failure to track down the last two on his vengeance list, he increased his pace and headed for the mountains.

When he rode into the mountains, he knew it was the place he was looking for. There was a strong stream running through them, and he followed it to a high waterfall that sent the water crashing down to a pool that he estimated to be seventy-five or eighty feet below. It was a natural place to camp, but there was very little sign of game—and there should have been animal tracks all around the pool. The Indians must have hunted the land out. *There's got to be some game somewhere in these mountains,* he thought. *If there is, I'll find it.*

The clearing around the pool might have been an excellent setting for a homestead, but it was much too open for one lone boy in the middle of Indian Territory. So he followed the stream down through the canyon until he found a steep ravine that led back up the mountain. There was a trickle of water that flowed down the middle of the ravine to join the main stream, so he urged his horses up the narrow defile. The farther up he climbed, the rougher it became until he decided it best to dismount and lead his horses the rest of the way. Finally he came to a ledge and a small clearing at the foot of a ring of pines that appeared to form a belt around the mountain. "This'll do," he decided at once.

He spent the following day building his camp. He found himself giving thanks that J.F. had thought to attach a hand axe to his saddle, for it made it much easier to build his lean-to with pine boughs cut from the trees. When he was finished, he was satisfied with his work, but he knew he needed some animal hides to line the inside to keep out the cold and rain. The next several days were spent completing his winter camp and a shelter for his horses. He then needed to lay in a supply of smoked meat to carry him in the event fresh meat was as scarce as signs indicated, as well as hides for himself and his shelter.

As he had feared, game was scarce in the mountains, so he was obliged to ride out on the prairie in search of antelope or deer. He felt confident, however, that with the arrival of colder temperatures, the animals would seek shelter among the valleys of the mountains. He was lucky on his second day out on the prairie to catch sight of a small herd of antelope. After tracking them for the better part of the day, he at last got within range of his Henry when the animals stopped to drink at a stream. He would have taken advantage of his Remington's greater range had he had more than only a few of the large-caliber cartridges left, and he was saving them in case he might get a shot at a bear, or even a buffalo. He was well satisfied with the Henry's performance, anyway, for he brought down two antelope before the rest of the herd sprinted away. It was a start for his winter camp. Since he had no knowledge of wild edible plants, his diet was going to consist entirely of meat and whatever berries he might find. To his young mind, there was nothing wrong with that, although he would have wished for biscuits and coffee if they had been available.

As the weeks passed and the weather grew colder and colder, and the deer still seemed reluctant to seek the shelter of the hills, he found it necessary to range farther and farther from his mountain camp. On one of these hunting trips, too far from his camp to return before dark, he made a bed for himself in a thicket of hackberry near a slow-moving stream. Early the next morning, he was awakened by the sounds of deer crashing through the brush on the other side of the stream. Being careful not to make any sudden moves that might alert them to his presence, he eased his rifle up beside him and searched the trees, trying to get a glimpse of the deer. In a few moments, he saw them emerge from the brush, bounding over smaller berry

bushes in their haste to escape whatever had frightened them. In a few seconds, they would be in the clear,
and he would be in position for an easy shot. He raised
his rifle to his shoulder and aimed at a spot a few feet
in front of a ten-point buck's nose. But he did not pull
the trigger, for at that moment he caught sight of the
reason for the deer's flight.

He carefully lowered his rifle as an Indian hunter,
armed only with a bow, ran from the trees before pausing to kneel and take aim. It would have been an easy
shot for John. The deer was no more than fifty yards
from him as it leaped across the narrow stream, but it
was obvious that the Indian had first claim on it, so
John remained still and watched. The hunter released
his bowstring just as the buck landed on the other side
of the stream, his arrow missing the deer by inches.
While John watched, the Indian quickly notched another arrow, but the deer had covered an additional
fifty yards by then, and the second arrow was short by
several yards. Thinking it pointless to let the deer get
away, John raised his rifle again and fired, dropping
the animal at once.

Startled, the Indian hunter stood frozen for a few
moments, unable to decide whether he should run or
prepare to defend himself. Unsure, he notched another
arrow and started to back away slowly, stopping again
when John emerged from the thicket. Surprised to find
it was no more than a boy, the Indian lowered his bow.
However, he was not prone to be careless, for the boy
obviously knew how to use the repeating rifle in his
hands, so the arrow remained notched on his bowstring.

"Your deer," John called to him. "He was gettin'
away—outta range of that bow—so I shot him for you."
Long Walker did not understand at first. He spoke
English, so he understood John's words, but he didn't
understand the boy's largesse. John motioned toward
the carcass. "He's your buck," he said again. "You saw
him first."

Long Walker's natural suspicions served to make
him wary of the white boy's intentions. He looked all
around him, to see if there were others, then took a
moment to study this strange white boy who had suddenly appeared out of the brush. Finally, he said, "You
shot the deer. It belongs to you."

"If you say so," John replied, "but I'm givin' it to you.
There wasn't no sense in lettin' it get away. And it looks
to me like you were onto that deer from back yonder
somewhere, so it's only right that you take him. I'll get
my horse and go after the rest of 'em."

Long Walker looked into the boy's eyes, searching
for any sign of deception. With his repeating rifle, the
boy had a distinct advantage over him, armed as he
was with only an ash bow. There was nothing he could
do to save himself if the boy's intentions were evil.
Although his face was hard and without emotion, Long
Walker could see no evil in his eyes. After a moment
more, he decided that John was sincere in his gift of the
deer. "I thank you for your gift. My village is not far
from here. If you will come with me, we will butcher
the deer and share it. My wife will roast the fresh meat
while we sit and talk. My name is Long Walker of the
Chickasaw Nation."

John hadn't considered the possibility of an invitation

to an Indian village. His first inclination was to refuse it, for he had no desire to visit anyone, red or white. He had no experience in making friends. The earnest look in Long Walker's eyes made him hesitate, however, for he didn't want to insult the Indian by appearing not to want to share meat with him and his family, so he nodded his head in acceptance and did his best to form a smile.

"Good," Long Walker said. "How are you called?"

"Chapel," John answered.

"Chapel," Long Walker repeated, and nodded his head in approval.

Together, they butchered the buck and packed it on John's horse. They washed their hands and arms in the stream, then walked back to Long Walker's village with John leading the buckskin. Greeted cordially by Long Walker's wife, Yellow Beads, John was shown all the hospitality a poor Chickasaw village could offer, which only served to make him uncomfortable and long for his mountain camp. Many more of the people joined in the feast of fresh venison than just his new friend's family, for all were curious to see the young boy riding a buckskin horse and carrying a repeating rifle. It was a long afternoon for John, and when he was invited to stay overnight with Long Walker and Yellow Beads, he declined to accept, saying he had to return to his camp to take care of his other horse. He could not divulge the main reason he would not stay—that he was not sure his horse and rifle would not be stolen during the night.

He returned to his camp in the mountains before dusk to find that everything was just as he had left it.

The day had certainly turned out differently than he had expected when he had left the day before, and the net result of his hunt was no fresh meat to cure and put away for winter. In the months that followed, he saw some of the Indians from Long Walker's village on occasion when they would leave their small farms to hunt. On several of those occasions, he donated a fresh-killed antelope or deer before riding back to his camp. Long Walker and his friends recognized that Chapel was a soul alone, in need of no companionship. They didn't know how he came to be without family at so young an age, for he never told anyone how he came to be in the Chickasaw Nation. One day he was just there. All agreed that his medicine was strong, and that although his body was young and growing, his mind was very old. When he had left the village on that first day, he had no thoughts of ever returning, but the necessity to buy coffee and beans when his meat diet became tiresome caused him to go to the trading post near the village. When he was there, he occasionally stopped to visit Long Walker, who always seemed glad to see him. Although it remained awkward for him, he soon became familiar with the other members of Long Walker's village, and it became easier for him to visit more often. When he had built his camp near the water-fall in the mountains, he had planned to stay only until spring. Spring became summer, and summer became fall, and it was not a good time to leave with winter coming on. He was content in his mountain hideaway. It would be twelve years before he decided it was time to move on. During that time he learned many things from the people of Long Walker's village. With his friend's help, he learned to fashion a strong bow and make his arrows as well. It gave him the opportunity to save precious cartridges when hunting small game, or when silence was necessary. He had always been a good hunter, but now he was as at home in the hills and on the plains as his Chickasaw friends once were before becoming one of the so-called civilized bands. It was a good life, even though there remained a restlessness in his soul that surfaced from time to time, reminding him that two of his parents' killers were still out there somewhere.

Chapter 4

There were no traces of the boy left in the powerful body of the man. When he reached age twenty-five, the same cold, piercing gaze of the boy who had hunted down and killed five desperate men was still present in his eyes, evidence of a boyhood that had never been. Thanks to the First State Bank of Sherman, Texas, he had been able to keep himself in cartridges and supplies as well as buy another horse when J.F.'s buckskin became too old to perform up to the big man's needs. His replacement, a gray gelding, was a stout horse with a strong heart. Although Chapel still preferred a buckskin, the gray was the best horse available to him at the time. The buckskin was allowed to run free in retirement, although he always returned to Chapel's camp at nightfall.

Gone, too, was his father's horse that had served him as a pack animal. Chapel found the old gelding dead one cold morning after a hard frost. It was not unexpected, for the old sorrel had been having difficulty climbing the rugged trail from the pool by the waterfall to Chapel's camp. With no desire to eat his father's faithful horse, he dragged the carcass around to the other side of the mountain, where he skinned it and left the rest to the buzzards. The hide served to patch an area of his roof where rainwater had found a way in. His money was closely budgeted, with none wasted on unnecessary purchases such as clothes. Like many of the Indians he had come to know, he dressed entirely in animal skins, sewn for him by Long Walker's wife. But Yellow Beads had seemed to suddenly grow older, her fingers stiffened by the cold winters. He wasn't sure how much longer she would be able to push her bone needle through the animal hides. He told himself that he might have to revert to white man's clothes.

Even after twelve years, he was still regarded as the strange lonely man with the cold, emotionless eyes. None of the men of the village had ever been to his camp in the mountains, which they could see in the distance from their village, a distance of about fifteen miles—and none had ever had an invitation. Some might think of him as a hermit, and certainly a lonely man, but he was satisfied with his life. It never occurred to him to worry about whether he was happy or not.

He was uncertain if the year was 1886 or 1887. It didn't matter that much to him, but he decided for the sake of curiosity, he would ask Edgar Deacon at the trading post, which Deacon now called a general store. He was on his way there now, it being a chilly day in early winter, and him in need of some supplies. He nudged the gray to pick up the pace when he was in sight of the village, some two miles away. In the next few minutes he heard the gunshots. There were several in rapid succession, pistols from the sound of them, in what he guessed to be a heated exchange. He gave the gray his heels again, causing the horse to break into a lope.

Riding past the outermost shanties of the Chickasaw village, he saw a crowd of people in the middle of the settlement, so he rode straight toward them. "Chapel!" Long Walker cried out when he saw his big friend approaching. "A marshal! He's been shot. I think he's dying!"

The crowd parted to let Chapel pass, most of them immediately relieved, thinking that he would take care of the trouble. "Who shot him?" Chapel asked, looking around the crowd for sign of a gunman.

In answer, several of the people pointed toward the north. "A white man," someone exclaimed excitedly. "He rode off that way!"

In the center of the gathering, a U.S. deputy marshal lay on the ground with two gunshot wounds in his chest. Two of the village's women were doing their best to help the wounded lawman, but the distress in their eyes told Chapel that they were losing him. He stepped down from his horse and knelt beside the dying man. As he looked to see how bad the wounds were, the deputy's eyes fluttered, then opened wide. "Ralph Landry," he gasped painfully. "He's wanted for cattle rustlin' and murder. I almost had him here, but he got the jump on me."

"You just hold still," Chapel said, "and we'll try to

see if we can help you." He said it hoping to offer encouragement, but he didn't give the deputy much chance of surviving.

The deputy seemed to be aware of it as well. "I ain't gonna make it this time," he forced out. "Stay away from Landry. He's a dangerous man." He paused to gather strength enough to say more. "Send somebody to Fort Smith to let 'em know what happened to me, Jim Polson."

"Jim Polson?" Chapel asked. "Is that your name?" The wounded man nodded. "We'll do that," Chapel said. "We'll let 'em know. I'll take you back, so you can tell 'em yourself." Then he realized that the deputy didn't hear him. He was gone. Chapel sat back on his heels, watching the life fade out of the deputy's eyes and thinking about the outlaws who had killed his parents. He hadn't thought about that in a long time, but now he wondered if this poor corpse had a family waiting somewhere for him to come home while he was out chasing down another mad dog.

Impatient for Chapel to act, Long Walker asked, "What should we do? There's no sheriff around here."

"I'll take him back to Fort Smith," Chapel answered. Then he looked up to meet Long Walker's eyes. "Along with that son of a bitch that shot him." He got to his feet and started toward his horse. "Who saw which way he rode outta here?" A young boy sang out that he saw him ride past the corner of his house and cut across the cornfield, heading toward the Washita River.

"Chapel, Fort Smith is three and a half, maybe four days from here," Long Walker informed him. "Maybe it's best to bury him here and let the other man go."

Chapel hesitated only a moment before deciding. "I told him I'd take him back, so that's what I'm gonna do. Right now, I'm goin' after the other one before he gets too far ahead of me. Find somethin' to wrap this deputy up in and lay him across his saddle. I'll be back as soon as I can." He stepped up in the saddle. "And, Long Walker, wrap him up good. That's a long way to tote a dead man."

The deputy's killer made no attempt to disguise a trail, leaving a wide swath of broken corn stalks in his wake. On the north end of the field, he kept going the way he had started, which Chapel knew would strike the Washita in about five miles. He urged the gray on, hoping to catch the outlaw before he made the river and maybe took some effort to lose anyone following. That was not the case, however. Chapel didn't overtake him before he reached the river, but the outlaw—Ralph Landry, he remembered the deputy saying—did not enter the river. Instead, he followed it west, leaving Chapel an easy trail to follow. *It's like he wants me to catch up,* he thought. *But how did he know anyone was following him?* As he loped along the riverbank, carefully watching the trees and brush before him, he thought it out and reasoned that Landry was probably sure the deputy was dead. And there didn't seem much possibility that anyone in the little Chickasaw village would come after him. *So he must figure he's pretty much in the clear.* Chapel found absolute proof of his speculation before the next bend of the river.

He pulled the gray gelding to a hard stop just before rounding the bend when he caught sight of a thin column of smoke wafting up through the cottonwoods before him. Dismounting quickly, he led his horse into the trees and looped the reins around the branch of a bush. With his rifle in hand, he made his way closer to the riverbank to a point where he could see the source of the smoke. *The son of a bitch stopped to eat,* he thought when he saw the outlaw tending a campfire. *That's how much he's worried about somebody following him.* He looked up at the sun. It was still early in the afternoon, too early to camp for the night. He raised his rifle to his shoulder and laid the front sight on the man's back. *I could make this easy,* he thought as he held the rifle steady. *He probably deserves killing. He killed that deputy back there.* It was tempting, but the feeling was different from the last time he had an unsuspecting man in his sights, twelve years ago. At that time, he was purely an executioner, with no thought but to avenge his parents and rid the world of the persons who took their lives. Maybe it was best to let a judge decide what fate this man deserved. "Damn!" He cursed himself for his pity. "I'll take him back to Fort Smith with the deputy."

Since the outlaw seemed to have just started his camp, Chapel figured he had plenty of time to decide the best way to approach him. There wasn't enough cover around him to slip in close to surprise him. He had selected an open area for his fire where he had a clear field of vision in all directions. With time to do it, he decided the best chance he had was to drop back and take a wide circle around the hills on the other side of the river, then cross back over and approach the camp from the west. If he was lucky, Landry would not think it was anyone after him, considering Chapel would be coming from the opposite direction. *Just might work,* he thought, and went back for his horse. Before stepping up in the saddle, he unbuckled his pistol, pulled it out of the holster, then put them both in his saddlebag.

Ralph Landry pulled a slab of salt pork from his saddlebag and sliced off a half-dozen pieces, dropping them in his frying pan one by one. "That damn Polson jumped me before I could eat breakfast this mornin'," he said to himself. "Well, he won't be chasin' nobody else, and that's a fact." He chuckled as if it were a joke. He was well pleased with himself. He had thought it bad luck that Jim Polson had picked up his trail after he robbed the bank and shot a teller in McAlester. Polson was a regular bulldog once he got the scent, and he had a reputation for getting every man he went after. "But he hadn't run into ol' Ralph Landry before!" he exclaimed. He had beaten the law again, and, armed with a Winchester '73, he felt invincible, even if those Indian farmers got up a posse, which he felt was very unlikely.

He got up from the fire and wrapped the rest of the slab of pork in a cloth sack. About to return it to his saddlebag, he hesitated when he caught sight of something moving a couple hundred yards up the riverbank. Still holding the pork in his hand while poised over his saddlebag, he stood frozen as he strained to see what manner of man was approaching his camp. After a minute, while the rider continued to close the distance between them, Landry declared, "It's a damn Injun." The rider was dressed in animal skins, and it was apparent he was alone. Landry dropped his bacon in the saddlebag, drew his Winchester from the saddle sling, and casually walked back by the fire, where he squatted on his heels and waited. *Most likely wanting something to eat*, he thought. *Well, he ain't gettin' a damn thing here.* "'Cept maybe a bullet up his hind end, if he's carryin' anythin' valuable," he declared aloud. He didn't realize his visitor was a white man until he swung his horse off the river trail and headed directly toward him.

"Good day to ya," Chapel called out. "I saw your fire and thought you might have a cup of coffee to spare." He took special note of the Winchester cradled in Landry's arms as he pulled the gray up before the fire. The man was wary. It was not going to be easy to capture him.

"Is that a fact?" Landry replied, his lip curled in a sneer. "Well, you thought wrong, unless you got somethin' to pay for a cup of this coffee. I just might be willin' to trade you some, though, if you've got somethin' that's worth a damn."

"Well, I might have somethin' you could use, at that," Chapel said. "Mind if I step down?"

"Nah, step on down. Whaddaya got?"

"I've got a genuine Indian cure for meanness," Chapel replied as he dismounted and turned to open his saddlebag.

"A cure for what?" Landry questioned, his caution relaxed, since Chapel's rifle was still in the scabbard, and he wasn't wearing a gun belt.

"Meanness," Chapel repeated as he took his pistol out of the saddlebag and turned to level it at the unsuspecting outlaw. "It's a .44 Colt. Takes the meanness right outta them." Startled, Landry couldn't react. "Now,

I'm takin' you back to answer for that deputy you just killed back there."

"Why, you son of a . . . ," Landry blurted when he realized he'd been bamboozled.

"Don't give me a reason to shoot you," Chapel warned when Landry started to shift his rifle around. "You'd best drop that rifle on the ground."

Still in a squatting position, and helpless to make a sudden move, Landry was nevertheless opposed to surrendering to the granite-faced man in buckskins. "You might think you've got the drop on me," he said in a contemptuous sneer, "but I can whip this rifle around before you can get off two shots. And one shot might not be enough to kill me. Maybe you oughta think about that."

"Drop the rifle," Chapel repeated. "You make a move with it, and you'll be dead before you even think about pullin' that trigger."

Landry stared at the imperturbable young man for a moment before finally saying, "All right, I'll drop it. You got the jump on me." He took the rifle in both hands and held it out before him as if preparing to lay it on the ground. "You don't look like no lawman I've ever seen before. When did you get on my trail?" He was counting on Chapel to relax his guard. When his rifle was almost on the ground, Landry made his move. Suddenly springing to the side, he whipped the rifle up and aimed it at Chapel. Before he could pull the trigger, a small dark hole suddenly appeared in the middle of his forehead, and he collapsed to the ground.

"Damn fool," Chapel pronounced, and reached down

to pull the rifle from his lifeless hands. "You'll be a sight less trouble to carry back to Fort Smith, though." He took a few moments to examine the Winchester, comparing it to the Henry he had carried since he killed J.F. twelve years before. He had heard talk about the Winchester, but living in the isolation of his mountain camp, he had never had the occasion to actually hold one in his hands. It had a good feel. The wood forearm was a definite improvement over his Henry, which had none, but the major difference was the rear-loading port. The magazine on his Henry had to be loaded from the muzzle end of the weapon. He glanced down at the corpse at his feet and murmured, "Mind if I try it?" He sighted on a dead limb on a tree across the river and squeezed the trigger. The limb split, half of it falling to the ground. Chapel quickly cocked the rifle and fired another round, which knocked off another piece of the limb. A partnership was immediately established. He walked over to his horse and pulled the Henry from the saddle scabbard, replacing it with the Winchester. The Henry was placed in Landry's saddle sling.

When he returned to Long Walker's village, he found the deputy marshal's horse tied at his friend's cabin with the deputy's body wrapped in a piece of canvas from an old army tent and tied securely to the saddle. There was still a sizable gathering standing around the cabin, waiting for Chapel's return. And when he showed up leading the horse with the outlaw's body across the saddle, a general murmur arose from the spectators. "I figured the man was as good as dead as soon as you set out after him," Long Walker said.

"I gave him a chance to give up," Chapel said. "He

didn't take it." His words were followed by a few grunts of approval in the crowd of spectators. "I reckon I'll be gettin' started for Fort Smith right away before those bodies start smellin'." Before he left, he made Long Walker a present of his Henry rifle, along with a box of cartridges. The rifle had been a good true partner to him, and he preferred to give it to someone who needed it, and someone he felt worthy of the trusty weapon. Long Walker was touched by Chapel's show of friendship. In the years since he had first met Chapel, the boy, and later the man, Chapel had never demonstrated anything more than a detached courtesy.

Chapel made a brief stop back at his mountain camp to collect all the things he needed to exist for however long he might be gone. What he left amounted to very little, since he lived a simple day-to-day existence. Based upon the cargo he was transporting, he thought it best to get under way as soon as possible before his goods began to spoil. The one thing he counted upon in his favor was the weather. If the cold held for a few days, he should expect the bodies to make it in reasonable condition—the deputy, especially, wrapped in canvas the way he was. He had his doubts about Landry, who was not packaged nearly as well—Chapel's old blanket with the singed edges was all he was willing to sacrifice for the outlaw's burial shroud. By Long Walker's estimate, it would take four days to reach Fort Smith. Chapel planned to make it in three at the most.

Riding until well past sundown on the first day, he stopped only when his horses began to tire. Because of his late start, he was able to travel only about fifteen miles before stopping beside a slowly moving stream. After he pulled the saddle off the gray, he lifted the bodies from the other two horses and laid them side by side a little downstream from his camp. Then he un-saddled the other horses. His supper consisted of a few strips of deer jerky roasted over the fire, washed down with half a pot of coffee. It was enough to sustain him.

Breaking camp at first light, he loaded his morbid string of packhorses and continued on a northeasterly course, assuming that, if he had figured it correctly, he would strike the Canadian River by the end of the day. Stopping only occasionally to rest his horses, he pushed on until they told him they needed a longer rest. Only then did he build a fire and roast some jerky for him-self. His concern was for the weather, for there seemed to be a warming trend setting in, which did not sound like good news for his cargo. There was a general clear-ing of the clouds that had cloaked the territory for more than a week, and the sun made an appearance before he loaded up his carcasses and started out again. Nightfall found him at the banks of the Canadian where the river ran on a more easterly course before turning back to the northeast.

When he unloaded his cargo that night, he was not certain, but he thought he detected the hint of an unpleasant odor. It was most noticeable from Landry's corpse, and when he laid it on the ground and pulled the blanket away, he could see signs that the body was bloating. "Damn!" he uttered in disgust when he saw evidence of early maggot infestation. "They must have gotten in the body while it was lying on the ground the night before." He considered leaving the late outlaw to the buzzards. "Why wouldn't they just take my word for it that he's dead?" When there was no answer from the deputy's corpse, Chapel said, "This is as far as I'm haulin' your stinkin' ass across this territory." He grabbed the corpse by the ankles and dragged it away from his camp, leaving it and his blanket in a gully. The Chickasaws had done a better job of wrapping the deputy's body, so he speculated that he might make it to Fort Smith before they could smell him coming.

The next day, he left early again, following the river toward its confluence with the Arkansas. Looking over his shoulder as he rode away, he saw a circle of buzzards already gathering over the riverbank behind him. Camp that night found him still a full day's ride from Fort Smith. Anxious to rid himself of the chore he had taken on, he was in the saddle again before sunup and pushing the horses to increase the pace. With one empty saddle now, he alternated the horses, letting each horse go without a load for part of the day. At the end of the day, nightfall caught him still short of the town on the banks of the Arkansas, so he was not to reach his destination until the following morning.

The weather turned cold again overnight, leaving him with a frosty morning to make his entrance at Fort Smith with his grisly load. Since it was his first time in the town, he had to ask someone for directions to the marshal's office. Everyone he passed paused to gawk at the strange sight plodding down the main street with the solemn rider, dressed in buckskins from head to toe, leading two horses, one with a body draped across the saddle. Although any one of the gawkers would have been glad to direct him, if only to find out where he was going, he chose a man sweeping the sidewalk of a hardware store.

"Mornin'," the proprietor of the hardware store offered while looking the odd stranger over with no attempt to hide his astonishment. "You looking for the sheriff or the undertaker?"

"I reckon I'm lookin' for the U.S. marshal," Chapel answered.

"John Council," the man replied. "His office is in the courthouse—that building down at the other end of the street." He pointed to a brick building with a wide porch on the front. The building was originally a barracks when Fort Smith was occupied by soldiers. The basement of the building was now used as a jail and notoriously known as Hell on the Border to outlaws who had spent time there. Upstairs over the jail was the courtroom of Judge Isaac C. Parker, who had come to be known as the Hanging Judge because of the number of outlaws who had swung from the gallows at Fort Smith.

Chapel had heard of him and was now caught wondering how his reception would be if they knew about the executions he had carried out as a boy. It had never occurred to him that most people would find it highly unlikely that a thirteen-year-old boy could accomplish what he did. *Well, this ain't gonna take long*, he thought. *As soon as I find this marshal, I'm done here.* "John Council, you say? Much obliged." He nudged the gray and left the store owner staring after the corpse draped over one of the saddles.

As was often his habit, John Council, U.S. marshal for the Western District of Arkansas, was standing at the window of his office, staring out the window—his way of thinking through problems that challenged him. The problem on his mind this morning was a recent lack of deputy marshals to cover the district that fell under his supervision. The attrition rate had been especially high during the past year with increased reports of robbery, cattle rustling, and killings in the part of his district across the river known as the Nations. "Now what?" he murmured when he saw what he thought at first to be an Indian pulling up to the hitching rail with what was surely a body. Not waiting to make sure, since he was fairly certain the man was coming to see him, he walked out of his office and down to the porch to intercept the stranger.

Chapel looked up to see the marshal cross the porch and start down the steps toward him. "You looking for me?" Council asked. "Who's lying across that saddle?"

"Are you John Council?" Chapel asked.

"I am."

"Well, I got one of your deputies here—said his name was Jim Polson," Chapel said.

No news could be more distressing to Council. Jim Polson was one of his most reliable deputies. "Damn," he cursed softly. "Who did it?" Then, before Chapel could answer, Council asked, "Who are you?"

"Chapel," he answered. "Feller ridin' that horse shot him."

"What fellow?" Council insisted. "Where is he?"

"Dead."

Council began to lose patience with the buckskin-clad stranger. "Damn it, man, can you talk? Who shot my deputy? Tell me what happened."

Chapel's stony expression remained on his face while he made an effort to give the marshal details. "Your man said the feller's name was Landry—somethin' Landry. I forgot his first name. That's his horse and stuff there."

"How'd you get involved in this?" Council asked, still trying to get the whole story out of the tight-lipped man.

"I told your man I'd see that he got back here, so you'd know about it."

"You still haven't told me what I need to know," Council continued. "You brought Polson's body back. What about Landry's body? Where is it?"

"In a gully back by the Canadian. It was startin' to stink." Chapel hesitated a moment, then repeated, "But there's his horse and stuff."

Council studied the big man's face for a few moments before asking, "Did you shoot Landry?"

"I gave him a chance to come peaceable. He didn't take it," Chapel answered.

Council continued to study the granite countenance of the somber man before him for a few moments more while running a sudden idea through his mind. He couldn't help wondering if he might be looking at Jim Polson's replacement. But first, he had to find out a little more about the man. "All right," he said, "you did a good job bringing Jim's body back here. I appreciate it. Tell you what—I'll have somebody take care of the body and the extra horses, and you and I can go over to the hotel and get a bite to eat. Whaddaya say?"

Chapel was not prepared for the invitation. He hesitated, reluctant to spend any more time than necessary for someone to take the body off his hands. Judging from Council's friendly expression, however, there appeared to be no intention of blaming him for the deputy's death, so he shrugged and said, "I reckon I could do that."

"Good," Council said. "You look like you've been living like an Indian for a while. You might enjoy some good home cooking, and they've got a good cook at the hotel."

It didn't sound like a bad idea at that, so Chapel waited while Council went inside the jail and got a guard to take care of the body and horses. As it turned out, it was satisfying, for Chapel had not sat down to a full table of food since his parents had been murdered. Beef stew with potatoes, carrots, and peas; oven-baked bread; and coffee, followed up with a generous slice of apple pie. He had forgotten such fare existed. The generous meal served to loosen the otherwise reluctant tongue of the stoic man, and John Council was able to get a more complete picture of the events that had happened in the Chickasaw Nation, as well as the character of the man he was considering whether to offer employment. Chapel sounded like the kind of man he needed, one who would go after a dangerous outlaw like Landry. And Chapel seemed honest enough. He had brought in the horses and the weapons that had belonged to Polson. It didn't escape his eye that Landry's saddle scabbard was empty while there was a Winchester '73 on the saddle of Chapel's gray. He figured it reasonable payment for going after Landry. "You got any family to speak of?" Council asked.

"Nope," Chapel replied as he spread a slab of butter across another piece of bread.

"No wife, no young'uns? Not even an Indian wife back there in the Nations?"

"Nope."

"You had any schooling?"

"Nope."

"So you can't read or write?"

Chapel shrugged. There had never been any need for it in his life to this point, but he answered, "I can read and write. My ma taught me, but it's been a while since I tried."

"That's all right," Council quickly responded, his mind made up. He was a perfect candidate—no wife, no family, accustomed to living off the land, and apparently fearless—so he made the move. "I'm offering you a job as a deputy marshal." He went on to explain the fee system and mileage payments for arresting outlaws, giving as an example Jim Polson's income of five hundred dollars for the prior year. "It's a damn hard job, and one that might cost you your life, like Polson, but it's a job that's steady, because it doesn't look like we're gonna run short of outlaws. Whaddaya say? It's better than living hand to mouth in Indian Territory." He waited for a minute, but Chapel was hesitant to answer. "I could arrange an advance for you to get yourself whatever things you need. Looks like you could use some clothes. Are those animal hides all you've got?"

"Yep," Chapel answered, still trying to decide what he should do. The money he had been able to hoard since he was a boy was rapidly running out, so the prospect of being paid was more than tempting. In the end, he agreed to give it a try for a few months to see if it was something he could do. The fact that he would be working in the Nations swayed him, but Council figured it was the dinner at the hotel. They shook on it, and Council said he would have him appointed by the governor of Arkansas. While he waited for the official order, he proposed to send Chapel over to Checotah in the Creek Nation on a trial run to pick up a prisoner being held in the town's jail. He figured it would be a chance to see if Chapel could bring one back alive to stand trial.

"You ain't wanted by the law anywhere, are you?" Council asked. When Chapel replied that he was not, Council opened his desk drawer and took out a badge. "I'm gonna go ahead and give you this, because I don't expect any problem with your appointment. It'll take a while before I get the official word back, and in the meantime, I've got a prisoner sitting over in Checotah in a storeroom they use for a jail. I need to have him brought back to stand trial for cattle rustling." He looked Chapel in the eye and asked, "Can you handle that job?"

"I reckon," Chapel replied.

"Good," Council said. "You bring him back in good condition and you'll get six cents a mile for going over there, and ten cents a mile for you and the prisoner on the return trip. It's about sixty miles to Checotah, so you can figure that up, but don't forget that I get twenty-five percent of all your fees. That's part of how I get paid." When Chapel frowned, but made no comment, Council did a quick calculation for him. "That comes up to nine dollars and sixty cents, and your part of it is seven dollars and twenty cents. That oughta take care of your expenses." Chapel nodded. He figured to make it in a day and a half each way, so it seemed fair to him. He had never had a job before, and the novelty of it appealed to him.

William Arrow Feather, the acting sheriff of Checotah, was relieved to see the deputy marshal arrive late one afternoon. The little settlement had no facility to house prisoners, and he was worried that Roy Wallace was going to find a way out of the feed storeroom he was being held in before the deputy showed up. "I'm glad to see you," he said in greeting Chapel. "You plannin' on startin' back in the mornin'?"

"I'm startin' back right now, just as soon as you get his horse," Chapel replied.

"You ain't even gonna get some supper and rest up your horse?"

"It ain't been that long since I rested him," Chapel said.

Arrow Feather shrugged indifferently and sent a boy to get Wallace's horse. "I'll get Roy ready to go," he said, and unlocked the padlock on the door of the shed. "Come on out, Roy. The deputy's here to take you to Fort Smith."

"It's about time," Wallace replied. "I can't wait to get outta this stink hole you call a jail." He walked outside, blinking against the late-afternoon sun. When his eyes became adjusted, he turned his full attention to the lawman who had come to transport him back to Fort Smith. When he looked into the lifeless gaze of the formidable figure studying him in return, he at once felt a tinge of fear tracing his spine. The man looked more like an executioner than a deputy, and he had the sudden urge to run. His first mistake was that he gave in to the urge, and suddenly bolted past William Arrow Feather, knocking the sheriff aside. His second mistake was in misjudging the pantherlike reflexes of the deputy, thinking a man his size would not be able to move so quickly. Chapel was behind the fleeing man immediately, and with one deft move of his foot, he tripped Wallace, causing him to land face-first on the ground. Before his body slid to a stop in the hard dirt, Chapel straddled him and roped his wrists together behind his back.

"That'll be the last time you'll take a notion to run," Chapel told him unemotionally. "The next time, you'll get a bullet in the back. My job is to take you in. Makes no difference to me if it's alive or dead." He saw no reason to tell his prisoner that John Council had stressed that he wanted the prisoner returned alive.

Wallace made no more attempts to escape, and had he been able to honestly evaluate his treatment on the ride to Fort Smith, he would have had to admit, he had suffered no undue hardship. There would be occasions in the months to come, when swapping experiences with other prisoners, when Wallace would recall the faraway look in Chapel's somber gaze, as if compassion could take no root in the desolate region behind his eyes.

That was the first of many successful assignments to follow over the next nine years, a period that established Chapel as Council's number one deputy, especially if the job promised to be riskier than usual. The times that Chapel worked with other deputies were very few, because of the solitary nature of the man and complaints from some deputies that his brooding demeanor made them nervous. But none could deny his dogged determination to hunt down an outlaw, nor his seemingly fearless approach to the job. Anyone who came into contact with him, on either side of the law, had to agree that Chapel was born to do the job he was doing. None really knew the anvil of death that had forged a young boy into a relentless hunter of men. As for Chapel himself, the sense of having failed to complete the revenge of his parents' murders faded to a dark closet in the back of his mind, where he kept it, never to be forgotten. And sometimes his dreams were haunted by the image of the two murderers who escaped him those many years ago. No one knew what went on in the brain behind those dark, lifeless eyes, for no one ever got close enough to Chapel to probe into his private thoughts. His only partner was his horse, and the years of hard riding caused him to retire the gray he had been riding and begin a new partnership with another buckskin, always his first choice.

Chapter 5

Deputy U.S. marshal Bill McDonald pulled his horse to a stop while signaling the jail wagon behind him to do the same. The formidable figure approaching him on a buckskin horse looked as if he might belong inside the locked cage with the three cattle thieves McDonald was hauling to Fort Supply. He eased his rifle up a little in his saddle scabbard while keeping a wary eye on the stranger. "Bob," he called back without taking his eyes off the rider, "keep your rifle handy. I don't like the looks of this jasper comin' to meet us."

"I hear ya," Bob Joyner answered. "You know him?"

"Nope, never saw him before." McDonald sat his horse and waited for the stranger to close the distance between them to about twenty yards before he held up his hand to stop him. The rider drew up when signaled. The three rustlers in the cage were half of a dangerous gang that had been hiding out in the Oklahoma Outlet, known as No Man's Land, a section of

unsettled Indian Territory that had attracted outlaws
from all over Oklahoma and Texas. There was a fourth
man on the back of the wagon as well: wounded deputy Jack Nevitt. His horse and the horses belonging to
the three rustlers were tied on behind the wagon.
"What can I do for you, mister?" McDonald asked.

"I reckon you'd be Bill McDonald," the stranger
replied. "Tell your man back there on the wagon to rest
that rifle. He ain't gonna need it for me."

"That so?" McDonald responded. "Who the hell
are you?"

"My name's Chapel. I'm a deputy marshal workin'
outta Fort Smith. I was sent over this way to find you."
He nudged the buckskin and moved up closer to
McDonald. "My boss said for me to offer my help if
you needed it to run down some of the outlaws in the
Outlet—thought you might could use some." He didn't
see any need to tell him his boss' real interest was to
find out if there was anything to concern him back in
Fort Smith. Bill McDonald's district covered southern
Kansas and northern Texas, but the marshal over there
had been doing a lot of talking about cleaning up the
Cherokee Outlet in Oklahoma. Since Oklahoma Indian
Territory came under Fort Smith authority, Chapel's
boss thought it a good idea to know just what the hell
was going on. Everybody knew the Outlet was a haven
for outlaws of all stripes, and McDonald was making
quite a name for himself in his campaign to rid the territory of all outlaws. John Council was convinced that
it was mainly the work of a Texas politician hoping to
gain a name for himself as a defender of law and order.
Whatever the reason, Council was concerned that it

might reflect on the efficiency of his office, so he sent his best man to find out.

"Is that a fact?" McDonald replied. "Chapel, huh? I've heard of you." He turned to tell Bob Joyner to relax. Back to Chapel then, he remarked, "I reckon I can use all the help I can get. We roused them three outta their hole, but half of their gang got away, the mean half, ol' Bevo Rooks and his three sons. They headed toward Texas, but they shot one of my boys up pretty bad. I've got to take him back to the army doctor at Fort Supply, so I had to let Rooks go. I expect he ain't plannin' to come back to this territory, anyway. He knows I'll get on his trail again, so if he's smart, he'd better keep goin' all the way to Mexico. My man ain't the only one Rooks and his boys shot. They killed a man and his wife over near the Texas border for no reason at all that I could see."

"How long ago was that?" Chapel asked.

"Two weeks ago. I thought we had 'em this time when we run up on them three in the wagon, and Rooks and his boys were with 'em. But they saw me comin', and sneaked out the back of a stand of cottonwoods before I could send Bob or Jack around to cut 'em off." McDonald cocked his head to remark, "The old man is slick. I'll give him that, and his sons are as mean as they come."

"When did the shoot-out happen?" Chapel asked.

"This mornin', couple of hours ago," McDonald answered.

"Well, I came to help, so I'll go on back the way you came. Their trail oughta be fresh enough to follow. Maybe I can catch up with 'em."

"You're gonna need to be damn careful goin' after that bunch of rattlesnakes by yourself," McDonald cautioned. "Like I said, that old man is pretty damn slick. Even if you caught 'em, you'd have your hands full tryin' to bring 'em in."

Chapel nodded thoughtfully before replying. He appreciated the warning McDonald had expressed, but he had heard of the notorious Bevo Rooks even though he had had no occasion to confront the outlaw in person. The fact that he had now shot a lawman made it more urgent to Chapel to bring him and his sons to justice. Chapel always worked alone; there was no question as to whether or not he would go after the four outlaws. "I'll go along now," he told McDonald. "You'd best get your man to the doctor." McDonald told him that the shoot-out had taken place about six miles back, on the Canadian River in a stand of trees opposite a wide sandbar in the middle of the river. "I'll find it and go from there," Chapel said. So ended his brief meeting with the deputy marshal who was reported to be clearing the Cherokee Outlet of murderers and robbers.

Bob Joyner pulled the jail wagon up beside McDonald. "I don't think that feller knows what he's gettin' into."

"Maybe not, but I've heard some talk about him and his work in the Nations. He's supposed to be as mean as the outlaws he goes after."

"He damn sure looks it," Joyner remarked. He turned then and asked, "You doin' all right back there, Jack?"

"I'm hangin' on," Nevitt replied weakly.

"I'm sorry you ain't got better company to ride with,"
McDonald said, referring to the three sullen prisoners
in the cage, "but we'll try to get you to the doctor as
fast as we can."

The grove of cottonwoods where McDonald and his
men had confronted the outlaws was easy to find. As
the deputy had told him, there was a wide sandbar in
the middle of the shallow water there. Evidence of the
camp was obvious enough, and Chapel figured they
must have been there for a couple of days at least. Small
coals were still flickering in the morning's campfire.
Chapel kicked some sand on them with his boot. His
only interest at this point was to pick up the trail of the
departing four who had escaped McDonald's raid, and
that, too, was easy enough to find. It was apparent that
Rooks and his boys had charged into the river and
crossed over to the other bank while their confederates
were no doubt in a gun battle with the lawmen. Standing on the riverbank, Chapel could see the tracks of the
horses on the sandbar. He stepped up in the saddle
and guided the buckskin into the muddy water.

There had been no attempt to hide their hoofprints
when they had emerged from the water on the other
side. They were obviously in full flight at the time.
Chapel urged his horse into a comfortable lope as he
followed the obvious tracks along the river. They led to
the west for more than a mile before turning to cross
a treeless prairie toward a range of hills to the south.
The thought crossed his mind that a man on a horse
could be seen a long way off on that open expanse
between the river and the hills, but the men he chased

had long since ridden this way, and they were riding hard at the time. He would be lucky to catch up to them by the next day. It had been some time since he had traveled in this part of the territory, so he was not sure how extensive a range of hills he was approaching. His concern was that Rooks might take more pains to hide his tracks once he reached the cover of the hills. It seemed more of a possibility when he came closer to the ridge, because there appeared to be another ridge behind the first one.

The tracks he followed appeared to be heading toward a rocky ravine at the base of a barren slope. The length of the horses' strides told him that they had still been at a full gallop at this point, and they were bound to be tired out. *Rooks would have had to find a good place to rest them,* he thought, *so that's why he headed for the ravine. Probably planning to keep riding until darkness forces him to camp.* He looked again at the hills he was riding toward, thinking again of his vulnerability on the open expanse of prairie. Rooks should be long gone from this place; yet he felt a need to be careful, even though the mouth of the ravine was still a good distance beyond the range of his Winchester.

That was the last thought he remembered before his world took a sudden spin. The impact of the .50-90 Sharps slug that slammed into his chest knocked him out of the saddle and landed him stunned on the hard ground. His whole body felt frozen, unable to move. He knew he was hurt, but he didn't realize he was shot until he felt the warm blood spread across his chest and back. The bullet had gone all the way through him. In moments, his rational mind righted itself, and he realized he had been bushwhacked. In a panic to get up to defend himself, he tried to rise to his hands and knees, but he was unable to move. He felt fire in his chest as if he had been speared with a hot poker. Soon his shirt was soaked in blood, and he was helpless to stop it. This was the way they found him when they rode out of the ravine.

"That was a helluva shot, six hundred yards if it's a foot," Crown Rooks shouted excitedly as Bevo and his sons pulled up to surround the wounded deputy marshal. "Let's see you match that with your Winchesters," he gloated as he stared down at Chapel, defenseless before them.

Father and sons all dismounted to inspect the body. Crown, the eldest son, grabbed Chapel by the shoulder and rolled him on his side to look at his back. Pleased with what he saw, he boasted, "Through and through; no wonder my Sharps can knock a buffalo down." He released Chapel's shoulder, letting him fall back flat. The sudden motion forced an involuntary grunt of pain from the wounded man, which in turn caused Crown to step quickly back. "He ain't dead," he exclaimed.

An interested bystander to that point, Bevo said, "Maybe not, but he might as well be. He looks damn near bled out now. Let's see why he was trackin' us." He knelt down beside Chapel and roughly searched his pockets. "Sometimes if they ain't wearin' no vest, they'll pin that tin badge inside a pocket, so it won't reflect the sun. Yep, there it is," he said after a moment. "He was trackin' us, all right. He's a damn marshal."

"Well, he ain't gonna do no trackin' no more," Corbett, the middle son, smirked. "He's a big'un, ain't he?

I believe you needed that buffalo gun, Crown." He knelt down to unbuckle Chapel's belt, then pulled it and his holster out from under him. His brothers soon joined in and stripped the helpless man of anything of value: boots, hat, any money they found.

"Well, I'll be damned . . . ," Corbett blurted. "Look at what I found." He held Chapel's gun belt out for his father to see. "Look at what that says."

"Hell, tell me," Bevo shot back. "You're the one that can read."

"C-H-A-P-E-L," Corbett spelled out, "Chapel. This son of a bitch is that he-bear deputy out of Fort Smith that's got everybody runnin' scared."

Bevo was so excited, he couldn't speak for a moment. "Well, ain't that somethin'? We got us Deputy Marshal Chapel hisself. There's a lot of bastards that would like to shake our hands right now." He stared out across the prairie, toward the Canadian River. "I don't see no sign of anybody else," he declared. "I think the son of a bitch was trailin' us by hisself. I always heard he went huntin' alone." He turned his attention back to the wounded man before him, studying him intently. Even when he was in pain and helpless, the notorious deputy marshal's face was deadly and defiant.

"Well, he sure as hell found us, didn't he, Pa?" Cotton, the youngest at fourteen, crowed.

"I reckon he did," Bevo replied. "I don't believe he's too happy about it, though."

Cotton pulled out his pistol and cocked it. "I'll go ahead and finish him off."

"Hold on, Cotton," Bevo ordered. He was still studying the wounded man intensely, somewhat disappointed that Chapel had not attempted to beg for his life. The deputy was as close to death as any man he had ever seen to still be breathing. Bevo enjoyed the fact that the lawman was dying, and he was reluctant to make his passage any easier. He knelt down beside the helpless lawman, and with his face no more than a few inches from Chapel's, he pronounced his death sentence. "I expect right about now, you're hopin' I let my boy finish you off, put you outta your misery, ain't you, Deputy Chapel? You look damn near bled out already. Wonder how long it'll take you to die, lawman? Oughta be some buzzards comin' to start eatin' on you before long. If I had to guess, I'd say it's about forty or fifty miles from here to Fort Supply, and there ain't as much as a stray Injun lodge between here and there." Getting to his feet again, he turned to his son, who was waiting with pistol cocked. "We'll just be on our way and leave this marshal to see if he's gonna be dead before the buzzards and the coyotes find him."

"Ah, Pa," Cotton protested, "lemme shoot him."

"And put him outta his misery?" Bevo replied. "Why would you wanna do that? We'll let him think about how smart he was to come lookin' for Bevo Rooks—out here with no horse, no boots, nothin', while the blood keeps runnin' outta him. Leave him be, right where he's a-layin'." He paused to point an accusing finger at Chapel. "You think about that, lawman, when the buzzards start a-chewin' on your hide, and you ain't got the strength to do nothin' about it." He stood up then. "It's time to go, boys. I heard there's cattle aplenty to steal down south of El Paso. Corbett, grab that buckskin's reins and tie him on behind you. Hook that gun belt over the saddle horn. Let's get goin'. I wanna make the other side of them hills before supper."

After a few moments more to get one last contemptuous look at the dying lawman, Bevo's three sons prepared to climb back on their horses. "When you meet the devil," Crown paused to crow, "tell him Bevo Rooks and his boys has got everythin' under control on this side." His comment caused a round of chuckles from his father and brothers.

He lay right where they left him for a long time after the sound of their horses' hooves had faded away before he attempted to move. It was hard to disagree with Rooks' evaluation of his chances. Weak and in severe pain, he knew he was dying, and he wondered how long it would be before he stepped through that dark doorway. The best thing to do, and in reality his only option, was to lie quietly and wait, hoping that the grim reaper came for him before the buzzards made their call. With one weak hand, he pulled his shirttail out and, balling it up, tried to press it against the hole in his chest. There was nothing he could do for the exit hole in his back.

As he lay there, thinking about the events that had led him to death's door, he felt angry over having blundered blindly into the ambush. *I won't make that mistake again,* he thought, then immediately smiled at the unintended macabre humor. A spasm of pain shot through his chest then, reminding him that he was still alive, so he resigned himself to wait patiently for the end. His surrender lasted for only a few moments, however, when he suddenly announced, "To hell with this. I ain't ready to die—not by a long shot."

With all the strength he could summon, he rolled over on his belly. After a few moments to catch his breath, he pushed up painfully to his hands and knees. Resolved to defy Old Man Death, he forced himself to crawl, vowing that he was not going to wait for the old fellow. *He's gonna have to come after me,* he thought.

Surviving on willpower alone, he crawled over the barren ground inch by painful inch until he became too weak to continue and had to collapse flat again to rest. His efforts had caused the blood to flow anew, but he felt helpless to do anything to stop it, so he just lay there, hoping to muster enough strength to start again. After a while, he summoned the determination to push on. His weary routine repeated itself for most of the afternoon, crawling until he was forced to rest, each segment of crawling becoming shorter while the rest periods became longer. The afternoon sun, still warm this late in the fall, seemed to suck up any additional strength he had left. Had he known that his afternoon's progress was not even as much as a mile, he might have given up long before he finally lay flat again, totally exhausted. The sun, the lack of water, the loss of blood, and his failing strength finally drained him, and he did not know if he could summon the willpower to go on.

He wasn't sure how long he had been lying there with his face in the sand when he became aware of a shadow over him. It did not remain, however. It seemed to swoop over him, only to return again and again. His feverish brain could not make sense of it at first until he suddenly realized the shadows were from the wings of a buzzard. "I'll be damned!" he exclaimed defiantly, and struggled to his hands and knees. "I ain't dead yet," he declared stubbornly, and forced himself to crawl. Drained of all the strength he had left, he soon collapsed, never hearing the shot fired, or the thump of the buzzard's body landing beside him.

Army scout Tom Turnipseed held his rifle ready to fire again, but his first shot had caused the other buzzards to draw away from the body lying on the prairie floor. He turned then and signaled for the cavalry patrol, already coming to meet him at a gallop. "I believe we found that feller the marshal said was out this way," he reported when the patrol caught up to him.

"What was the shot?" Lieutenant Chad Harrington asked.

"Buzzard," Turnipseed replied, and pointed to the bodies of the man and the buzzard lying side by side.

"Is he alive?" Harrington asked as he urged his horse forward.

"I don't think so, Lieutenant," Turnipseed responded. "I just now spotted him myself. He don't look very alive, though."

When they pulled up before the man lying still on the ground, they dismounted and gathered around the body. "Damned if he ain't a mess," Sergeant Milton Evers remarked. "Wonder how far he crawled before he died." He knelt down beside the body and rolled it over on its back. Pulling the bloody balled-up shirttail from the wound, he exclaimed, "Looks like somebody shot him with a buffalo gun or somethin'. Stripped him of everythin'. I'd say it was Injuns if they hadn't left his hair."

Harrington knelt down to see for himself. "Yep, he must be that deputy out of Fort Smith McDonald told us about, so I guess we'd best take his body back with us. Sergeant, load him on one of the horses."

"Yes, sir," Evers replied, and turned to decide which trooper would carry the corpse behind his saddle. "Pollard," he decided, "give me a hand here."

"Yes, Sergeant," Pollard responded reluctantly. He knew he got stuck with the body because he was the smallest, and it would therefore result in the least weight on the horse. He knelt down and took hold of Chapel's shoulders, preparing to lift as soon as one of the other troopers grabbed his feet. "Whoa!" he exclaimed when Chapel's eyes blinked for a second. "He ain't dead!"

"You just got spooked," Evers said, causing the other men to laugh at Pollard's expense. "It's just his body drawin' up. Hell, throw him up on that horse."

"I ain't foolin' you, Sergeant," Pollard insisted. "This man's still alive. I can see blood pumpin' in the vein on his neck."

"Let me see," Lieutenant Harrington said, and knelt down beside Chapel again. Taking his wrist in his hand, he felt around for a few moments before finding a weak pulse, but it was a pulse. "Pollard's right. This man's alive."

"Barely," Sergeant Evers said. "You might as well say he's dead."

"Well, it sure as hell isn't gonna help him any to bounce him all the way back to Fort Supply on the back of a horse," Harrington said. "Sergeant, send a couple of men back to the river to cut a couple of poles for a travois."

Tom Turnipseed, an interested spectator, remained seated in his saddle as two troopers loped off toward the river. He shook his head slowly and muttered to himself, "That man's dead."

Much to Turnipseed's surprise, the dead man opened his eyes before the two troopers returned with travois poles. Confused, Chapel said nothing at first while he stared up at Evers, who was inspecting his wound. When Evers realized that the wounded man was awake, he said, "Take it easy, fellow. You've got a nasty-lookin' hole in your chest. We're gonna take you back to the surgeon at Fort Supply, but you're gonna have to hold on for a while, cause it's a two-day ride. Can you do that?"

"I can," Chapel replied weakly.

It was a rough ride back to Fort Supply, and a lively betting pool was created among the troopers of the patrol to see who could come closest to predicting the hour of his death. Of the fifteen enlisted men on the patrol, only three were betting that Chapel would be alive when they got back. Tom Turnipseed was not in on the pool, because he didn't have the dollar required to bet. Had he been able to chip in, he would have bet on the injured man. As he told Sergeant Evers, "That man was dead when them buzzards was flappin' their wings over him. And he came back, just like that Lassiter feller in the Bible that was raised from the dead."

"Horseshit," Evers said. "Nobody comes back from the dead. Anyway, that fellow in the Bible was Lazarus, not Lassiter."

"All the same," Turnipseed said, not convinced he was wrong.

The soldiers did the best they could for him, giving him water and offering food, but Chapel could not eat. It seemed an eternity to him before the cavalry patrol finally arrived at Fort Supply. In a feeble voice, he thanked Lieutenant Harrington and Sergeant Evers for their efforts to keep him alive long enough to get to the surgeon. Dr. Waters took one look at him and expressed his amazement that he was still alive. "You can take him into the infirmary and put him on the bed next to that other fellow the deputy marshal brought in," the doctor said. "After we clean him up, I need to get him into my surgery right away."

It didn't take long for Dr. Waters to realize there was little he could do for Chapel. The large-caliber bullet had torn straight through his body, doing extensive damage to muscle and bone, but luckily it had gone out his back. Waters cleaned both wounds and probed both chest and back to try to see the extent of the damage. He could only guess, but it appeared that no major organs had been damaged, which seemed impossible. But he managed to stop the bleeding. When Chapel was lucid again, Waters told him there was nothing more he could do for him. "You've lost a helluva lot of blood, so we'll just try to feed you enough to build it back up. I guess it'll be up to you as far as how fast you recover, and I have to be honest with you—I don't know if you'll ever fully recover."

"Much obliged, Doctor," Chapel said. "I ain't tryin' to tell you your business, but I expect I'll recover all right." In his mind, there was no question; he had to recover, for he could not die until he had settled with Bevo Rooks and all three of his sons.

"I hope you're right," Waters said.

When Sergeant Evers told Tom Turnipseed the doctor's prognosis, the scruffy-looking scout replied, "He'll make it, all right. He's done come back from the dead one time."

Recovery was not quick and it was not without pain, due to the severity of the wound. Three times during his stay in the infirmary Chapel took a turn for the worse when the doctor figured his constitution had been weakened to the point of giving up. But three times the determined patient rallied, causing Waters to comment that he had never seen a man face death so many times and refuse to surrender. "He's one helluva strong man," he said to Tom Turnipseed, who periodically asked about the patient.

"He'll be back," Tom insisted. "He's done took a look on the other side and come back once. There's somethin' he's got to finish doin' on this side." He was convinced of it.

It was a matter of weeks before the stoic deputy marshal defied the damage done by the .50-90 Sharps slug and began to return to health. Once his body was whole again, the recovery was rapid, and one month to the day he was brought to Fort Supply, he left his hospital bed for good. Dr. Waters was not ready to discharge him, but Chapel gave him no choice. So, on a cold day in November, Chapel left Fort Supply to return to Fort Smith, a journey that would take him ten days. Dressed in boots and clothes furnished by the army, riding a borrowed horse, and with rations to last him the trip, hopefully, he rode out the front gate, only to confront Tom Turnipseed.

Waiting patiently, Turnipseed sat on a paint pony with a sorrel tied behind. The sorrel was carrying a light packsaddle. "Figured you might could use a little company on your trip," Tom said in greeting.

Chapel, who never needed company, was surprised the simple scout was offering to ride with him. "'Preciate the offer," he said, "but I don't need nobody."

Turnipseed was prepared for Chapel's reaction, expecting the somber deputy to refuse his help. "The hell you don't," he replied. "It's a full week, maybe a couple days more, from here to Fort Smith, and there's still some bands of Injuns out that way that don't know they're supposed to be on the reservation. You ain't got no gun, and nothin' to cook with that I can see, and there can't be much salt pork and crackers in them saddlebags."

"I don't need much," Chapel insisted. "I'll get outfitted when I get back to Fort Smith."

"*If* you get back to Fort Smith," Tom pointed out sarcastically. "I'm goin', either with you or right behind you, so there ain't much you can do about it. You can't shoot me. You ain't got no gun. And I know you're about twice my size, but you still ain't strong enough to go to tusslin' with anybody. So whaddaya say? We partners?"

"I don't generally have partners," Chapel said.

"Well, you got one now," Tom insisted. "Whaddaya say?"

"I reckon you're goin' to Fort Smith with me, but what about your job scoutin' with the army?"

"They can get along without me. They got a bunch of scouts, even though there ain't none of 'em as good at it as me." He was not really bragging, for in his mind, he was merely stating a fact. "First thing we gotta do is get you on a decent horse to ride. That damn mare the army was so kind to loan you don't look like she could tote you to Fort Smith. She looks older than I am. I went by the stables early this mornin' and picked up this sorrel—told the soldier on duty it was for Lieutenant Harrington." He paused to chuckle while he recalled the incident. "He didn't know if he should let me take the horse, but I didn't give him a chance to think about it. I told him I didn't care if he let me take the horse or not. I'd just go back and tell the lieutenant he said he couldn't have the horse." He paused to chuckle when he recalled it. "That sure as hell changed his tune. We can shift that army saddle over to the sorrel, and put that little packsaddle on the mare, but let's ride a ways from the fort in case that soldier asks somebody about it."

Chapel was not sure how he felt about the proposed partnership. He had always been detached, a loner, depending upon himself and no one else. That was the way he liked it, and the way he intended it always to be. His recent brush with death had caused him to withdraw even further into himself, and he was not yet ready to forgive himself for blundering into the ambush that sent him to the hospital. He had been careless, a fault he could not forgive easily, and he felt he needed solitude to work through it. Possessing a practical mind, however, he had to consider the sensibility of accepting Tom's offer for all the reasons the strange man had given. The part that puzzled Chapel was why Tom insisted on accompanying him. He was unaware of the man's fascination for what he firmly believed was his return from death—and the fact that, realistically, he had taken on a disciple instead of a partner.

When it appeared that the dispassionate lawman would no longer object to the arrangement, Tom continued to take charge of the trip. "One thing we gotta do pretty quick is some huntin'. You're gonna need some fresh meat to get your strength back. That little bit of bacon and hardtack sure ain't gonna carry you very far. I bet they didn't give you no coffee, neither. Did they?" When Chapel shook his head, Tom remarked, "I didn't think so. Well, I got plenty of coffee beans in that pack. Hell, by the time we get to Fort Smith, you'll be ready to fist-fight with a mountain lion." He was so sure of what he said that Chapel began to believe him, so he resigned himself to having a traveling companion, a rare situation for the loner he had always been. *And what a companion,* he thought, looking at the almost comical appearance of the man—with his long gray hair blowing wildly out behind him when he rode, and the angular face reminiscent of a horse's long face, half covered with a scraggly beard. The eyes were sharp and alert, however, for the old man never seemed to miss much.

Chapter 6

The first couple of days proved to be hard on the recovering patient, so they stopped to rest on the third day. The decision was made on the morning of that day when a small herd of antelope was sighted crossing the Cimarron River. Tom set out after them and was lucky enough to stalk them from downwind. He was able to get within range for one shot before they became aware of the danger and bolted. He returned to the camp with a healthy doe, and the rest of that day was spent resting, eating, and smoking the meat.

The following morning found Chapel ready to ride. Rested and fed, he was already feeling his strength returning. As each mile passed, he was able to stay in the saddle for longer and longer days, and by the time they reached Okmulgee, he felt well enough to go back to work as a deputy marshal. They figured they should reach Fort Smith in two days' time. Although still of the opinion that he preferred to work alone, Chapel had to admit to himself that he had become accustomed to Tom's presence and his nonsensical babbling, most of which was conversation to no one but himself. By the morning they left Okmulgee, Chapel had decided that he actually liked his weird companion, and he was aware that Tom had made his trip back a hell of a lot easier for him. The sometime cavalry scout had made no mention of his plans once Chapel was back to report for duty again, so on their last night in camp before starting for Fort Smith the next day, he asked Tom what he was going to do.

"Why, I don't know," Tom replied. "I can usually find somethin' to do. When I can't, I go back to Broken Knife's village in the Osage Nation." He paused and shrugged indifferently before saying what was really on his mind. "I was kinda thinkin' you might need a posseman to help you—you know, till you get back on your feet good." Tom knew that, when sent out in the territory after an outlaw, most deputy marshals took a wagon with a cook and at least one posseman with them. After spending more than a week on the trail with Chapel, he was well aware that this was not his style, but he thought it worth a mention.

To Tom's surprise, Chapel said, "I'll think about it." That was all the discussion on the matter. The thing working on his mind was that Bevo Rooks was somewhere out there, probably heading for Mexico. Chapel could not be at peace until he had put him and his evil seed in the ground. The immediate problem to overcome was his physical state. He knew he was in no condition to go after the four killers. It would take a little time before he could set out with confidence. The next problem was a matter of money. The Rooks clan had stripped him of everything—horse, weapons, supplies and ammunition. He was going to be forced to delay his plan to find Rooks. None of this did he confide to Tom.

It was early afternoon when the two unlikely partners rode into the town of Fort Smith and headed straight to the courthouse. Standing at a window in his office down the hall from the courtroom, U.S. marshal John Council looked down as the two riders pulled up to the hitching rail and dismounted. "Well, I'll be damned . . . ," Council uttered, and took his cigar out of his mouth so he could press his face closer to the glass. He had received a telegram more than three weeks before telling him that his deputy was dying in the hospital at Fort Supply. "I reckon they just didn't know Chapel." He walked over and opened his office door, then sat down behind his desk and waited.

"I don't reckon I'll be long," Chapel said to Tom before leaving the scout with their horses. He climbed the steps and walked past Judge Parker's office to the open door at the end of the hall.

John Council got to his feet and stepped forward to meet him when he came in the door. "I swear, I wouldn't believe it if I wasn't seein' it with my own eyes," he said, favoring Chapel with a wide grin. "I thought you were dead."

"I thought I was, too, for a while there," Chapel replied, his face devoid of emotion. "I figured I'd best get back to work."

"Are you sure you're ready to go? You're lookin' a little peaked." He moved back behind his desk and waved Chapel to a chair. "Sit down, Chapel, and tell me what the hell happened out there in the Outlet." He listened intently while his deputy made a verbal report. When he had finished, Council stroked his chin thoughtfully. "It's a mighty good thing that cavalry patrol came along when they did."

"I reckon," Chapel replied.

"I saw you out the window just now," Council went on. "Noticed you had somebody with you. Who's he?"

"Somebody I picked up along the way—Tom Turnipseed. He's a good man. I don't really know if I'da made it back here without his help. He's hopin' I might sign him on as a posseman."

"You sure you're ready to come back to work?" Council asked again.

"Don't see any reason not to," Chapel replied. "I just need to get a horse and some supplies, a saddle and a rifle. I lost everythin' but my shirt and pants when they shot me."

"I'll make you out a voucher so you can get outfitted," Council said. "We can take it outta your salary for the next few months. Looks like you already got a horse." It was customary for deputy marshals to provide their horses themselves.

"He's kinda on loan," Chapel said, "sort of a permanent loan from the army." He shrugged and added, "He's a pretty good horse, but I'm partial to buckskins. After I get caught up with my pay, I'll most likely find me another one." He got up to leave.

Council got up with him and walked him to the door. "I'm glad to see you back. When you're ready to go, I've got a few jobs I'll put you on that won't put much of a strain on you, serving a couple of subpoenas, and one witness to a holdup I need to find. I'll take it easy on you till you get yourself fit again."

"I'm fit now," Chapel said, "at least enough to take any job you need me for. As soon as I buy another rifle, I'll be ready for anything." Even as he said it, he knew he was going to be broke for a year after he replaced everything he had lost. If he had been able to arrest one of the Rooks gang, he would have received six cents a mile for the trip out to the Cherokee Outlet from Fort Smith, but no arrest, no fee. The piddling little jobs that Council proposed for him now would not be much help to get him out of debt.

"We don't wanna rush it," Council said. "You need to get your health back."

With a decent secondhand saddle and a new Winchester rifle, Chapel and Tom proceeded to a stable on the eastern edge of town to leave their horses for the night. "Where's the buckskin?" Will Porter asked upon seeing Chapel ride in on a sorrel.

"I lost him," Chapel replied. "We may be here for a couple of days—I ain't sure—but I'll pay you tomorrow. I ain't got no money on me right now. All right?"

"Sure thing, Chapel," Will said. "You've been boardin' your horses here for a long time." For anyone else, Will would have demanded money up front, but in truth, he had always been intimidated by the menacing deputy marshal who never seemed to smile. On the other hand, he had never failed to pay his bill. He turned then to the less intimidating man who had ridden in with Chapel. "How 'bout you, mister?"

"I'll vouch for him," Chapel said before Tom could answer. He had no idea if Tom had the money to stable his horse.

"Good enough," Will quickly responded.

"I'll pay up front," Tom said, surprising both Chapel and Will.

After unloading the horses, they took their saddlebags and weapons and walked some fifty yards down the street to a weathered old boardinghouse where Chapel made his Fort Smith headquarters in an eight-by-ten-foot room on the back of the house. "Damn," Tom couldn't help but exclaim, "you might as well be livin' in a jail cell."

"I don't stay here much," Chapel said, "so I don't need much more than a place to sleep. It does fine for that. You can spread your blanket on the floor beside the cot." The situation had become a bit awkward now, for he wasn't sure Tom was still counting on remaining with him. And he was waiting to see if he would announce that he was going to return to Fort Supply and his old job of scouting for the army.

"Fine and dandy," Tom said, apparently happy that he was not thrown outside to find accommodations for himself. The situation reminded Chapel of once before when he had thrown a scrap of meat to a stray dog, and the dog consequently adopted him. The partnership lasted for six months before Tom realized there was no real need for him in Fort Smith. So one morning he announced he was going to visit some old friends in the Osage Nation in Indian Territory. Chapel had been given some mundane jobs to do close to Fort Smith in spite of his insistence that he was ready to ride on any

assignment. Such duties as serving subpoenas, or finding witnesses offered no need for a posseman to accompany him. Tom knew he was out of his element in a
busy town like Fort Smith, but it was a reluctant farewell on his part, for he truly believed he had seen
Chapel return from the dead. Consequently, he also
believed it would be good luck for him to be associated
with a man that special, and he had hoped that one
day Chapel would tell him what was on the other side
of that dark door. He was convinced that the tight-
lipped deputy had seen the next life but had promised
not to speak of it when he came back to this life. "Well,"
Tom finally remarked, "you know where to find me—
Broken Knife's village—if you was ever lookin' for me."

"I reckon I haven't thanked you properly for all you
done for me," Chapel said, finding it awkward to express his appreciation, "but I won't forget it."

They shook hands, and Tom climbed on the paint
pony and wheeled it toward the river. His departure
was somewhat of a relief for Chapel. Even though he
liked the simple man, he had abided Tom only because
he owed him.

Pearl Mae Rooks looked out the window of the shanty
that had been her home for the last several years when
she heard one of her sons bellowing like a lost calf.
That would be Corbett letting her know they were back,
and it was the signal for her to start cooking something
for them to eat. "Huh," she uttered when she saw the
small herd of cattle they were driving. "Looks like they
did all right this time." They had been gone three
nights to rustle Mexican cattle, and at least they weren't

returning empty-handed. She picked up her coffeepot and walked to the back porch where the pump was located. She took the can of water sitting there for the purpose, and poured it down the pump to prime it. Cranking the handle up and down, she cursed the lack of immediate response from the rustic pump. It was running dry. She had warned Bevo time and again that one day soon, somebody was going to have to walk to the river to fill her coffeepot. And when that day came, he could get it himself or do without.

"Damn house oughta been built closer to the river in the first place," she grumbled to the reluctant pump when it finally drew up some water. The first thing she did was refill the primer can and set it on the porch rail beside the pump. It made no difference if the first to come up was cloudy and brown. It would still prime the pump next time. When the water cleared a bit, she filled her coffeepot and returned to the kitchen to place it on the stove. "Leave me here to take care of this place. They're lucky I fix the sorry lot of 'em any coffee," she muttered. The cabin was in a sad state, but her menfolk were hardly the kind to work on the place; her sons were as worthless as their father. Bevo had told her when he first carried her off from her home in Kansas that he wasn't the working kind. He had said there were plenty of working fools out there so they could steal what they needed, and that was the way it had been ever since. The first three years of their union— they never did have a church wedding—she spent having babies while they moved around the territory to keep ahead of the law. After a few years on the run, she insisted on establishing a base, so she could stay put and take care of her babies. She found that she was content with Bevo gone most of the time, leaving her free of his pawing and fondling. And as the years went by, he reached the point where it didn't interest him as much, anyway. As each son grew old enough, he went off with his father to rustle cattle, hold up stagecoaches, steal anything of value, and kill anyone who got in the way. She had to admit that her husband had greater influence over her sons than she did. They were all a sorry lot. She had been able to teach Corbett to read a little, but he soon lost interest in it. His brothers wouldn't even try. Both were of the opinion that their father had never had any need for reading and writing. Why should they? *It had been a good life for a while,* she suddenly thought, *when the boys were still too small to accompany their father.* "But I'm damn sick and tired of it." She often had thoughts of packing up her few belongings and going back to her father's home in Kansas. Bevo and the boys were usually gone for such long periods of time that she might as well be permanently without them. It would bring her a great deal less worry. *I'll think about it some more,* she told herself.

Hearing her men approaching the rough pole corral, she pulled her coat on and shifted the gun belt she always wore to settle more comfortably on her hips. She was a tall, rawboned woman, almost as tall as her husband. She thought that was probably the reason they had produced three big men. Her hips were unusually wide, so she wore her .44 pistol in the middle, centered between her legs. It was easier for her to draw it if the need arose to kill a snake, and although it was sometimes in the way when she was cooking or working the garden, she felt undressed without it. *They'd better damn sure be thinking about butchering one of those cows,* she thought, *because I sure as hell don't have anything to cook but some dried beans.* She went out on the porch then to watch them drive the cattle in.

Seeing his mother on the porch, Cotton, her youngest, yelled, "Hey, Ma! I shot me a Mexican yesterday!"

"Is that a fact?" Pearl Mae replied without emotion. The taking of a human life held no sense of alarm for her. It was a dog-eat-dog world that she lived in, and the occasional killing was just a cost of doing business, the business they happened to be in at any rate.

"Yeah," Corbett scoffed, "a little ol' boy about twelve years old. He didn't even have a gun."

"Hell, I didn't know that," Cotton said. "He coulda had one."

"Caused us to hump it pretty hard to get back across the river," Bevo said. "I oughta broke a stick across his back. Drive them cows on in there," he directed his sons, and wheeled his horse toward the cabin. "I hope to hell you've got some coffee on."

"It's on," Pearl Mae said, "but if you're wantin' some supper, you'd best kill one of them cows."

"Crown," Bevo called to his eldest, "cut one of them calves out and butcher it. Let Cotton shoot it. He's so damn anxious to shoot somethin'." He turned back to his wife then and remarked, "Ever since I wouldn't let him shoot that deputy up in Injun Territory, he's had the itch to shoot somebody. I'm glad he got that Mexican boy, even though his shot mighta had a bunch of 'em on us if they'da heard it." He stepped down from his horse and followed his wife into the kitchen.

He sat down at the table and waited while Pearl Mae set a cup of coffee before him. "I swear, I'm gettin' tired of travelin' all over this territory. I'm ready to stay put in one place."

"Well, if you're gettin' ready to set yourself down on *this* place, you're gonna have to dig a new well, 'cause this'un's goin' dry," she said. "And you need to fix the roof over the kitchen. We don't get much rain, but when we do, I have to cook with water drippin' on my head."

"Hell," Bevo said, "don't tell me about it. Talk to the man who built the place."

"Well, I reckon I will if he ever shows up around here," she replied. Then they both chuckled at the joke, for the original owner of the cabin was buried on the other side of the corral, along with his wife.

"We ain't stayin' here much longer," Bevo told her. "I'm leavin' this damn dry-ass country and headin' north. I'm thinkin' 'bout findin' a place up where there's some better grass and set us up like honest ranchers. Get me a rockin' chair, and watch the boys take care of the place. When I find the right piece of land, we'll build us a house, and me and the boys will come back here to pick us up a sizable herd of cattle to drive up there and get us started in the ranchin' business, all pretty and proper."

"This ain't the first time I've heard that tale," his wife said, unimpressed.

"You'll see," he told her. "I ain't done nothin' my whole life but try to stay one step ahead of the law, and I'm ready to stay put in one place." She cocked a curious eye in his direction. Maybe he meant it this time, but she doubted it.

* * *

The months that followed Chapel's full recovery saw him become more involved with the business of the Federal Court, with little time to dwell on his obsession with finding Bevo Rooks. Even after working long enough to repay Council for resupplying him with a replacement for the army saddle and new weapons, he was not able to get away long enough to look for Rooks. To make his task more difficult, there had been no reports of the notorious patriarch of the Rooks clan anywhere north of the Mexican border. The months continued to pile up until almost three years had slipped by since Tom Turnipseed and Chapel had parted company. But Chapel saw Tom on several occasions when he had cause to ride through the Osage Nation and Broken Knife's village. And each time he saw him, the wizened old scout informed him that he was ready to ride with him anytime he needed a posseman. On one of those visits, Chapel found that Tom had built a shack for himself, and although it was little more than an enclosed shed, it was home as far as Tom was concerned. He was proud of it, and he insisted that Chapel should stay overnight.

It was not Chapel's preference, but he figured he owed it to his simple friend to accept his hospitality. Tom roasted some deer meat he had killed the day before, and the two men ate their fill while sitting around the fire and drinking coffee in front of Tom's new home. As usual, Tom asked if there was any news of the whereabouts of Bevo Rooks. The question always seemed to push Chapel into a pensive mood and cause Tom to quickly change the subject. It was obvious to him that his friend was never going to be free of his hunger for vengeance. It was late in the evening when Chapel finally spread his blanket beside the fire and went to sleep.

Possibly the talk about Bevo Rooks and the time spent recovering from the wounds suffered at his hands caused Chapel's sleep to be troubled by dreams of frustration, for he woke Tom in the wee hours of the morning with excited bursts of anger. Tom was amazed because he had never seen Chapel excited about anything, and he wondered if he was communing with someone he had seen when he had been dead.

The following morning Tom was eager to question his friend. "What was you dreamin' so hard about last night?" he asked. "You was sure doin' a lot of talkin' to somebody."

Chapel was immediately guarded in his response. "Talkin' about what?"

"That's what I'm askin' you," Tom replied. "You were talkin' to your ma and pa, sounded like, and maybe there was somebody tryin' to kill 'em or somethin'."

"I don't remember nothin' like that," Chapel insisted. "It musta been just crazy dreams."

Tom refused to let him pass it off that easily. "You was contacted by dead folks you saw when you died, warn't you?"

"No, damn it," Chapel replied. "I told you. I wasn't dead. You've got to get that outta your head once and for all. Nobody dies and comes back to tell about it."

"What about the fire?" Tom insisted, remembering bits and pieces of the sleep talking. "And somethin' about a horse gettin' burnt up?"

When Tom kept probing, convinced that his friend

was harboring something that gave him bad dreams, Chapel finally told him about the murders of his mother and father, and the burning of their home on the Red River. "That was a long time ago," he said. "I was just a boy." He locked his lethal gaze onto Tom's eyes then and said, "Now I've told you somethin' that nobody else knows, so I'm gonna ask you to swear to me that you'll never tell another livin' soul."

"I swear," Tom said. He was truly shaken by the grim man's confession. When thinking about it later, he knew he understood the cause of the man's grave disposition at last, and it had a sobering impact on him. At the same time, he felt privileged to be the one other person who knew Chapel's devastating past, and he felt closer to him than before. Of course, he fully expected that the somber hunter would never soften his granite countenance, even around him. As far as Chapel was concerned, he had told Tom more than he had ever intended to tell anyone, and he cursed himself for doing it. It would be a long time before he returned to visit his friend.

One morning in early spring, John Council sent for Chapel. "I know I've been working you pretty hard all winter and I promised I'd give you time off to do some hunting," Council said, "but I've got a situation over in Atoka that needs to be handled right away. A damn crazy Choctaw half-breed named Billy Red Wolf robbed an MKT train over there last week. I sent Marvin Whitley, a damn good man, over there to arrest him. I just got a wire from the sheriff that Whitley was shot and killed—shot in the back by Red Wolf. The sheriff's a fellow named Wilson Little Foot, and he said Red Wolf and a friend of his have the whole town afraid to come out of their homes. There's nobody to send over there but you. Every one of my other deputies is in the field. You're the only man available."

Looking at Council with his customary imperturbable gaze, Chapel asked, "So what's the problem?"

"Well," Council said, hesitating, "can you ride? I know you just got back yesterday."

"That's what I'm paid for, ain't it?"

"Good man. If you start out right away, you can get to Checotah by tomorrow night. The next morning you can catch the train and be down in Atoka around one or two that afternoon. Whaddaya think?"

"Sounds reasonable," Chapel replied, "but I might as well angle across. It's a little farther than Checotah, but I can make it to McAlester in two days and catch the train there if the timing's right. McAlester ain't but about forty miles from Atoka."

"That's a harder ride, but if you think that's better, then it's up to you." There was no talk about lining up anyone to go with him. Council knew he would elect to go alone. "Chapel," Council cautioned, "be damn careful. The sheriff says that pair is wild as hell, and now they've got a taste of blood."

He made the ride to McAlester in less than two days and went straight to the little train depot. Even though it was past dark, the telegraph operator was still there. He told Chapel there was a southbound train due in the morning at seven o'clock. That worked out fine for Chapel. It would give his horse some much-needed rest. He had asked a lot of the sorrel over the seventy miles from Fort Smith, and he was pleased to see the horse respond.

"I'm fixin' to go home, since there ain't no trains scheduled through tonight," the telegraph operator said. "You fixin' to go down to Atoka?" Chapel nodded in reply. "I figured as much. They must have some wild ones actin' up down there. I talked to the engineer on a northbound train that came through here last evening. He said he saw two fellows ridin' up and down the middle of Court Street, shootin' off their pistols at anybody they saw. He said he didn't waste any time driving that engine outta there—thinks it mighta been the same two that robbed a train a couple of weeks ago. There was already one deputy marshal sent down there. He came through here about a week ago."

"He's dead," Chapel said.

"Oh," the clerk responded. "I'm sorry to hear that—seemed like a nice feller." He paused to shake his head slowly as if feeling real sympathy. "So now you're goin' down there," he said.

"That's a fact," Chapel replied, and headed for the door.

"Mister, I wouldn't want your job."

"Not many people would," Chapel replied as he went out the door. "I wouldn't want yours."

It was a little after eight o'clock when Chapel arrived at the Atoka station. The train was not pulling a cattle car, but the deputy was able to load his horse into an empty freight car for the short ride. There was no ramp at Atoka as there had been at McAlester, so he had to persuade the reluctant sorrel to jump from the freight car. Once that was accomplished, he led the horse up the street to the sheriff's office. He was the only person on the street, which was far from the usual scene at that hour of the morning. None of the stores appeared to be open, and after walking along the silent street, he was beginning to wonder if everyone had deserted the town. Tying his horse in front of the small board building that served as the sheriff's office, he stepped up to the door and found it locked. There appeared to be a light inside, so he knocked. After a few moments, he noticed someone peering at him from the front window, so he motioned for him to open the door.

Sheriff Wilson Little Foot slid the bolt on the door and opened it only because he recognized the dominating figure that was Chapel. Still holding the shotgun he had picked up as soon as he heard a knocking on his door, he stepped back when Chapel entered. Puzzled by the unusual reception, Chapel greeted the sheriff. "What the hell's goin' on here, Sheriff? Where is everybody?"

"Chapel," Wilson pronounced, "I'm damn glad to see you, even if you're too late to do us much good. I'm hopin' the trouble is over and the town will get back to normal now."

"What do you mean?" Chapel replied, still baffled. "What's over? I was told Marvin Whitley was killed. Have you got the killer in the cell in back?"

"No, I ain't got nobody in the lockup. What I mean is, Billy Red Wolf and his worthless friend, Lem Tucker, has finally left town after raisin' hell for the last three days."

"You mean you just let 'em ride outta town without tryin' to arrest 'em?" Chapel knew that Wilson Little Foot was a sheriff in name only. Before this, there had never been a need for any real law enforcement in the normally peaceful little town, but still it was hard to believe Wilson had made no real effort to arrest the killers.

"There wasn't nothin' I could do," Wilson insisted. "They was both armed to the teeth, shootin' up the town, and I didn't have no help. When they shot your man, Whitley, down, I knew I couldn't go up against them. So I reckon I did what everybody else did—locked my door and sat here with my shotgun ready. They left one night, and I thought they was gone for good then. But they just went over the border to one of those whiskey towns to get more likker. Then they came back again. Whitley wasn't the only one they killed. They shot Fred Ziegler, the blacksmith, when he tried to stand up to them." He looked at Chapel with pleading eyes. "I'm just not willin' to stick my neck out for the little bit of pay these folks give me."

"Then I reckon you ought not be wearin' that badge," Chapel said. He had no patience for cowardice in any form.

Wilson rankled a little at the remark. "I reckon that's easy to say if you wasn't here in the middle of it."

"I'm here now," Chapel stated flatly. "Where can I go to look for these two murderers?"

"Billy Red Wolf lives with his mama and papa in Low Dog on the Kiamichi River. I don't know where Lem Tucker hangs out. He ain't got no family that I know of."

Chapel nodded. He knew where Low Dog was. "Has anythin' been done about Marvin Whitley's body?" he asked.

"Floyd Rich picked it up, his and Fred Ziegler's, too. They're at his funeral parlor behind his barbershop. I reckon we can bury them now that the trouble's over."

Assuming he had all the useful information he was likely to get from Wilson, he left the sheriff and headed for the barber-undertaker's shop. As he walked, he noticed a few people here and there, cautiously emerging from the buildings like frightened mice. They favored him with blank stares. Like Wilson Little Foot, Floyd Rich was very cautious about opening up to Chapel's knocking. The lawman was intent upon setting out for Low Dog, so he didn't waste much time with Floyd. After identifying himself, he told the undertaker that he had come to collect Whitley's weapons and any other personal items he might have had on him.

"He didn't have any weapons," Floyd said. "They took his rifle and pistol belt off his body, right in the middle of the street. The only personal items he had were a pocket watch and a pretty good briar pipe. I reckon his family might want them back. The watch wasn't much good, but it runs. I was thinking about keeping it for my fee."

"I expect I'll take it and the pipe back with me. I don't know if Whitley's got a family or not, but if he does, they might want to keep somethin' of his." When he saw the look of disappointment in Floyd's face, he said, "I'll see that the Marshals Service wires you your fee."

When Floyd went into the back of his shop to re-trieve the items, Chapel turned upon hearing a foot-fall on the stoop. In a moment, the door opened and a woman walked in. She was middle-aged and some-what dowdy. There were tears in her eyes. Chapel knew before she spoke that she must be the blacksmith's wife. Not comfortable with grieving widows, he started to pass by her on his way out, but she stopped him with a hand on his arm. "I saw you get off the train," she said. "Someone said they thought you might be a federal marshal."

"Yes, ma'am," Chapel said, "I'm a deputy marshal."

"Then you know what's happened here," she said. "Those men killed my husband. His body is lying back there beside the marshal's body. Are you here to catch those murderers?"

"Yes, ma'am. That's what I came here for. I'm sorry 'bout your husband. I'll do my best to track his killers down." He pulled away and started for the door, but she was not finished.

"There's more they must not have told you," she said, pausing a moment when a sob threatened to over-come her. "They took my daughter, my baby. She's only twelve years old, and they took her away." Unable to hold back the tears any longer, she succumbed to a series of long, painful sobs.

Momentarily stunned by the woman's plea, Chapel was taken by a whirlwind of compassion and anger—compassion for the poor woman, and anger at the sher-iff and the town in general for taking no action to stop the abduction. "Damn," he cursed without thinking, then quickly looked into her eyes with the dark, baleful gaze that usually spelled trouble for someone. "I'll get 'em," he said, and from the tone of his voice, she knew it was a promise.

He stormed out of the barbershop then, knowing he could afford to lose no more time, but he took a moment to visit the sheriff. "You gutless son of a bitch," he charged as soon as Wilson opened the door. "You let those bastards ride outta here with that little girl. I'll by-God see that you lose the job of sheriff when I get back to Fort Smith." Willing to waste not a second more on the cowardly sheriff, he spun on his heel and stepped up in the saddle. Humiliated and hurt, Wilson Little Foot was left to stand stinging from Chapel's angry tirade.

Chapter 7

It was more than twenty-five miles to Low Dog, and he intended to make it there before dark. He started out along Muddy Boggy Creek for about a mile before veering to the northeast to strike the Kiamichi. Memories of a distraught thirteen-year-old boy came to cloud his mind as he followed the Muddy Boggy. And he was once again reminded that there were two who had gotten away. With other business to take care of now, he tried to put those thoughts in the back recesses of his mind again.

It was late in the afternoon when he guided the sorrel toward the little gathering of huts known on the Kiamichi as Low Dog. Chapel was well familiar with the settlement, for it had been a favorite hangout for some of the local troublemakers for years, and a source of irritation for the few Choctaw families that had settled there. He reined his horse to a stop before riding into the center of the settlement, thinking it best to look the scene over first. All seemed peaceful as the evening approached, with only a few people about. Most of the people were inside. Chapel knew where he would go first. He had been there before. Giving the sorrel a gentle nudge with his heels, he rode in on the rough trail that served as Low Dog's main street.

"Chapel," the old man quietly acknowledged when he saw the lawman dismount at his door. His face weathered and rutted like the bluffs of the river he lived beside, Joseph Red Blanket walked outside to meet the deputy. "Long time since I saw you," Joseph said. "I figured a lawman would show up here soon."

"Hello, Joseph. You're lookin' fit," Chapel said, purely out of respect for the gray-haired old man, who seemed to have aged a dozen years since he had seen him last. Of the families who lived here, Joseph's had been the most cooperative with the law. Most of the others were not really hostile, but they were often reluctant, or perhaps afraid, to give any assistance to the white lawmen who sometimes rode into their village looking for outlaws. "I'm lookin' for a couple of fellows," Chapel said.

"I figured," Joseph replied. He did not have to be told whom Chapel was looking for. He, like many of his neighbors, was reluctant to inform on members of their tribe when it was a matter of some of the young men getting drunk and raising some mischief. But Billy Red Wolf had caused problems for his family and neighbors for too long. And now, word had gotten back to Low Dog that Billy and his white friend had done more than mischief. "Billy Red Wolf?" Joseph asked.

"Yep," Chapel replied. "He and another fellow killed two people over in Atoka. One of 'em was a deputy marshal, and they kidnapped a twelve-year-old girl. I figured they mighta come back here to Low Dog."

"They're here," Joseph said, his expression sad and gray, a reflection of many disappointments in the young men like Billy Red Wolf in his tribe. "They set up a tent a short ride up the river."

"Did they have a white girl with them?"

Joseph nodded solemnly, then spoke. "Yes, they had the girl. I saw them when they rode through here. They weren't trying to hide anything. I think they were still too drunk to care. I would have tried to help the little girl, but I am too old now, and they had guns."

"You were wise not to try," Chapel said. "It's my job to arrest them. You've helped me find 'em, and that's more than a lot of your people would do." He shook hands with Joseph and climbed into the saddle again, eager to find Red Wolf's tent before darkness set in.

He had ridden no farther than a quarter of a mile when he caught a glimpse of white canvas between the trunks of the trees about seventy-five yards ahead. Dismounting, he tied the sorrel's reins to a sizable bush, cranked a cartridge into the chamber of his rifle, took a coil of rope from his saddle, and proceeded to make his way from there on foot. As he drew closer to the tent, he realized there was little need for stealth, for the loud laughter and boisterous talk were evidence enough that the two murderers were drunk beyond caring who or what was approaching. *Oughta make my job a lot easier*, he thought as he stood erect and walked boldly into the camp, his rifle leveled before him and ready to fire.

He found the two outlaws sitting before a fire in front of the tent, each with a bottle of whiskey in hand. "All right," he announced, "this party's over. I wanna see your hands in the air." Oblivious to his presence until he spoke, both men struggled drunkenly in an attempt to get to their feet. One quick jab with Chapel's rifle butt knocked Billy over backward to land on the edge of the fire. His partner, thinking more quickly, and maybe a little less drunk, drew his pistol, but he was slammed with two rapid rounds from Chapel's Winchester. He managed to squeeze his trigger once before he fell dead, the bullet ripping the canvas of the tent. Chapel turned his attention immediately back to Billy, who was rolling around on the ground, trying to put out the flames that had caught on his coat. Chapel stuck the barrel of his rifle a couple of inches from Billy's face and warned, "You're under arrest. You give me any trouble and you'll get the same as your partner."

"You broke my nose, you son of a bitch," Billy moaned, blood soaking into his mustache from his injured nose. "You're lucky you caught me dead drunk."

"Maybe you'd rather have a bullet through your brain," Chapel threatened. He reached down and drew the pistol out of Billy's holster, then tossed it into the brambles. In the tense moments before, there had been no time to look about the camp, but now he demanded, "Where's the girl?"

"In the tent," Billy said.

"Hello in there," Chapel called. "Miss? You all right?" There was no answer from inside the small tent. Chapel turned Billy over on his belly and tied his hands together behind his back, then looped the rope around his ankles to make sure he wasn't going anywhere.

"She ain't likely to answer you," Billy slurred contemptuously. "She ain't been talkin' much for a spell now."

Chapel hurried inside the tent. The child was there—at least her corpse was. Bloodied and bruised, her half-clothed body bore the sickening evidence of the repeated violations that had tortured her until finally, mercifully, death came to take her life. Chapel was staggered for a moment, overcome by the horrific scene before him. When he recovered his senses, his first impulse was to beat Billy until he extinguished the life in him. He stormed out of the tent to stand over the trussed-up murderer, his fists tightly clenched in anger. He cocked his rifle and remained standing there for a long moment before he regained control of his emotions and released the hammer.

Billy, thinking moments before that he was about to join his partner in hell, turned his head in an effort to look up at his captor. "I reckon I'm under arrest," he smirked. "You gotta take me in for trial. Ain't that right, Marshal?" When Chapel didn't answer him, Billy taunted, "She was a sweet little gal as long as she lasted." That was enough to elicit a response from the usually stoic lawman.

"Shut up, you sorry piece of shit!" Chapel roared, and for emphasis delivered a sharp kick in Billy's ribs. Leaving his prisoner to writhe in pain, he walked back to retrieve his horse. When he returned, he found Billy trying to drag himself over to the fire with the idea of burning his ropes in two. Using the length of rope that bound his wrists to his ankles for a handle, Chapel dragged him over to a tree and secured him for the night.

There were other tasks to be done before starting back to Atoka with his prisoner. The foremost, and one he did not look forward to, was to try to clean up the little girl who had been so brutally murdered. He couldn't let the girl's mother see her daughter as he had found her. A search of the tent produced a few articles of her clothing that were free of bloodstains, no doubt having been removed before the brutal assault by the two men. For a washcloth, he picked up one of the men's shirts. Then he gently lifted the body up in his arms and went down to the edge of the water to clean as much of the blood as he could off her face and torso. He paused and gritted his teeth when he heard Billy call out. "Hey, Mr. Lawman, you ain't tryin' to take a little peek at her, are you? She ain't bad lookin', is she? I mean for a little slip of a girl." Chapel had never had a stronger urge to kill someone, but he had already resigned himself to do his duty as a U.S. deputy marshal and take his prisoner to trial.

After he had done the best he could for the girl, he wrapped her in a blanket, then turned his attention toward collecting the weapons and horses of the two outlaws. There was the question of the man he had shot. He decided not to take the body back to Atoka. He had already forgotten the man's name, and he didn't really care. He was probably wanted for something somewhere, but he didn't want to bother with him, so he dragged his carcass down the bank and dumped it in a gully.

The night passed without incident. He slept lightly, but enough to rest himself for the day ahead. Reluctantly, he gave Billy a little bit of bacon for breakfast and untied his hands long enough to let him relieve his bladder before loading him on his horse for the ride back to Atoka. The morning was not kind to the sullen half-breed. A combination of hangover and a throbbing nose, plus some aching ribs, took much of the cockiness out of him. Chapel started out, leading Billy on his horse, and the girl on the other horse tied behind Billy's. It was a sober parade that passed through the little gathering of huts called Low Dog, and there was at least one spectator standing out in front of each hut—all of them staring without expression. When he passed Joseph Red Blanket's hut, the old Choctaw nodded solemnly. Chapel touched his hat brim with his finger in return.

The somber column rode down Court Street in Atoka in the afternoon. Unlike the day before, the town seemed to have come alive again with people out and about, all curious to see Billy Red Wolf in the custody of the stoic lawman. Foremost in the crowd was the tearful mother of the slain girl. Unable to stand the sight of her once-beautiful daughter as Chapel lifted the body from the horse, she collapsed in the arms of one of her neighbors. Floyd Rich quickly took charge of the girl's body while several of the townsfolk helped the grieving mother compose herself. As soon as she was able to stand again, her first thought was to attack the man who had raped and killed her daughter. Before anyone could stop her, she flew into Billy with fists flailing, causing Chapel to grab her around the waist and carry her back to her friends.

"Is that the best you got?" Billy taunted the wretched woman. "Hell, your little girl put up a better fight than that."

"Shut your mouth!" Chapel ordered, and lifted his rifle up to threaten the insolent half-breed.

A witness to the scene, Sheriff Wilson Little Foot spoke up then. "I reckon you wanna put him in my jail till you take him back to Fort Smith."

"I don't reckon I want to, but there's not much choice," Chapel replied.

Still smarting from Chapel's previous criticism, Wilson was in no mood to cooperate with the deputy marshal. "Well, I ain't got nobody to guard him all night, so maybe you'd best start back to Fort Smith right now if you're plannin' to get him to trial."

"Why, you sorry bastard . . . ," Chapel exclaimed. "I'll take over your whole damn jail if I need it." He felt a burning sensation in his chest where the wound was still healing, a throbbing he sometimes felt when he was riled. Then he reminded himself of the grief suffered by the slain girl's mother, and he wanted to offer his condolences before she was led away by her friends. "I'm real sorry about your daughter, ma'am. I'm sorry I wasn't there in time to save her."

Chapel's sentiment brought a snicker from his prisoner. Billy, feeling safe in the hands of the law, couldn't resist the urge to taunt the poor widow. "Yes, ma'am," he called out to her, "I'm sorry 'bout your daughter, too. After 'bout the fourth or fifth time I jumped her, she stopped fightin' so hard. Hell, I thought she was enjoyin' it. Come to find out, she'd died."

It was the fuse that set Chapel off. Suddenly his anger overcame his restraint, and he was consumed by a fiery rage over the worthless piece of human filth. Walking back to where he had left Billy standing in the street with his hands tied behind him, he sent Wilson Little Foot a scorching glance. "You won't have to worry about holding him in your damn jail." Then, glaring directly into Billy's eyes, he pulled out his Colt Peacemaker and stuck it in his face. "This is your trial, you son of a bitch. I pronounce you guilty as charged." When the pistol discharged, the crowd gathered around him gasped involuntarily. Billy slumped to the ground, dead, a bullet through his brain. The crowd, stunned by the sudden execution, drew away from the angry lawman, afraid that his rage might not have been satisfied. For a few long moments, the busy street was rendered deathly silent, with no sound other than a snort or whinny from the horses. Of those gaping at the enraged deputy, Sheriff Wilson Little Foot was the first to break the eerie silence. "You ain't got the right to kill a prisoner like that," he murmured loud enough to be heard by the people standing closest to him.

The sheriff's sentiment was not shared by the crowd, however. Walter Hoffman, who owned the hardware store, spoke up then. "Well, I say three cheers for the deputy. They'da hung that mad dog, anyway. Anybody who did what he did oughta be shot down like a dog." His statement spawned a wave of similar comments, all endorsing the actions of the lawman.

As for Chapel, the ever-somber face gave no evidence of the turmoil engaging his brain at that moment. He knew he had abused his duties as a representative of the law, and he regretted the loss of temper that had caused him to do so. Though he had no regrets for killing Billy Red Wolf—no man ever needed killing more—he did regret the rage that had robbed him of his self-control. Judging from the general reaction of the folks who had suffered Billy's terrorizing of their town, everyone appeared to support the execution. His foremost thought now was to put the dust of Atoka behind him, anxious as he was to close the incident. On his ride back to Fort Smith, he would give a lot of thought to how he was going to explain Billy's death in his report to John Council. Seeing the undertaker coming back from his shop, Chapel said, "I got one more body for you to take care of. I'll see that they send you your fee from Fort Smith as soon as I get back—for Billy and the lady's child and husband."

"There ain't no fee," Floyd Rich said. "I'll take care of Richard and Mary Ann, and it'll be my pleasure to dig a hole out on the prairie somewhere and dump Billy's worthless body in it."

"Much obliged," Chapel said. "There might be some money in Billy's pockets, but I doubt it. I'll leave you his pistol and rifle to help with the expenses." Floyd nodded his appreciation. "I reckon I'm done here," Chapel said, and stepped up in the saddle. "I've got a long ride back." Floyd's offer to take care of Billy's body was appreciated as well, since it was policy that the deputy would be obligated to pay for the burial of any fugitive he had killed.

* * *

Riding the sorrel and leading the two horses that had belonged to Billy and his partner, Chapel would figure to take four days to make Fort Smith. If pushed, he could have made it in three, but he was in no hurry to get back, since he had no prisoner to be concerned with. So he set out on an old trail that struck the Kiamichi River and generally followed it north. He left the trail after two days to skirt the western side of the Winding Stair Mountains and strike the Poteau River, then follow it on into Fort Smith. By the time he reached that town, he had made up his mind to simply report that upon attempting to arrest the two outlaws, he had been forced to kill them both. It was not enough, however, to remove a slight stain on his conscience for having shot an unarmed man, even one as vile as Billy.

It was sunny but chilly on the afternoon he arrived in Fort Smith. Chapel speculated that winter might be reluctant to give up its grip. It was no more than idle speculation, however, for he was indifferent to the weather. Proceeding directly to the stables, he turned his horses out, and with his saddlebags and rifle, plus the weapons he had not given to Floyd Rich, he headed toward the courthouse.

John Council seemed startled when Chapel walked into his office. "Chapel!" Council exclaimed. "I see you made it back." He attempted a nervous smile.

Chapel was at once puzzled by the marshal's greeting. It seemed uncharacteristically uncomfortable, but he shrugged it off. "I need to have some money wired to Atoka for burial expenses for the victims of those two outlaws. I told the undertaker I thought we might pay for it. I didn't bring no bodies back with me." He placed the captured weapons on the floor at the end of the desk. "But here's their weapons, and their horses are at the stable."

"Ah, right," Council stammered. "Let me go see about that. Sit down, and I'll be right back." While Chapel took a chair, Council hurried out of his office, closing the door behind him, leaving his deputy still puzzling over his boss' attitude—as if he'd been caught doing something illegal.

When Council returned, he was accompanied by two policemen. Officers of Judge Isaac C. Parker's court, they were both familiar to Chapel. He had seen them in court many times, but he was now mystified by their presence here. Both men nodded to him when they came in, but they remained on either side of the door while Council returned to his desk. "We've got a little problem, Chapel," he said. He reached into his desk drawer and pulled out a telegram. "I got this wire from Atoka four days ago. It's from Sheriff Wilson Little Foot. He claims you shot Billy Red Wolf in cold blood, while the prisoner was tied up and in custody. He said there wasn't any problem with providing witnesses, 'cause you shot him in front of a street full of people. He said Billy wasn't trying to escape or anything. I'm wonderin' what you've got to say about that."

His strange reception was crystal clear now. Chapel glanced behind him at the two officers standing by the door. "What are your two boys for, John? Are you arrestin' me?" Both policemen responded with awkward expressions, clearly uncomfortable with the situation. Chapel turned back to his boss. "Yeah, I shot him, and I reckon I'd probably do it again if I had it to do over."

His answer left Council in need of further explanation. "Well, yeah, that's pretty much what the sheriff said, but I was hopin' you could tell me a little something more about *why* you shot him."

"He shot up the town, killed a deputy marshal and another man, and he raped and killed a twelve-year-old girl. He needed killin', and he was headin' for a hangin', anyway."

"Yeah, but that ain't your job, Chapel," Council stressed. "Your job is to arrest him, and Judge Parker will decide if he needs to be hung or not. It's understandable if you're caught in a gunfight, or have to kill somebody to keep from gettin killed yourself. But if what Little Foot says is true, that wasn't the situation. Now, damn it, the judge told me to take you into custody until we get a chance to look into it." His last statement caused the two policemen, all too aware of Chapel's reputation, to shuffle nervously.

"I reckon you gotta do what you gotta do," Chapel said without emotion. "I reckon takin' me into custody means throwin' me in that stinkin' jail in the basement."

"If there was someplace else, I'd use it," Council said. "It's Judge Parker's orders, but he said he intends to have your trial right away. He's already sent a marshal over to Atoka to investigate the witnesses. Probably won't be more than a week before he lets you go."

"Or hangs me, or sends me to Little Rock," Chapel said, referring to the state penitentiary. He got to his feet, which caused both policemen to drop their hands on their revolvers. "Take it easy, boys," he said with a baleful glance in their direction. "I'm just taking off my gun belt." He unbuckled the belt, laid it and his rifle on Council's desk, then took his badge off and placed it beside them. "I'd 'preciate it if you'd take care of these for me."

"I'll look after 'em," Council said, then nodded toward the guards to take him away. "I'm sorry, Chapel. I'm just following orders."

It was certainly not the first time Chapel had been in the foul confines of the jail, but he had never been subjected to its unhealthy conditions for an extended stay. At each end of the building was a large fireplace. Since they were not in use, they served as urinals for the prisoners in an effort to encourage the stench to go up the chimney. Large tubs were placed in the fireplaces for the purpose, but it was still common to smell the odor of urine upstairs in the courtroom. It was a ghastly joke that those prisoners awaiting a date with the hangman found the gallows a welcome relief. It was especially difficult for a man like Chapel, who spent almost all of his life camping in the free air of the prairies and mountains. To make matters worse, there were no individual cells. The basement was divided into two large rooms by a solid masonry wall across the middle. Consequently, prisoners of all ilk, from petty thieves to rapists and murderers, were corralled together like sheep in a pen. In view of that, Council had ordered the guards not to reveal Chapel's identity. Although there were not at present any inmates he had personally caused to be there, most of them probably knew his name.

Prisoners were curious about the new inmate at first, but the stone face, devoid of emotion, when combined with the imposing physical appearance, was sufficient to discourage questions. The jail population decided it was best to leave him alone to sit with his back against the wall, or to pace around the common room, offering conversation to no one. At night, he slept on a straw mattress on the flagstone floor, his blanket soaked by the dampness of the floor. It was not long before he began to have thoughts of escape, although no one ever escaped from the jail, primarily because the conditions called for guards to watch them day and night.

The week that Council had estimated turned out to be two weeks, but finally the day arrived when Chapel was called up to Judge Parker's court. Haggard and filthy, the prisoner washed himself as best he could in one of the two sinks provided, but there was nothing he could do to clean his clothes. One of the first persons he saw when the guards escorted him upstairs was John Council. The marshal recoiled, stunned when he witnessed Chapel's appearance. Chapel's reaction was no more than a solemn nod as he was led into the courtroom.

What followed was not the ordinary trial in Parker's court. There were no witnesses, no jury, and no lawyers. The only deposition given was that of the deputy marshal sent to Atoka to investigate the incident. The deputy, a man named William Sifford, worked in the eastern part of Judge Parker's district and therefore had no personal experience with Chapel. Judge Parker had chosen to send him to interview witnesses to the shooting, hoping to get a report without prejudice.

When Parker walked into the courtroom at precisely nine o'clock, the bailiff called for all to rise. Parker immediately seated everyone again and busily looked through a folder he had brought with him. When finished shuffling a few pages, he looked up to give a stern eye toward the grim countenance of Chapel. "You look like our accommodations have been less than healthy for you, Mr. Chapel."

"Reckon so," Chapel replied.

"I want to stress the seriousness of the charges against you," Parker said. "This complete disregard for a prisoner's rights cannot be tolerated in this court. What you have done is an affront to the judicial system of the state of Arkansas. Do you understand that?"

"I do, Your Honor." Chapel was fully aware that the hearing was just that, and no trial at all. There was no question as to his guilt. This hearing was to determine how he would be punished.

"All right, let's get on with it. Deputy Marshal William Sifford, take the stand, please." Sifford stepped up and swore that the testimony he was about to give was the unbiased truth as testified by the thirty-six citizens of Atoka he had questioned. Judge Parker had already read Sifford's full report, so he asked him to simply give a general summary of what he had found.

"Well, sir," Sifford started, "like it says in my report, I interviewed thirty-six citizens of Atoka. All of 'em was witness to the shooting, and all of 'em but one, the sheriff, said it was justified."

"Explain to me how a cold-blooded execution could be considered justified," the judge said.

"Well," Sifford went on, "the prisoner, Billy Red Wolf, and another fellow had shot up the town and scared the daylights outta the people for a week. He shot the deputy marshal who had been sent there to arrest him. Then he shot Fred Ziegler and kidnapped and raped to death Mr. Ziegler's daughter, Mary Ann."

"I see," Judge Parker said. "There is certainly no doubt that the prisoner deserved to be tried for his heinous crimes, and Mr. Chapel did his duty in arresting him. But that does not justify a public execution without benefit of trial."

Sifford scratched his chin whiskers thoughtfully before answering. "I think the folks over there thought it was justified because of the prisoner's lack of remorse and his taunting the widow of the man he killed, who was the mother of the little girl, too. The woman collapsed at one point, and the prisoner still laughed about how he had raped the little girl. The folks agreed with Deputy Chapel that the only way to stop the mental torture suffered by Mrs. Evans was to put a bullet in Billy's brain. In fact, they thought Chapel oughta be given a medal for what he done."

Parker paused for a few minutes before telling Sifford he could step down. Then he looked directly at Chapel and asked, "Do you have anything you want to say?"

"No, sir," Chapel replied. "I guess the deputy pretty much told it like it happened."

"All right," Parker said, "this is my ruling on this matter. There is no question that the prisoner, Billy Red

Wolf, was guilty as charged. However, even in cases as vile as this one, it is the right of all accused persons to receive a fair trial in a court of law, no matter what their crime is." Looking directly at Chapel, he continued. "As a representative of this court, you should know this, and it is your sworn duty to uphold the law. I am aware of your excellent record over the nine years you have served this district. In view of that, I have decided not to sentence you to internment in the state penitentiary in Little Rock. However, your failure to uphold the laws that you have sworn to enforce cannot be excused. I therefore sentence you to be immediately discharged from the United States Marshals Service. This case is closed." He banged his gavel once and left the courtroom, leaving Chapel a free man.

Chapel got up from his chair when both John Council and William Sifford hurried over to talk to him. "I did my best to talk the judge into letting you keep your job," Council said, "but he wouldn't budge—said it would be a bad precedent to set."

"I can understand how he feels," Chapel replied. "Hell, I shouldn't have done it, but like I told you before, I'd most likely do it again."

"Come on by my office with me and pick up your weapons and saddlebags," Council said. "I got your traveling money for going over to Atoka to get Billy Red Wolf, six cents a mile. I went ahead and got that approved before they had this hearing and disallowed it."

"I can sure use it."

After waiting for Chapel and his boss to finish that little piece of business, William Sifford extended his hand. "I just wanted to shake your hand. Those folks over in Atoka know why you shot that son of a bitch, and so do I. Good luck to you."

"I 'preciate you speakin' up for me," Chapel told him. "Good luck to you, too."

A few minutes later when he left Council's office, he walked down the hall, knowing it was the last time he would ever again set foot in the building, or see the man he had worked for over the last nine years. He guessed he had regrets; he really couldn't decide. His indifferent mind was not prone to dwell on things that were over and done, or on what might have been. He lived in a present-day world, never worrying about tomorrow, so he decided to go back to his room at the boarding-house, heat up a tub of water, and wash off the stink of Parker's jail. *When I get up in the morning, I'll decide what I'm gonna do for that day. I'll let the rest of my life come to me day by day.*

Chapter 8

It was a day and an event like no other in the history of the United States. April 22, 1889—an estimated fifty thousand eager homesteaders gathered on the Texas and Arkansas borders of Oklahoma Indian Territory. Most came from Kansas and Missouri, but there were people from all over the country, come to try their luck at claiming a place to call their own. Clear and dry, it was a perfect day for the celebrated land rush.

Link Cochran stood waiting beside Loafer, his six-year-old bay gelding, at the front of a long line of thousands of other folks that stretched for miles along the Oklahoma border. Like all of them, Link waited impatiently for the sound of the army bugle that would signal the start of the race into the Unassigned Lands of Indian Territory. Some said there were as many as ten thousand people who had gathered in this one stretch of the border to take advantage of the government's offer of free land. Link knew for sure that it was more people than he had ever seen in one place. Men on horses, entire families in covered wagons, men on foot— all waited anxiously as the clock crept toward twelve noon on this bright, sunny day in early spring. More people would be coming on the railroad, in cars packed to overflowing. Beside him in the line, Link's sister, Martha, her husband, Sam Anderson, and their two children watched in nervous anticipation as the bugler took a moment to wipe his mouthpiece, getting ready to respond at once when his commanding officer gave the signal. In the back of the wagon, Luella Cochran, Link's other sister, busied herself making sure everything was tied down securely in preparation for a wild and bumpy ride.

Link glanced over at Sam, who shook his head and smiled in response. "I got about two minutes till," Sam said, looking at his watch.

Link nodded and put a foot in the stirrup. Loafer stamped his front feet impatiently as Link stepped up to settle himself in the saddle. Horse and rider were ready for the race soon to begin. They were about to start on an adventure that would determine the pattern for the rest of their lives. It was a true family endeavor with the three surviving members of John and Lydia Cochran's family: Martha, the eldest, her sister, Luella, and her brother, Link, the youngest. New land in Oklahoma Territory seemed to offer the promise of prosperity that Kansas had failed to provide.

Like so many of the other participants in this race for land, Sam and Link had already picked the parcel they wanted—a section along the Cimarron River about fifteen miles from the Guthrie Station. They had scouted it out months ago, before the government had forbidden civilians to enter the territory to be given away. And Link was confident in Loafer's strength and speed to make sure no one would beat him to it. In his saddlebags, he carried the stakes to mark their claim. Sam and the others would follow behind as quickly as they could.

"I bet you beat everybody, Uncle Link," nine-year-old Sammy called out proudly.

"Loafer'll give 'em a run for their money," Link called back. "He don't like to eat nobody's dust."

"Ride like hell," Sam said. "We'll be right behind you."

Martha smiled and gave her brother a wave of her hand as the final seconds ticked slowly by. "Be careful, Link."

At last the moment came. The sweet, clear notes of the bugle sounded out "Recall." And the rush was on! Charging across the grassy slopes of the Cimarron Valley, the horde of settlers raced neck and neck, leaving a great cloud of red dust behind. In short time, the men on horseback pulled away from the wagons, with those on foot bringing up the rear. Link's faith in his bay proved to be justified, for Loafer seemed intent upon keeping his nose ahead of the others. After a quarter mile or so, the great pack of Boomers began to fan out to head toward the parcels they had their hopes on. Sam's wagon was far behind him now as he urged Loafer on with no one in his way.

Although the gritty horse gave no indication of surrender, Link knew he had to rest him as they raced along the banks of the river. Satisfied that he had a good lead on the riders who had picked the same course he had taken, he pulled Loafer to a stop, dismounted, and led the horse to the water's edge. It was clear to him at this point that there were only two riders to cause him concern, the only two who had continued to follow him from the start, and he had opened a considerable lead on both of them. As soon as Loafer had finished drinking, he began walking, leading the tired horse. He was soon overtaken by both men, whipping their exhausted, lathered horses mercilessly. They gave him no more than a curious glance as they thundered by. Though extremely difficult to do so, Link resisted the urge to jump in the saddle and start out after them. The plot of land he and Sam had their eye on was still some miles away.

After a couple of miles walking, he decided it safe to remount, so he climbed back up in the saddle and urged Loafer to a comfortable lope, not wishing to demand more than that just yet. Within a couple more miles he came upon one of the men who had passed him, standing beside a completely spent horse at the water's edge. The rider, a gaunt, heavily bearded man, looked up as Link loped by. "I reckon I'll stake my claim right here," he called out.

"Well, then, good luck to you," Link returned, and continued on his way.

In another mile, he came upon the second rider, who was evidently not content to stake his claim at the end of his horse's endurance. Instead, he continued to flail away at the exhausted animal with his reins, but the horse had nothing more to give, and finally came to a stop just as Link caught up with him. The man looked at him with what Link could only describe as an angry glare. Link offered no words, but nodded as he passed him by. He had no use for a man who would mistreat his horse like that.

Moving steadily on, he began to feel a sense of heightened excitement as he recognized familiar features of the land, recalling his scout months before. If he remembered correctly, the river took a horseshoe-like bend just beyond the bluffs he now approached. When he rode over the rise beyond the bluffs, he found the tract of land just as he had remembered it—with one exception. When he had been there before, there had been no wagon and tent in the cottonwoods near the bend of the river. His initial reaction was simple astonishment, followed immediately by anger. There was no way a wagon could have beaten him to this spot if it had started out when he did. The only explanation was that the party, which looked to be three men, were sooners and had come into the territory illegally before the official start of the race—and from the looks of their camp, probably a day or two before. In the days before the start of the race, there had been talk of the probability of some people slipping into the Unassigned Lands illegally to grab choice tracts in the designated town sites as well as the farm and ranch land. Even worse, it had been rumored that many unscrupulous men had arranged to have themselves appointed as deputy U.S. marshals with the sole purpose of getting the pick of the land. The army and government officials were the only people allowed into the unassigned lands before the race. This included, of course, U.S. deputy marshals. Feeling the bile rising in his system, Link refused to take the defeat quietly. He nudged Loafer to descend the gentle bluff, heading toward the camp.

"We got company, Pa," Crown Rooks said when he spotted the single rider heading their way.

Bevo Rooks raised his craggy gray head, squinting his eyes to look where his eldest son pointed. He pushed the rest of the piece of bacon he had been chewing into his mouth and wiped his hands on his shirt. "Well, let's see what he wants," he said, getting to his feet. "Corbett, you just stand easy till we see what he's got to say," he told Crown's brother.

"You reckon he's a marshal?" Corbett asked.

"Ha," his father grunted. "All the damn marshals is in Guthrie, settin' on the choice town lots they staked out for theirselves. He ain't no marshal." The three of them walked toward the edge of the camp to confront their visitor. "Good day to ya, young feller," Bevo called out when Link had approached to within a few dozen yards. "What can I do for ya?"

Still angry at having been cheated out of his choice of land parcels by a pack of obvious sooners, Link replied, "Well, you can explain how the hell you got on this piece of land before I got here."

His question brought a wicked grin to Bevo's face. "I reckon me and my boys just ain't the kind to dawdle around when we've got someplace to go," he said. "Ain't that right, boys?"

Link nodded toward the wagon and the tent beyond. "I don't see no wings on that wagon yonder, and, from the looks of that tent, I'd say you've been here at least since yesterday. You've got no right to this piece of land."

"Is that a fact?" Bevo replied. "Well, I don't see as how you've got much to say about it one way or the other. We were here first, and I don't expect there's much you can do about it. Now, we've got work to do, fixin' up our place, so why don't you just ride on outta here while you still can?"

Standing beside his father, Crown dropped his hand to rest on the handle of his pistol. It did not go unnoticed by Link, who reacted quickly enough to draw his rifle from his saddle sling. While holding the Winchester leveled at Bevo, he backed Loafer away several steps. "I wouldn't do anything rash if I was you," he warned Crown, "unless you want your old man cut down."

"You got no cause to draw that rifle on us," Bevo said. "We settled here peaceable. We ain't the kind to look for trouble. We just beat you to this spot, so you'd best quit your bellyachin' and go on and find you another'n."

"This ain't the last of this," Link warned. "I'm filing on this piece of land. We'll let a judge decide who got here legally." He continued to back slowly away while keeping a sharp eye on the three of them, ready to shoot the old man at the slightest move by one of the sons. He never heard the shot that smashed in the side of his head, dropping him to the ground to lie dead at his horse's feet.

"Hoo-hah!" Corbett exclaimed excitedly.

Cotton Rooks, Bevo's youngest son, charged out of

the tent, his rifle in hand. "Hot damn!" he shouted. "Got him in the head! That's gotta be, what, Pa? Fifty yards, I bet—helluva shot!"

"More like forty," Crown allowed.

"It was a good shot," his father admitted, "but I was beginnin' to wonder if you was asleep in that damn tent. You waited long enough after he pulled that rifle on me."

"Ah, hell, Pa," Cotton said, still proud of his marksmanship, "I wasn't gonna let him shoot ya, but I knew I had to knock him off with one shot, or he mighta got one off hisself."

"You done good," Bevo conceded as they approached the body. "We'd best get rid of him before somebody shows up lookin' for him." He squatted beside Link's body and started searching through his clothes for anything of value.

"'Pears like we got us a fine-lookin' horse," Corbett said, admiring Loafer openly. "Good saddle, too."

"I shot him," Cotton said. "I oughta be the one who gets the horse."

"I'll be damned," Crown objected. "I s'pose you think you oughta get that rifle, too."

An argument started immediately over the distribution of the spoils, but it was stopped short by the father before it became violent. "I'll say who gets what later," he ordered. Looking at Crown then, he said, "Right now I want you and Corbett to drag that carcass over to the other side of the river somewhere and dump it outta sight. Cotton, you take that horse over with ours and put that saddle in the tent." Hands on his hips, he stood for a moment, looking down at the corpse. "He mighta been on his own, but I got a feelin' there might be somebody comin' along after him with the rest of the family." He had sworn to Pearl Mae that he was dead serious about finding a section of land and building a proper homestead on it. When the government decided to open this land for homesteading, free of charge, it was ripe for his plans. He and his sons had slipped into the unsettled area of Indian Territory two days before it was legal to do so, and they had set up camp on what he considered a choice piece of land. A man who claimed to work for the federal marshal had spotted their camp. He told them they would have to pack up and leave, and make a run for the land with everybody else. Bevo was explaining to the lawman why rules didn't apply to him, while his eldest son, Crown, was in the process of thrusting a long skinning knife into the man's back.

It was a little before dark when Sam drove his wagon past the bluffs and started over the rise beyond. Like Link before him, he was taken aback by the scene that met his eyes. He quickly pulled the horses to a stop while he and the women stared at the camp in the cottonwoods by the river. At first confused, he halfway expected to see Link coming to greet them, but he was perplexed by the wagon and tent already there. Not knowing what to think, he turned to meet his wife's puzzled look. "Something's wrong," she uttered. "Where's Link?"

"What is it, Mama?" seven-year-old Jenny asked.

"Nothing, child," Martha answered. "You and Sammy stay back in the wagon." When Jenny obeyed, Martha gave Sam a worried look and said again, "Something's wrong. Are you sure we're in the right place?"

"I'm sure," Sam replied. "This is the spot Link and I scouted. I don't see how those folks coulda got here with that wagon before Link did." As he said it, the people seated around the campfire caught sight of them and got to their feet. There were four of them, all men, and all carrying a rifle in one hand. "Uh-oh, they don't look too friendly," Sam remarked.

"Sooners," Luella snorted in disgust. "That's what they are. They look like they've been here two or three days."

"Maybe we should just pass on by," Martha said.

Always more aggressive than her older sister, Luella said, "I wanna know where Link is. If this is the right spot, then why isn't Link here?"

"Lou's right. We've got to find out what happened to Link," Sam said, although not really eager to get any closer. "Could be he went to the wrong place, but I don't see how. This is the spot. We'll at least ask them if they've seen Link." He reached down behind the seat and pulled his shotgun within easy reach. With a cold lump in his throat, he started the horses and headed them down toward the camp. He pulled the horses to a stop when he was within easy talking distance.

Bevo Rooks strolled casually up beside the wagon seat while his three sons fanned out to cover the wagon on both sides. "Evenin', folks," Bevo offered.

"The name's Brooks, and this here's my claim. What can I do for you?" He then waited for Sam's response.

Sam was struck with the immediate feeling that he was in a risky situation. Although there was a smile on the old man's face, it was a face as cruel as an Arizona cactus, and certainly anything but neighborly. He wondered at once if he had put them all in danger by approaching the camp, but it was too late to remedy that now. Glancing at the three younger men, he saw the same sarcastic leer on each face, a reflection of their father's attitude. Still, he decided to state his concern. "My brother-in-law shoulda been here before us," he started cautiously. "We were figurin' on filin' on this piece of land."

"You don't say?" Bevo responded. "It is a choice spot, ain't it? That's the same reason me and my boys picked it."

Encouraged by the lack of hostility in the old man's response, Sam was emboldened to say, "I can't see how you fellers got that wagon in here ahead of him. It don't seem possible."

"Oh, it don't, does it?" Bevo replied. "Well, I reckon your—who'd you say he was? Your brother-in-law? Maybe he ain't fast enough, or maybe he got lost."

"You're sayin' you ain't seen him at all?" Sam asked.

"There was that one feller," Crown Rooks spoke up then. "He stopped here a while back, but he rode on up the river. I bet that was your brother-in-law."

"I expect you're right, son," Bevo said. "I done forgot about him." Grinning back at Sam and Martha then, he added, "He said he was gonna look a piece upriver for his land."

Sam felt Martha press closer to him. There was something sinister in the facial expressions of the four men leering at them. He suddenly shared his wife's apprehension over their situation, and he felt his heart skip a beat when he glanced at the horses grazing near the river. The foremost thought at that moment was to remove his family from what could become a deadly encounter. When, in the next moment, one of the younger men started to casually move toward the back of the wagon, Sam decided it was time to go. "Well, I reckon we'll go on and see if we can catch up with Link," he said, and popped the horses with the reins.

As the wagon lurched into motion, Cotton, who had gotten around behind it, discovered Luella and the children in the wagon. "Well, lookee here," he commented gleefully. "What's your hurry? You oughta stop for a while so we can have a visit."

"Not with the likes of you," Luella responded defiantly.

Her response delighted Cotton, who laughed loudly, amused by her prickly attitude in contrast to the obvious fright the couple in the wagon seat had conveyed. He was joined by his brother Corbett, and the two ran after the rapidly departing wagon for a short distance, hurling sarcastic comments and invitations to spend the night there.

Bevo chuckled as he watched his boys chasing after the wagon; then a more serious thought came to mind, and he turned toward Crown. "Son, them folks might be scared off for good, and they might not. I want you to get on your horse and ride back to Guthrie to that claim office and file on this piece of land, just in case they're figurin' on beatin' us to it."

"All right, Pa," Crown said. "I'll head out first thing in the mornin'."

"No, damn it," Bevo responded. "You'll leave right now."

"But it's fifteen miles or more back to Guthrie," Crown complained, "and it'll be dark before too long."

"It ain't gonna hurt you to ride in the dark," Bevo said. "I want you to be the first one at the door when they open that office in the mornin', and don't forget to register it under the name of Brooks."

"I won't, Pa," Crown replied obediently, and went to get his horse.

Afraid they were not out of danger yet, Sam flailed the team of horses, urging them to exit the bend in the river as quickly as possible. "I'm worried about Link," Martha said in anguish, relieved to be leaving the four behind. "Those men frighten me." She looked back at her sister then. "Lou, you shouldn't antagonize men like that. They look like they'd just as soon murder us for lack of something else to do."

"They can go to hell, as far as I'm concerned," Luella replied. "They're nothing but a bunch of damn sooners."

"Lou, please watch your language in front of the children," Martha scolded.

"Nothing they don't already know," Luella said. "Isn't that right, Sammy?" She reached over and playfully punched him on the shoulder.

Sam had become quite used to the minor squabbles

between the two sisters, but there was something of a more grave nature on his mind, so he interrupted. "I'm sorry to have to tell you this," Sam replied, looking back behind them to make sure they were not being chased, "but that was Loafer back there with those other horses. I'm sure of it."

"Oh, Sam!" Martha gasped. "If something has happened to Link . . ." She could not finish her statement.

"Are you sure it was Loafer?" Luella asked, equally alarmed.

"I'm sure."

The thought was too much a shock for Martha to think clearly at that moment, and she could not permit herself to consider the full implication of her husband's words. "Sam, what can we do?" she implored. "Do you think those men harmed Link?"

"I'm pretty damn sure they did, and I'm afraid it was worse than just harming him, but there was nothin' I could do back there. I couldn't risk you women and the kids. I'm sorry, truly sorry, if they murdered Link, but I don't see how they coulda got his horse without killin' him." Looking into the shocked faces of his wife and sister-in-law, he promised, "I ain't gonna let Link die in vain. I swear it. I'll find a way to make them pay for what they've done."

"What are you gonna do?" Martha begged, her eyes now filled with tears for her brother.

"Ain't nothin' I can do right now," he said. "It's gonna be dark before long, and I've got to find us a place far enough away from them to camp. Then I'm goin' back there to make sure they ain't got no ideas about visitin' us."

"Oh, I don't know about that," Martha remarked. "Those men look evil. I don't think you should take any chances with them. I don't want you to leave us alone, either. Damn it, Sam, I'm frightened."

"I'm gonna get you someplace safe first. And don't you worry, I ain't gonna take any chances. I just want to be sure they're in their camp tonight, and I owe it to Link to make sure he ain't tied up somewhere back there." The matter was left at that point while Sam continued to drive the horses up the river until he came to a spot that looked shallow enough to ford while enough light remained to permit a safe crossing. On the opposite bank, he pulled the wagon in among some cottonwood trees that offered a screen from any passersby on the other side. It took a great deal of effort to affect an air of normalcy to spare the children the tragic events of the past hours, but Martha had Jenny and Sammy collect wood for a fire while she anxiously went about helping Luella cook their supper. Sam concerned himself with watching the opposite bank and the way they had come.

Luella went about the business of making supper silently, knowing how much it upset her sister when she made bold statements about retaliating against the sooners. As tall as her brother, Link, she was a raw-boned woman, and a spinster at age thirty, having never met a man worthy of being her husband. Like Martha, she agonized over the fate of her brother, but until there was definite word, she resolved to remain calm for the sake of the children.

Supper over, bedtime for the children came with no sign of anyone trailing them. Yet Sam was not willing to leave his family until the night wore on and a full moon rose high in the starry sky. He wasn't sure what good it was going to do to try to spy on the camp back down the river, but he told himself he could never forgive himself if Link was being held captive by the four men and Sam had made no effort to effect his escape. His honest concern was to know that the four sooners were still in their camp, and not on the way to do him and his family harm.

When he decided he could hesitate no longer, he loaded his shotgun, gave it to Luella, and asked her to stand guard while he was gone. "I'm goin' back, but I'll stay on this side of the river and see if I can find out anythin' about that bunch of crooks. You keep your eye on that bank over there and blast anythin' that comes across. When I come back, I'll give you a couple of whistles so you don't shoot me." He then whistled two low notes to demonstrate. "It ought'n take me more than an hour to make my way back there on foot."

She shook her head bravely and took the shotgun in hand, knowing she would give anybody who tried to harm them a warmer welcome than they were looking for. "You be careful," she whispered, "I'll take care of Martha and the kids." He nodded, knowing she would defend his family with every ounce of her strength. He gave Martha an encouraging smile then as he slipped away from the wagon and started back down the riverbank at a trot.

With his mind still reeling from the shock of the day's tragic events, Sam made his way as quickly as he could along the river, constantly watching the other bank for any sign of the four who had taken over his land. He admitted to himself that he was afraid. Those four looked capable of murder without conscience, but he knew he had to make some effort to find out what had happened to Link—if not for his sake, at least for Martha's and Luella's. The cheerful enthusiasm that had brought them to this day of great expectations had been slashed like the gutting of a carcass, turning their dream of a new beginning into a nightmare. *I wish to hell we had stayed in Kansas,* he thought. Then his conscience reminded him that he owed it to Link to make some effort to avenge his brother-in-law instead of giving in to the impulse to simply run away. He reached down to feel the handle of his .44 revolver to bolster his courage, then picked up his pace.

Breathing heavily, he stopped after what he figured to be about forty-five minutes' time and stared at the moonlit bank across the river, thinking he remembered driving his wagon past the lone cottonwood leaning over the water. The tree, no doubt a victim of a strong windstorm, was not far beyond the four claim jumpers' camp, if his memory served him. He had to be close. With a thought toward being more careful at this point, he proceeded as quietly as possible toward a thick stand of willows near the water's edge.

It was dark in the midst of the willows, with the light from the full moon filtered by the branches, causing him to watch his step, lest he stumble and make a noise that might alert the camp. Pausing every few steps to listen, he reached a point where the light of the campfire on the opposite bank suddenly became visible. It stopped him cold. He dropped to one knee and stared at the point of flame shimmering through the cottonwood trunks. Aware of his rapidly beating heart, he tried to calm himself. *They can't possibly hear me,* he told his anxious mind. As soon as the thought struck him, he heard the sound of laughter from the camp. It seemed to freeze him where he knelt, unable to decide what to do. What *could* he do? The impulse to turn and retreat was too much to overcome. *At least I know they're in their camp and aren't planning on looking for us,* he told himself. *The main thing is that I'm sure my family is safe.* With those thoughts to justify his actions, he turned and hurried to retrace his steps.

In the spotty darkness, his desire to quickly vacate the scene caused him to almost fall when he stepped over a log, but he caught himself in time to regain his balance, only to trip over an apparent second log next to the first. He crashed down headfirst in a pocket of dead willow branches and leaves. Fearing that the noise of his fall might have been heard across the river, he remained flat for a few seconds, listening. Fortunately, there was no sound of alarm from the camp. After a couple of minutes with no challenge from the claim jumpers, he got to his hands and knees, preparing to stand again. It was then that, glancing back at the log that had tripped him, he looked into the cold face illuminated by a single shaft of moonlight through the trees. *Link!* The stark countenance of his brother-in-law stared up at him with wide-open eyes that had gazed into the dark beyond when the impact of the .44 slug had torn through his temple. Sam's initial reaction was to recoil from the corpse while he fought to control his emotions. He could not seem to breathe for long seconds. They had murdered Link, just as he had feared. Still on his hands and knees, he tried to think what to do. There were no thoughts of exacting revenge at that moment. He could try to slip in close enough to shoot at them with his pistol, but what if he missed? Even if he didn't miss, the other three would likely kill him, and what good would that do Martha and the kids?

There's nothing I can do against them now, he decided. *The only thing I can do is go to the law for justice.* The question then was what to do with Link. He felt he couldn't leave him there to be eaten by scavengers. He should at least have a proper burial. He took another long look at the body. It wouldn't do for the women and children to see Link like that, with his head smashed and covered with dried blood. Still, he could not desert him. His mind made up, he got to his feet and considered the task before him. Had he had tools available with which to dig a grave, he would have buried him there. Since there were no tools, he crouched over Link's head, shoved his hands under the shoulders, and lifted. It was a strain, but the body, already stiff, tilted up like a log as Sam struggled to bring it up on its feet. Holding Link upright, he moved around and bent over to let the body fall across his shoulder. He felt the full weight of his brother-in-law as the body settled to ride stiffly on his shoulder. Getting his feet squarely under him, he started out of the willow thicket, placing each foot carefully to avoid stumbling.

His mind swirling with indecision and confusion, Sam trudged back the way he had come. After a while the body seemed to bend a little, but the weight soon began to tire Sam out. Finally, when he had gone as far as he thought he could without resting, he decided to bury Link there. It would be better, anyway, he told himself. That way, Martha and the children would be spared the sight of Link's ghastly appearance. So he knelt down on one knee and let the body down as gently as he could manage. Looking around, he decided upon a place near the tree line, but not so close as to run into roots. "I'll be back, Link," he said softly. Then he hurried off to get a pick and shovel and break the sad news to those waiting at the wagon.

It was a short but mournful ceremony held over the grave of Link Cochran, twenty-two years of age, attended by his sisters, his brother-in-law, a niece, and a nephew. It was close to three o'clock in the morning by the time they had prayed over the grave and Martha stepped back while Sam finished filling it in. In typical fashion, Luella took another shovel and helped. She had wrapped Link's body in a blanket, so a tearful Martha wouldn't see him in his final state but would remember him always as the adventurous, fun-loving brother who was eager to build a home with her and Sam.

With the burial over, it was time to decide what they should do now. Sam made some halfhearted comments about taking his shotgun and paying the claim jumpers a visit. Luella at once volunteered to accompany him. Martha, her eyes red from crying, immediately rebuked them both for even thinking of it. "You will do no such thing!" she scolded. "Those men are outlaws and murderers! I've just lost my brother. I'm not going to lose my husband and my children's father."

Relieved that she was of such a mind, Sam gave in. "All right," he said, "we'll go back to Guthrie to find a judge. There's got to be some law there. We'll demand justice, for Link's murder as well as those outlaws stealing our claim." Luella kept silent, knowing it would amount to suicide to even think about confronting the four desperadoes.

There was no thought of continuing on in hopes of finding a plot of land as good as the one they had lost. Sam and Martha were inclined to return to Guthrie immediately. "What if they find Link's body missing in the morning?" Martha worried. "They'll know we found him." It was a question that caused them all concern, so they decided to hitch up the wagon and start back in the half-light before dawn. No one but the children slept that night, and their sleep was brief.

With eyes red from lack of sleep and nerves on edge with worry over who might be following them, they rolled into Guthrie before eleven in the morning, astounded by what they saw. In the short time they had been gone, a whole city had been born. Thousands of people had already staked lots. Streets had been laid out, there were hundreds of tents already up, and construction was under way for permanent buildings. The Federal Land Office was easily identified by the long line of people waiting to file their claims. Next to the land office, a large tent had been erected, bearing a rough sign that proclaimed it to be the courthouse and sheriff's office. Sam guided his team of horses toward it.

Like every other business in the overnight city, the sheriff's office was busy trying to get established amid the near chaos of the rush for city lots. "Sheriff ain't here," Sam was told by a man sawing lumber for a partition between the sheriff's desk and the circuit court space. When Sam explained why he was looking for help from the law, the man suggested that he go talk to Judge Barnes. "Maybe he can help you, but I can tell you right now there ain't nobody available to ride back down the river with you. There's too much to do right here in Guthrie."

With already an overwhelming load of disputes between claimants to settle, Judge Norman Barnes had little time to spend with Sam. "In the first place," Barnes informed him, "I'm a judge. I can rule on the validity of a claim, but only on evidence of some wrongdoing. It's the sheriff's or a deputy marshal's job to arrest the accused. I just try 'em. From what you're telling me, there were no witnesses to the shooting. It's just your word against the party you're accusing. Even if I believed your side of it, there's nothing I can do to help you."

"This is more than just somebody jumping a claim that me and my brother-in-law rightfully have a claim on. Those men murdered my brother-in-law, shot him in the head, and dumped his body in a willow thicket."

Judge Barnes shook his head in empathy for the wronged man's plight, but there was nothing he could do to help him. Although he did not express it to Sam, he was more inclined to believe it had been a case of a fight between the two parties that ended up with one person getting shot. "I'm afraid there's more than a few incidents of lawlessness out there, but it's impossible to cover all that territory. The sheriff has no jurisdiction outside of Guthrie. He won't be of much help to you, either. The only advice I can offer is to find a federal marshal. Maybe one of them could investigate your complaint."

As he exited the judge's chambers, Sam found the man who had been working on the partition wall awaiting him. "My name's Clary," he said. "I couldn't help hearin' what you were talkin' to the judge about. Mister, it sounds like you and your family deserve some kinda help in findin' justice. But I can tell you, you ain't likely to get no help from a deputy marshal. There's about four or five of 'em right here in town, and there ain't a one of 'em interested in workin' for the law. They just got themselves appointed deputies so they could get the jump on everybody lookin' to snap up the best town lots."

That wasn't very good news to Sam. "I reckon I expected somethin' more from the government, the army, or somebody to keep law and order," he commented.

Clary had one more thing to say before Sam returned to his wagon. "I can tell you somewhere else you might try for help," he said. This captured Sam's attention, causing him to pause at the tent flap. Clary continued. "There's a feller that stays near an Osage village most of the time—name's Chapel. Judge Barnes wouldn't hardly tell you about Chapel, but that man might help you clean them outlaws outta your claim."

"Why would he help me?" Sam asked, at once thinking of a hired gunman, or a bounty hunter. "Who is he?"

"Not many folks know much about Chapel," Clary said. "He used to be a deputy marshal in the Indian Nations, workin' outta Fort Smith, but they kicked him out 'cause they said he shot a man he had arrested for rapin' a twelve-year-old girl. The story goes that Judge Parker didn't send him to prison 'cause they figured the man he had arrested had it comin', so they just discharged him."

"What makes you think he might help me?" Sam asked, still skeptical.

"I don't know that he will," Clary replied. "He's a strange feller. But they say he has a strong dislike for outlaws that take advantage of folks who can't help themselves. I know one thing—he don't help nobody for the money. If he decides he wants to go after somebody, it's more'n likely 'cause he thinks they deserve to be caught." Clary stood watching Sam closely, aware that he was giving his advice some serious thought. "He's livin' in Chief Broken Knife's village. I can tell you how to get there if you wanna talk to him."

Sam was still skeptical. It seemed highly unlikely that this Chapel fellow spent his time chasing after outlaws and punishing felons that were not caught by the local law enforcement officers. It seemed more likely to him that the man might be no more than a legend created by the runaway imagination of a lawless community of folks. Sam expressed as much to Clary. "Oh, he ain't no legend," Clary insisted. "He's real, all right, but he ain't no do-gooder, and he sure as hell ain't what you might call a guardian angel. I saw him, myself. I was at Fort Gibson, over near Muskogee, when he brought a man in who'd been sellin' whiskey to them Osage Injuns and turned him over to the army." He shrugged his shoulders then and said, "Like I said, I'll tell you how to get to that Osage village if you're thinkin' about goin'. Looks to me like you ain't gonna get no help from the law."

Sam talked the idea over with the women at length before they finally made their decision. Clary's word was not much to go on, and it seemed hardly likely that this mysterious ex-marshal, Chapel, would have any interest in helping them. The only reason he might, they felt certain, would be if he were well paid to act on their behalf. And they were not prepared financially to pay a high-priced gunman. "We've got Link's money," Martha said, referring to a small sum of money they were carrying in the wagon that belonged to her late brother. "It's not much, a little over a hundred dollars, but maybe it would be right to use his money to avenge his death."

"I don't know," Sam commented. "That ain't much money to offer a gunman to go up against four outlaws." The urge to return to Kansas, to try once more to farm that plot of dust they had left, was getting stronger. He thought of the land he and Link had scouted, where the Cimarron flowed through rolling grassy hills, and the plans he had made to raise his family there. It was difficult to give up on those dreams. He could have tried to find another piece of land, but it was too late now to find a desirable plot. In reality, there was but one choice left to him, and that was to return with his shattered dreams to Kansas.

From the first, Luella's vote was to go find Chapel and fight for the land that rightfully belonged to them, avenging her brother's death in the process. Possibly the man was nothing more than a gun for hire, but working with a gunman was preferable to her to letting Link's death go without vengeance. Martha was not as enthusiastic. She had been silent for a while, but when she spoke again, it was sufficient to surprise them. "Let's go see if we can find this Chapel character," she said. "Maybe he might help us get our claim back." Her statement brought a firm nod and a smile from her sister.

Their decision made, they remained in Guthrie only as long as it took Sam to move up to the front of the long line at the Federal Land Office. Not really sure they could legally file on the claim, they nevertheless thought it in their best interest to try to do so. After all, they had gotten to the land as the first legal claimants. As Sam expected, their plot had already been filed on by someone named Brooks. When Sam protested that Brooks was there illegally, the clerk told him it would have to be settled by the court. But he also warned that the decision usually went to the party that was established on the land. "More than likely," the clerk said, "it's gonna be a case of his word against yours, and it'll be hard to prove Brooks sneaked into the territory before the official start of the race."

With prospects becoming dimmer and dimmer, Sam returned to the wagon to give the women the results. They decided that their only choice, outside of some miracle of help from the legend Chapel, was to return to their little farm in Independence, Kansas. And from the directions Clary gave them, the Osage village was not that far out of their way.

Chapter 9

Clary's directions to the Osage village took them east along the Cimarron to a point where it doubled back to form an S, with high bluffs on the southern side. From there, Sam and his family struck a trail due north that led them to the Arkansas River. Broken Knife's village was on the northern bank of the river. The journey took more than four days at the best rate he could manage to coax out of his team of horses. Both Sam and Martha questioned the wisdom of traveling that distance to talk to a man who Clary said might not even help them. Luella expressed her opinion that it was at least worth looking into. The farther they traveled each day, the more they began to think they were on a fool's mission. The only justification for their actions, they decided, was the fact that they were going back to Kansas if all else failed.

Their arrival in the Indian village of huts and tepees just before noon caused a turnout of the entire camp, since the people were not accustomed to white visitors. By the time Sam pulled the horses to a stop before one of the larger huts, the wagon was surrounded by a crowd of curious men, women, and children who appeared to be astonished by these unlikely visitors. Sam's initial thought upon surveying the inquiring faces gazing up at them was that this had been a grave mistake, and a poor decision by the three of them. Feeling Martha press close to him, he knew she shared his uneasiness. Just as his discomfort began to progress into fear, he was relieved to see a white man coming to greet them. A few seconds later, when the man approached to within twenty yards, he was not so sure he was a white man, and his apprehensions returned. "What a wretched-looking man," Martha whispered. Sam could not disagree. His hopes for any help from this quarter quickly evaporated. He hardly looked the image of a guardian angel. Dressed in dirty buckskins from head to toe, a bear claw necklace around his neck, and a grease-stained derby set at a rakish angle atop long gray hair that had yellowed with age, he strode casually up to the wagon. "You folks lookin' for the big land rush?" he asked, flashing a grin that revealed a couple of gaps where teeth had once rooted. "'Cause you sure as hell missed it." Not waiting for Sam's answer, he walked around and peered into the back of the wagon, his stare met by one from Luella. "See you got a couple of pups in the back," he said to Sam when he walked back to the wagon seat. "These folks here is Broken Knife's people—Osage. When you came up in that wagon, they was kinda hopin' you was bringin' the bacon and flour the Injun agent promised."

Dismayed to have traveled so far to be met by one with such a shabby appearance, Sam was not sure what to say to the grinning man staring up at him. He may have been a deputy marshal at one time in his life; Sam couldn't say. It had to have been a good many years before this day, though, because he seemed hardly the man Clary could have remembered. Finally Sam managed to speak. "Chapel?"

The man cocked his head to one side. "You lookin' for Chapel?" he asked. "What for?"

"Are you Chapel?" Sam asked again.

The man threw his head back and chuckled. "Hell no," he remarked as if everyone should know. "I'm Tom Turnipseed. Whatcha want with Chapel?"

Impatient with the man's questions, yet relieved that he wasn't Chapel, Sam replied, "I just wanna talk to him. Is he here?"

"Nah," Turnipseed said. "He don't stay here. He stays by hisself down the river a piece. I can take you down there. Lemme get my horse."

"Much obliged," Sam said. They sat there waiting, surrounded by curious Indians who were crowding around them. From the back of the wagon, Sammy and Jenny exchanged timid greetings with some Osage children. Martha almost wished she and Sam were driving a wagon filled with the promised supplies. The children looked in need of flour and bacon.

When Turnipseed returned, leading a pinto pony with no saddle, he spoke to the people in their native tongue, explaining that the wagon was merely a white family who were probably lost—and had not come with the promised bacon and flour. The disappointment was obvious in their faces as they stood back from Sam's horses. "Come on," Tom said to Sam, then jumped upon the pinto's back and started out along the riverbank.

Sam followed the strange man for what he estimated to be about a mile and a half before he caught sight of a couple of horses grazing near the water, and a small tent almost hidden in the cottonwood trees that lined the banks. There was no sign of anyone about the camp, but Tom led them straight toward the clearing and the tent. At the edge of the clearing, he pulled the pinto to a halt. "Looks like you been doin' some huntin'," he said, and slid off his pony's back. Both Sam and Martha looked back and forth across the clearing but could not determine whom Turnipseed was addressing. "I brought some folks to see you," Tom went on.

"What for?"

The folks in the wagon heard the response but still saw no one. "I don't know," Tom replied. "They just said they needed to talk to you."

Sam stared hard in the direction from which the voice had come before finally discovering the man kneeling behind a screen of berry bushes at the water's edge. He was apparently butchering the carcass of an animal. He could still make out no more of the man's appearance than the hazy outline of a pair of broad shoulders. Feeling uncomfortable with the encounter, Sam finally broke the silence that had swallowed the few words spoken so far. "Mr. Chapel? My name's Sam Anderson. I'd like to talk to you, if you don't mind."

Chapel didn't respond at once while he studied the man and woman seated on the wagon seat, now with the heads of two small children pushing through between them. He had watched their progress from about a quarter of a mile as they had approached his camp, and he could not say he was glad to see them. Families in covered wagons had always been a sign of trouble to him, either at the time he saw them, or in time soon to come. Finally, when it seemed to Sam that the shadowy figure screened by the berry bushes had not heard him, Chapel finally replied, "What about?"

Martha and Sam exchanged uneasy glances. They had not known what kind of reception to expect from this mysterious recluse, but so far, it appeared to be considerably less than a welcome one—and they had not even stated what their purpose was in seeking him out. Feeling a bit perturbed for having to talk to a berry bush, Sam started to climb down from the wagon, but he hesitated a moment with his foot on the hub of the wheel. "All right if I get down?"

"Why not?" Chapel replied, looking at the tall woman who had already climbed out of the back of the wagon.

"Well, I didn't wanna . . . ," he started; then, feeling foolish for having asked, especially upon seeing Luella, he stepped down to the ground. "Feller, name of Clary, said maybe I should talk to you."

"Clary, huh?" Chapel responded. "Little weasel-faced fellow that works for Judge Barnes?"

"That's the man," Sam replied. "He said you might help me and my family." He glanced at Tom Turnip-seed, who stood close so as not to miss any of the conversation, an expectant smile upon his whiskered face.

"Is that a fact?" Chapel responded. "Now what would give Clary an idea like that?" He placed his skinning knife down on the hide of the antelope and rose to his feet. Looking at Tom, he said, "Go ahead and cut you off a piece."

"Much obliged," Turnipseed said, and wasted no time in dropping down beside the carcass to slice off a piece of fresh meat. Then he hurried over to set it over the campfire, using a spit propped there for the purpose.

Tom's eager response to Chapel's invitation to eat went unnoticed by Sam and the women, their attention drawn instead to the imposing figure that emerged from the brush. Dark eyes that seemed to measure them under a heavy brow, wide, high cheekbones, and a square jaw gave him a moody look that reminded Sam of a granite cliff. He didn't doubt for a moment the stories Clary had told about Chapel.

"You folks hungry?" Chapel asked in a low voice devoid of emotion.

Surprised by the gesture, Sam hesitated for a moment, looking back at his wife. "Well, we haven't eaten since early this mornin'," he said. "I reckon we could use somethin' to eat. Much obliged."

Martha nodded eagerly. She knew the children were probably hungry, and the aroma coming from Tom's roasting antelope was hard to resist. "That is certainly very generous of you, Mr. Chapel," she said. "We have coffee we can brew to drink with it." She scrambled over the seat into the back of the wagon to fetch her coffee mill and a sack of beans. She handed the coffeepot to Jenny and told her to fill it from the river. When the coffee was busy boiling over the coals of the fire, she brought out a large skillet and laid strips of fresh antelope in it to fry. "I'm sorry I didn't know we were going to have dinner," she said. "I could have made some biscuits to eat with the meat you so kindly provided." Stepping in where her husband had seemed to be awkward in the meeting with the stoic man, Martha directed Jenny to fetch cups for Chapel and Tom. "And don't forget to bring some of that sugar," she called after her daughter. She looked up at Chapel, who had been watching her every move to that point. "Maybe Mr. Chapel likes sugar in his coffee." Then, giving him a friendly smile, she said, "*Mister* seems so formal. Do you have a first name?"

"Yes, ma'am," Chapel replied, but did not offer it.

Pausing for an awkward moment, Martha nevertheless regained her confident air. "Well, my name is Martha, and my husband's is Sam. This is my sister, Luella." She pointed to the children in turn and said, "Jenny and Sammy."

Amused by the lady's attempt to ease things up a little, Tom said, "He just goes by Chapel. Don't nobody call him anythin' but that."

"Oh," she replied, and hesitated for just a moment. "Well, that's certainly fine, isn't it?" She turned her attention back to her skillet. *It's like trying to talk to a bear*, she thought.

Luella remained silent while she witnessed her sister's attempt to make polite conversation with a man who seemed to have never participated in any communication beyond primordial grunts. At the same time, she found the granite-faced hunter somewhat intriguing and wondered if there was something a little deeper in his being that he purposefully preferred not to reveal. Her initial impression was that he was the man needed for the job.

"What did you wanna talk to me about?" Chapel asked when Martha had poured his coffee. With Sam standing silently by, Martha related the events after the official start of the land rush, and the fact that they had not been able to get the land they planned to because someone had cheated. Chapel listened with no show of interest, even when she told him that these men had murdered her brother. When she had finished, he asked dispassionately, "Why did you come to me? Why didn't you go to the law? I'm sorry for you folks, but I ain't the law."

"We tried that," Sam exclaimed, "but that judge over in Guthrie said there were too many disputes to handle for the one deputy marshal who's still doin' his job. All the others are only interested in stakin' claims for themselves. He said it might be six months before he could even get around to us."

"Did you file with the land office on that piece of land you said you wanted?" Chapel asked.

"Yes, I did," Sam answered, "for what good it did." He went on to tell him what the clerk had told him about his chances.

"Well, that's what you shoulda done if you're thinkin' about havin' the judge rule on who rightfully owns the land."

With frustration fully setting in upon Sam's brain at this point, he protested passionately. "I can understand the delay in ruling on the land, but what about Link's murder? Why can't somebody do somethin' about the cold-blooded murder of my wife's brother?"

"I understand how you feel," Chapel said. He nodded toward Martha then. "I'm sorry about your brother, ma'am, but I can't see how it has anythin' to do with me. I ain't the law in this territory."

Although totally dismayed by the stoic man's lack of interest in their plight, Sam could understand his position. After all, why would a stranger four days away from the problem want to get involved in their troubles? "Well, I reckon I thought it wouldn't hurt to try," he said, then looked at Martha and shook his head. "I don't know if the law could help us, anyway. Nobody actually saw that Brooks fellow shoot Link—him and his three sons—all of them lookin' like they'd enjoy killin' someone." He started to say more, but Chapel interrupted him.

"Who?" he exclaimed, Sam's comment having triggered something in his brain. "Who'd you say?"

"He said the fellow's name was Brooks," Sam replied. "I don't remember his first name. I reckon I didn't even remember his last name. When I saw the man, I thought he said his name, but I didn't remember it. At the time, I didn't care what his name was."

"Brooks," Chapel repeated, then said, "B. Rooks. You say he had three sons with him, is that right?"

It was the first hint of animation in the grave, emotionless face. "That's right," Sam said. "He said they were his boys. Each one of 'em lookin' like they would just as soon slit your throat as look at you. You know 'em?"

Chapel knew them, all right. He knew them well. At least he had a feeling that he did. And if he was right, the last time he had been on their trail was three years before, when they had shot his horse out from under

him and left him to die in the middle of the prairie with
a hole in his chest. There was a score left to be settled,
but Bevo Rooks and his boys had not been heard of
since then. *So now, after all this time, he shows up in Oklahoma Territory,* he thought, finding it hard to believe
the boldness of the man. "I know him," he replied
softly. "We'll be startin' back to the Cherokee Strip first
thing in the mornin', so you might as well make camp
here tonight. Cut you out what you want of that meat.
Tom, you can take the rest of it back to the village."

"You goin' back to Guthrie with 'em?" Tom Turnipseed asked. "Goin' after Bevo Rooks?"

"I am," Chapel replied.

"Can I go with you?"

"Hell no."

"Ah, come on, Chapel. I won't be in the way. I can
help you out." Tom's pleading seemed to be falling on
deaf ears. "I can help these folks get their place set up
after you take care of Rooks."

Astonished witnesses to the banter between the
menacing-looking ex-marshal and the ragtag clown of
a man, Sam and the women were not sure what had
just happened. Chapel's complete reversal had come
about so suddenly that they were still not sure he meant
he really was going to go back with them to seek justice and help them win their land. "Are you sayin' that
you're goin' back there with us?" Sam had to ask. Chapel merely nodded to confirm it. Sam was naturally
pleased to know their plea for help had been answered,
but at the same time he was still a little anxious over
what might lie ahead. He was smart enough to know
that Chapel had changed his mind only after allowing

the possibility that it was someone named Bevo Rooks and his sons on the claim. There was obviously some bad history between Chapel and the Rooks family. At this point in their partnership, Sam was a bit leery about asking the dispassionate Chapel to explain. Another matter that he hesitated to broach was the question of money. Chapel had not mentioned how much he would require to act on their behalf. It might be more than the money that Link had left with him for safe-keeping.

Thinking along the same lines as her husband, Martha was less apprehensive than Sam. They had agreed to use Link's money to avenge his death, but they could not afford to spend all of their savings, if the price was indeed that high. And Martha knew that thorny matter had to be settled before they traveled the first mile back to Guthrie. "We're pleased that you are going to go back with us, Mr. Chapel," she said, "but we need to know what your price will be."

Chapel met her plaintive gaze with a blank stare, as if judging her for the first time. "I ain't thought about it," he answered.

"I reckon we'd best know before we get started," Sam said, knowing he should have spoken of it before.

"All right," Chapel said, then paused for a minute to think about it. "I'll need two boxes of .44 cartridges for my rifle and a sack of coffee beans. I reckon I can handle the rest."

"I can do that," Sam said, "but what about your fee?"

"That *is* my fee."

"Mister," Sam exclaimed, "we've got a deal." He looked at his wife and sent her a wide grin of relief.

"I think we can do a little better for you than that," Martha offered. "We can at least feed you while you're helping us." She smiled at him, then added, "Of course we'll buy you the sack of coffee beans, too, if you want."

"What about me?" Tom Turnipseed asked. He had been forgotten in the negotiations.

"What about you?" Chapel replied, his expression as wooden as ever.

"You never said if I could go with you or not."

"You're gonna take 'em back to Johnny Duncan's tradin' post on Antelope Creek." He turned to Sam then. "That's where we can buy my cartridges and anything else you folks might need. Tom knows the way. I'll catch up with you there. It'll be quicker'n the way you came, too."

Concerned, Sam glanced at Tom, who was grinning smugly; then he looked back at Chapel. "I thought you were goin' with us," he said.

"I'll be along in a couple of days. I'll catch up with you by the time you get to Duncan's. Like I said, Tom knows the way, and it'll be about a day shorter than the way you came."

Martha Anderson became concerned early on about the wisdom of their decision to employ the services of the curious man called Chapel. He had seemed so detached when they had first solicited his help, only to suddenly completely reverse his decision. There was something about him; he had an aura of death about him, especially in the depth of his gaze when his dark eyes settled upon her, and she imagined how a fawn must feel under the lethal gaze of a mountain lion.

Luella, on the other hand, always the rebel, found Mr. Chapel fascinating in an ominous way, and she welcomed him as an ally. In his intense interest in this man Rooks and his sons, would he abandon her family to serve his own desire for revenge? Tom Turnipseed had told them of the near-fatal wound in Chapel's chest, a souvenir of his last encounter with the notorious outlaws. Neither she nor her husband could understand how a family of known outlaws could claim a parcel of land in the new territory, even though attempting to register it under a fictitious name. Surely there would be some response by the U.S. Marshals Service, especially if someone was suspicious enough to realize how easily the name Brooks could be created from B. Rooks. But Turnipseed had commented that there was no law to speak of outside the new towns like Guthrie. She feared her innocent family might be caught in the middle of a gun battle. Chapel was dangerous. Of that there was little doubt, but what of the seeming buffoon of a man wearing the ridiculous derby hat who guided their wagon back toward Guthrie? In contrast to the silent Chapel, Turnipseed seemed to ramble on constantly, even when he was the only participant in the conversation. Yet, he apparently knew where he was leading them, and he was more than willing to help with the horses and the setting up of camp—and he was very respectful toward her and Luella. So she counted him as harmless. It was a lot to weigh upon her mind as Tom pulled up on the trail ahead and waited for them to come alongside.

"That cabin yonder is Johnny Duncan's place," he said, pointing toward a clump of cottonwoods where a creek emptied into the river. Neither Sam nor Martha had spotted the cabin from the wagon seat until Tom had pointed it out. "I'll ride on ahead and tell 'em we got women and children, so they need to watch their manners." He gave his pinto a kick and galloped off, leaving Sam and Martha to exchange puzzled glances, hardly comforted by Tom's comment.

Expecting a party of rough, uncivilized ruffians, they were pleasantly surprised to find a rather round, jolly-looking man of perhaps fifty or sixty years of age—by appearance, he could have been either—for his head was barren of hair and his cheeks red with the flush of alcoholic spirits. Standing beside him, and a head taller, was an Osage woman in a calico dress. They were both smiling warmly. A few feet away, Tom stood, waiting to direct Sam. "Pull her right over there between them two big trees," he called out. "That's handy to the creek. We'll camp here tonight and wait for Chapel."

"Welcome, folks," the little round man spoke up. "My name's Johnny Duncan, and this here's my wife, Ruby. Glad you stopped by." Ruby greeted them with a pleasant smile.

"Glad to meet you," Sam replied. "Our name's Anderson, Sam and Martha, and our sister, Luella Cochran." When two small heads peeked out around the canvas, Sam added, "And Sammy and Jenny."

"Well, bring 'em on inside when you get your horses took care of and your camp set up," Johnny said. "I think I might still have a few pieces of peppermint candy left. I got most anythin' else you might need, too. Got some cornmeal, and that's somethin' scarce as hens' teeth. If you folks been travelin' in that wagon for a long time, you might wanna let my wife fix you somethin'—some corn cakes and side meat, hot coffee and some fall peas—just twenty-five cents apiece." He paused for a minute while Luella and Martha looked at each other, wondering if they wanted to risk it. "Ruby's a mighty fine cook," he went on. "Tom can tell you that. Right, Tom?" Then, rubbing his ample belly, he chuckled and said, "You can tell that by lookin' at me."

"Well, I suppose I should fix our supper," Martha said, "but it would be nice to have somebody fix *my* supper for once." She looked at the still-smiling Indian woman and quickly said, "Maybe Luella and I can help Ruby with the cooking."

Ruby shook her head with her patient smile still in place. "No, I fix." She promptly turned around then and went to the kitchen.

"Twenty-five cents apiece seems fair enough for grown-ups," Sam commented. "Ought'n it be a little cheaper for children?"

Duncan chuckled before responding. "A body might think so, but I've seed some young'uns that could pack in a heap of chuck." Looking at nine-year-old Sammy, he said, "Like that little feller there. I bet you can outeat your daddy, can't you, boy?" Sammy visibly puffed up a little at the thought, but made no reply. "You folks come on into the store when you get settled," Johnny said, and turned to follow his wife inside.

Sam and Tom, with Sammy's help, took the horses to the creek for water while Martha and Luella busied themselves in the wagon. "We'll need a fire in the morning," Martha called after Sammy. "You'd better look for some wood before it gets dark. Jenny can help."

"Yes'um," he yelled back.

While the men watered the horses, Sam said to Tom, "When Johnny was bragging about his wife's cooking, I didn't hear you say anything when he said you'd back him up. Is she as good a cook as he says?"

Tom grinned. "Nah . . ." He tilted his derby up halfway and scratched his head while he considered the question. "I mean, she's all right, I reckon. I've et her cookin' a few times, and I ain't caught a bellyache yet."

"I was afraid we mighta been better off feeding ourselves," Sam said, "but I do think it'll be good to give Martha and Luella a night off."

Johnny Duncan went into the kitchen to talk to his wife. He found her sifting through a sack of cornmeal, picking the weevils out. "Those folks look green as grass," he said. "We might make a little money off 'em if Tom don't spoil it for us. I think I'll get him to drinkin' some of that rye whiskey I got last month, and he'll be asleep before he knows what hit him."

Ruby did not reply. She had seen her husband take advantage of innocent travelers before, selling them worthless cures for lame horses, buffalo grease guaranteed to make a wagon run smoother and faster, miracle salve to keep a woman's skin from drying out in the Oklahoma sun. She could feel his eager anticipation.

"Cook up some of that side meat that's startin' to turn," he said. "Oughta charge 'em more'n twenty-five cents for supper. Hell, there's ten cents' worth of worms in that meat."

* * *

"There you go," Sam said when he laid the money on the table, "one dollar and fifty cents. I'm paying for Tom's, too." Turnipseed grinned and nodded his appreciation. They sat around a long plank table in the kitchen, and Ruby served the plates. Everyone pitched into the simple fare, which proved to be palatable in spite of its integrity. Only the children seemed less than enthusiastic, and finally Sammy made the statement that killed his little sister's appetite for good.

"There's something wiggling on my plate," the youngster reported, and he started poking at it with his fork.

Seated next to him at the table, Tom reached over and picked the wiggler out of Sammy's plate. He held it up for all to see before dropping it on the floor and smashing it with his foot. He chuckled and said, "He's a tough one. Made it through the fryin' pan and still kickin'." That was enough to curtail Martha's appetite as well. She was accustomed to occasionally finding weevils in her flour, but she had never cooked any wormy meat. Both Tom and her husband seemed indifferent to the worm on Sammy's plate, and they continued to clean their plates with enthusiasm, as did Luella.

After supper, Johnny asked Sam what supplies he might need. Sam explained that he was well stocked at present, but there were some things he had agreed to provide for Chapel. "So we'll be doing a little business later on when he gets here," he said.

"Fine and dandy," Duncan replied, "I'll be glad to help you any way I can."

As darkness fell in the shade of the cottonwoods,

Sam decided it was time to retire for the night. Martha and the kids had already returned to the wagon to help Luella prepare the beds. Sam's only concern at the moment was how to keep Martha from smelling the alcohol on his breath. At Duncan's urging, he had taken a couple of drinks of whiskey, but in spite of Johnny's persistence, he had drawn the line at two. "Little woman keepin' a tight rein on you, huh?" Johnny asked.

"I guess you could say that," Sam replied, "but I expect I'll be a little better off in the morning without an aching head."

"You're probably right," Johnny conceded. "I'll walk out to your wagon with you. I need a snort of fresh air before I go to bed." They started across the clearing between the store and the trees where the wagon was parked. "By the way, Sam, I was gonna mention this to you. I noticed your axles squeaking a little when you pulled in. I might have somethin' that'ud take care of that for you. Give you a lot longer life outta them axles."

"I doubt he'll need it."

Both men jumped, startled by the voice behind them in the shadows. Duncan recovered first and complained. "Dagnabbit, Chapel, You scared the hell outta me. I wish you wouldn't walk up on a man like that. You could get yourself shot."

"You ain't totin' a gun," Chapel replied frankly. He emerged from the heavy shadows, leading a buckskin horse.

Knowing his chance to sell Sam some of his worthless

remedies was destroyed with Chapel's arrival, Johnny quickly remarked to Sam, "That's right—them axles didn't sound all that bad. You most likely don't need no buffalo grease on 'em." He turned his attention to Chapel then. "Sam, here, says you'll be needin' some supplies."

"I'll be needin' some .44 cartridges if it's a fair price; else I'll get 'em in Guthrie."

"And a sack of coffee beans," Sam reminded.

"And a sack of coffee beans," Chapel echoed. "I'll be in directly, soon as I take care of my horse." While Johnny returned to open up his store again, Chapel turned to Sam. "He'll sell you somethin' you don't need," he warned. "You folks get some sleep, 'cause we'll be pullin' outta here at first light. We can make a few miles before we have to rest your horses. We'll eat breakfast then. That all right with you?"

"Whatever you say," Sam replied. Chapel started to walk away, but Sam stopped him to ask, "You think maybe it'd be a good idea to buy some of that buffalo grease he was talking about?"

"Nah," Chapel replied. "It ain't nothin' but the same grease you've got in that can on the side of your wagon, with a little bit of buffalo shit mixed in it."

"Oh," Sam responded, thankful that the dark shadows hid the flush of embarrassment on his face. "I suspected as much," he lied.

"I'll tell you in the mornin' how much you owe Duncan," Chapel said as he walked away, the buckskin gelding following along behind him, and Tom Turnipseed following the buckskin.

Always eager to make conversation with Chapel, Tom remarked, "You're back ridin' a buckskin." Chapel didn't answer, thinking it rather obvious that he was in fact riding a buckskin, a horse he had traded two other horses for. Tom went on. "That was a buckskin you was ridin' when them Rooks boys dry-gulched you."

"That's right," Chapel said.

"That sorrel you was ridin' when I brought you back from Fort Supply was a pretty stout horse. How come you traded it away?"

Chapel was well aware that Tom was really not that interested in the horse he rode. It was his way of reminding him that he had helped him back to Fort Smith after he was wounded, but Chapel went along with it. "I like buckskins." This was all he said, but he had always favored the breed. It was his opinion that buckskins were stronger horses; they had harder feet and better bone, and most of the time when other horses were ready to quit, his buckskin could keep going. The best one he had owned was lost to Bevo Rooks, and that provided almost as much reason for running the bloody villain down as his own near-death injury. The thought of it caused his mind to call back the vision of that fateful day when he was left lying on the prairie to slowly die—and Bevo Rooks' sentencing him to die slowly. The terrible scars on his chest and back began to ache slowly, with each beat of his heart, and his desperate need for vengeance rose up inside him.

It had been some time since Tom had ridden from Fort Supply to Fort Smith with Chapel, but the detached, somber silences common to his big friend still occurred on occasion. He sensed one of them now, so he knew the chance of conversation was remote until Chapel came back from wherever it was that haunted his mind—all the more evidence that the moody ex-lawman had actually passed over death's threshold and returned. To Tom, Chapel's moody lapses were even more eerie in the darkness, so he finally said, "I'm goin' to the store to get me some likker. You be along?" Chapel merely grunted in reply.

By the time Chapel walked into Duncan's trading post, Tom had already relaxed his vocal cords with a couple of shots of Johnny's whiskey. "Uh-oh," he sang out. "It's a damn good thing Chapel ain't still wearin' a badge, or you'd get arrested for sellin' whiskey in Injun Territory."

"Hell, I don't sell it to the Injuns," Johnny lied, eyeing Chapel nervously. He still wasn't sure whether the ex-deputy cared or not, but he preferred not to chance the possibility that he might. "You want a little shot?" he asked.

Chapel nodded. "One shot, then I need two boxes of .44 cartridges. Scoop me up one of those bags of coffee beans, and I hope they ain't as green as the last ones I bought from you." He paused then to glance at the items on the shelf behind the counter. Then, before Johnny could ask if there was something else, he said, "That'll be it. How much you askin'?"

"I ain't makin' no money a'tall on these folks," Johnny complained. "If it was just you, you know it'd be the regular price, but there's no harm done if I make a little bit more on them folks. That's fair, ain't it? I don't expect they'll ever buy nothin' from me again. So

where's the harm?" He gazed plaintively at the menacing man-hunter for what seemed to be an extended
length of time, but Chapel's intense stare never wavered
until Johnny gave in. "Hell, all right, I'll charge 'em the
same as I always charge you. But damn it, I can't make a
livin' chargin' these cheap prices."

When Chapel finally responded, it was to say, "Your
prices are higher than what I can get cartridges for at
Bob Dawson's place up the river."

"Yeah, but you have to ride twelve miles up the river
to Dawson's," Johnny protested. He had had the same
argument with Chapel before, but the stoic man never
wavered.

They were on their way early the next morning with
Chapel and Tom out in front, matching the leisurely
pace of the team of horses pulling Sam's wagon. Luella
walked beside the wagon, as she often did. Chapel
planned to make camp north of Guthrie that night if
Sam's horses were up to it. It was midmorning before
they stopped to rest the horses and fix a late breakfast.
Young Sammy helped again with the unhitching of the
wagon and the watering of the horses, after which the
horses were hobbled and left to graze while Martha
mixed up pan bread in her big skillet to fry in the grease
left by the bacon. When it was ready, she called everyone to breakfast.

There was very little conversation among the breakfast participants, save for some rambling remarks from
Tom Turnipseed about the drove of settlers that had
taken over the Cherokee Outlet. "All that territory they
opened up to settlers used to be set aside for the tribes

of the Nations to hunt," he informed the Andersons. "And buffalo, why, there was so many buffalo on these grasslands you wouldn't never think you could ever kill 'em all. But not no more. Ain't that right, Chapel? Chapel could tell you." Chapel did not reply.

I bet he could, Luella thought, *if he ever decided to talk*. She glanced at the always-morose man sitting cross-legged, Indian fashion, a little apart from the circle, eating the breakfast Martha had cooked. *It's like having a dead man at the breakfast table*, she thought, then glanced at Martha, wondering if she was having the same thoughts. *I wonder if he ever smiles*. Martha caught her glance and answered with a raised eyebrow. Chapel was a stranger, and would always remain one, she decided. And they were probably fools to have enlisted him to help them. They all might be killed as a result of returning to claim the parcel by the river. *And yet, here we are, following along after this strange man, instead of doing the sensible thing, which is to avoid trouble*. His penetrating gaze shifted up to meet her eyes at that moment as if he had read her thoughts. She boldly returned his gaze for a few moments before looking away.

Sam spoke up then. "Are you figuring on going into Guthrie, Mr. Chapel?"

"No need to," Chapel replied, "if you can find that piece of land again. We'll just follow the river west until we come to your land—oughta find it before dark tomorrow if that map you drew is near right."

"You think we oughta go into Guthrie first to the land office? Maybe they sent a marshal out there to look into it," Sam said.

"We could do that, I reckon," Chapel said, "if it'd make you feel any better." He was well aware of Sam's concern about what was about to take place, and he didn't really blame him. He had a wife and kids to worry about, but Chapel doubted very seriously that a response from anyone in law enforcement had occurred. Evidently Sam had not yet realized that Chapel's sole interest in this endeavor was in the destruction of a nest of vicious killers, in the same way he might destroy a nest of hornets. Sam's land claim was secondary to that, and it was of little interest to him once he had accomplished what he had come to do. He had to admit, however, that he was slightly curious to see how big a town Guthrie had become since its recent birth. "We'll make camp tonight where the Cimarron takes a big swing to the north," he decided. "If we stop there, we'll only be a little over an hour's ride from the new town. Will that suit you?"

"Yes, sir," Sam replied. "That would be just fine. I'd like to see if anything has been done to settle our dispute."

The decision was met with a small sense of relief on Martha's part. She had already imagined a deadly gunfight, with bullets flying all about her loved ones, and it was something she wanted no part in. Since there were four of the claim jumpers to deal with, she assumed Chapel was expecting Sam to be a part of the fighting. And this she was against. Sam had no business in a gunfight, especially against notorious outlaws like the Rookses. She was resolved to have Sam talk to the federal land representative. Then if he said they had no legal claim on the land, maybe they would decide to turn around and head back to Kansas, and say farewell to the baleful Mr. Chapel. These thoughts were enough to give her some hope as they hitched the horses up in preparation to continue on toward Guthrie.

Chapter 10

It was even bigger than he had heard. Chapel was amazed by the development of a city of thousands of people where he had hunted for deer six months before. Hundreds of tents were in place, but there were also many buildings finished or under construction, and the streets were laid out and bustling with folks coming and going. There was a board structure replacing the tent that had housed the land office when Sam and the women were there last, and it was still open even at the late hour when Chapel and Sam rode in. Tom sorely wanted to ride in with them, but he agreed to stay with the wagon after Sam promised to bring a bottle of whiskey back for him. He even loaned Sam his pinto to ride into town.

When at last they were able to talk to a clerk in the land office, they were told that the particular piece of land they inquired about was under a disputed claim between Brooks and Anderson, but Brooks had prior rights to the land because he was the first to occupy it. When told by Chapel that the alleged claimant was in fact a man named Rooks who was wanted for cattle rustling and murder, the clerk said he would notify the U.S. Marshals Service to investigate the accusation.

"Again, words," Sam complained when they left the building, "but will they actually do anything about it?" Chapel merely shrugged in response. He had expected nothing more from the little office swamped by complaints and requests from hundreds of people. "Well, let's get back to the wagon and tell Martha and Luella what he said. First, I'll go right over there to that saloon and get Tom the whiskey I promised."

"I'll wait outside," Chapel said, and took the reins for both horses. Then he followed Sam to a large tent with a wide board over the entrance and a sign proclaiming it to be a saloon.

"Damn!" Crown Rooks blurted, unable to believe his eyes at first. He rubbed them frantically, trying to clear his blurry vision left by too much whiskey. He backed quickly away from the corner of the saloon, thinking he had surely seen a ghost. *It's the whiskey*, he thought. *It ain't the same man.* "Couldn't be," he murmured to himself. "I put a hole the size of a quarter right through that son of a bitch." Just then, the flap of the tent opened as Sam came out, and the light from inside the busy saloon shone upon Chapel's face. In a panic, Crown stepped backward until he almost fell over a tent rope. When he tried to regain his balance, his stumbling caught the attention of the solemn man holding the horses. Frightened when Chapel turned to look his way, Crown grabbed his pistol and started firing as fast as he could pull the trigger and cock it again. In his haste to destroy the ghost he thought had come back to haunt him, and hindered by his drunken blur, his shots were wild and wide.

As soon as he had seen Crown move for his pistol, Chapel dived at Sam, knocking him to the ground, and in one continuous motion, rolled the two of them off the edge of the board stoop. By the time he was able to pull his revolver from his holster, Crown had emptied his pistol and was running for his horse. Chapel got off three shots before Crown managed to get behind his horse for cover, one of them catching Bevo's eldest son in the left arm. "Go back to the wagon!" Chapel shouted to Sam before he scrambled to his feet and jumped in the stirrup. The buckskin sensed the urgency and leaped to a gallop while his master threw his leg over and settled in the saddle. Confused and shaken, Sam struggled to his feet, still holding on to Tom's whiskey and staring wide-eyed after Chapel until he could no longer see him in the darkness. As curious folks filed out of the saloon to see what the shooting was about, he did as he had been told and headed back to the wagon.

With hooves thundering on the hard prairie ground, Crown Rooks whipped his horse mercilessly, the image of the cruel dark face still fresh in his mind's eye. It was a face he had never expected to see again, and it still held the same defiance he had witnessed on the day they had left him to die a slow death on the prairie. He realized now the mistake it had been not to let Cotton finish the dying deputy marshal off when they had the chance. Now he had come back to stalk them. The pain from the bullet wound in his arm was throbbing in time with his racing heart, like the rapid ticking away of ominous seconds.

Frequent looks over his shoulder revealed no sign of the dreaded lawman in the darkness, but he knew that Chapel was coming. Pressing his horse for more speed, he galloped into a wide creek and pulled the already-tiring horse sharply to his left, splashing along the shallow creek in an effort to hide his trail. When he came to a grove of cottonwoods, he left the creek just before it emptied into the river, and frantically urged the laboring animal up the bank and into the trees. Pausing only briefly to listen and peer into the darkness behind him, he had no thoughts toward ambushing his pursuer—only thoughts of escape. Such was his fear of one who had defied death to come searching for him. With his shirtsleeve now soaked with blood, he had no inclination to rest his weary horse, so he forced the animal into the river and crossed over to continue his race for his father's camp. Because of his panic to get away, he was not now sure of his way home, so he had no choice but to follow the winding Cimarron until reaching the camp.

Behind the frightened fugitive, Chapel was forced to stop his pursuit when he reached the creek. There was barely enough light to tell him that Crown had not ridden straight across, for he could find no trace of tracks on the opposite bank. It was now a question of whether the fleeing man had gone upstream or down-, and there was nothing to give him a clue either way. He could not say that he had gotten a good look at

Bevo Rooks' three sons on that day more than three years earlier, but he felt certain that the man who shot at him was one of the brothers. If not, what reason would there be for him to take the shot? He saw it as bad luck that he had been spotted by one of the Rooks clan, because they were now forewarned, making his task much harder.

Frustrated that he had lost the trail in the darkness, he nevertheless decided to follow the creek to the point where it met the river in hopes that he might find Crown waiting for him to show. He was not sure, but he thought he might have gotten one slug into him, so once he reached the Cimarron, he cautiously approached the bluffs. But there was no one there, and he was forced to admit that Crown had gotten away. The element of surprise was lost, since he had been unable to stop him before he warned Bevo, but he knew where the old man and his sons were. Sam could take him there. Disappointed in the night's outcome, he turned the buckskin around and headed back to the wagon.

Sam and Tom walked out to meet him when he approached the camp on the bank of the river. Anxious to hear what had happened, they both spoke at once, Tom the more insistent. "Did you get him?" he asked. "Was it one of them Rooks?"

"I'm pretty sure it was," Chapel answered, "but I lost him in the dark. Doesn't matter, I'll find them tomorrow evenin'." He dismounted and led his horse back toward the campfire glowing beside the wagon.

"I expect you could use a shot of this whiskey Sam brought back," Tom declared.

"No, thanks," Chapel replied. "I think I need some coffee and somethin' to eat instead."

"I'll get you some," Luella volunteered.

Chapel looked at the obviously worried woman standing beside Luella, with little Jenny hanging on to her skirt. "Thank you, ma'am," he said to Luella when she handed him a cup of coffee. Then he glanced at Sam standing by, waiting for more details about the attack outside the saloon, and Sammy looking at him expectantly, and he made a decision. "I think it best for you and your family to stay on here until this thing is finished, one way or the other. Maybe you can give me that map you drew, and I can find your claim with that. If I had to, I could most likely find it by just following the river till I come to their camp." In the flickering light of the fire, he could readily see the instant relief in Martha's face.

"Maybe you're right," Sam quickly agreed.

Chapel thought some more about it, then suggested, "Tom can stay back with you and maybe do some huntin' to help out with your food supplies."

"Ah, wait a minute, Chapel," Tom protested at once. "I need to go with you. There's four of them Rooks. You'll be needin' some help. I don't wanna wait back here."

"We'll be all right," Sam said. "We've got enough provisions to last."

"That's right," Martha agreed quickly. "We're close enough to town that we should be all right." Her opinion of the indifferent man was altered slightly in his show of concern for their safety. Maybe she had been wrong, and there was a slender thread of compassion running through the granite exterior, although she was not ready to concede any change in his single-purpose demeanor—and the man had still never smiled. "Please take Tom with you if he wants to go. You may need his help."

Luella filled a plate from the pot still sitting in the coals of the fire from supper, placed a couple of pan biscuits on it, and brought it to Chapel. As was his habit, he walked a short distance away from the others to sit down and eat. This time, Luella followed him and sat down opposite him with a cup of coffee for herself. Puzzled by her move, he gazed at her, waiting to see what she wanted. "Go on and eat your supper," she told him. "I'm not going to bother you."

"What do you want?" he asked, still puzzled.

"I don't want anything," she said, "except this cup of coffee." What she wanted, in fact, was to get a closer look at this perplexing man, wondering how much of what Tom had told them about him she could believe. Watching him now, she could readily see that he was uncomfortable with someone watching him eat, or was he just uncomfortable with women? She could certainly understand that he had acquired a reputation as a relentless hunter. He surely looked the part, with his cold, dark eyes and his chiseled features, but she somehow sensed that there was something inside his hard shell that might approach decency. "Were you ever married?" she asked. Her question caused his hand to pause halfway to his mouth as he stared at her, astonished by her blatant demeanor, and he didn't know how to answer her. She smiled. "It's a simple question," she said. "Either yes or no. Don't you know if you've ever been married?" When there was still no answer from him, she realized the reason for his lack of response. "You've never been around women much before, have you?"

"That's a dumb question," he finally replied. "Course I have." He failed to understand the real meaning of her question. He had been around women before, his mother and some Indian women, but never in the circumstances she meant.

She was certain that she had guessed correctly, however, and satisfied with her probe of his mind, she got up to leave. "I'll go and let you eat in peace," she told him.

"'Preciate it," he replied, thinking what a strange woman she was.

Martha stood by the fire, waiting for her sister, when Luella came back to place her cup in the dishpan. Fixing her gaze accusingly upon her, she asked, "Lou, what are you doing?"

"I'm putting my cup in the dishpan," she said. "Then I'm going to take the dishes over to the river to wash them as soon as ol' Smiley over there finishes."

Not amused, Martha responded. "You know what I mean—getting cozy with that notorious gunman."

Luella laughed. "Is that what I was doing? Getting cozy?"

"Lou, that man is nothing but trouble. It's best to keep as much distance as possible between all of us and him. I'm just worried about you. This is not a man you want to tease, even if you're just playing, which I find hard to believe, even for you."

"All right, *Mother*," Luella said. "Thank you for being

concerned. I'll try not to incite him into raping and murdering us all."

"All I'm doing is warning you," Martha insisted. "There's no telling how many people that man has killed." She could see by the smirk on her sister's face that her warning was probably a waste of time. Luella would do what she damned well pleased, just like always.

Bevo Rooks looked out across the river, then let his gaze sweep eastward across the gentle rise in the prairie floor beyond the bluffs. It was something he had done frequently since Crown had come back from Guthrie in the wee hours of the morning, his horse ridden half to death. With a shake of his head, he turned and walked back to the fire where Crown was chewing on a slice of bacon, washing it down with coffee. Bevo paused a moment to look at the rag tied around Crown's arm. "Ain't bleedin' no more," he observed.

"No, sir," Crown replied.

"You're dead sure it was that damn deputy that shot you?"

"Yes, sir," Crown answered. "It was him, all right, and he sure as hell saw me. That son of a bitch oughta be dead."

"I told you to let me finish him off," Cotton said.

"Shut up, Cotton," Bevo snapped, then turned back to his eldest. "Who shot first, you or him?"

Crown hesitated, unwilling to admit that he had pulled his gun in a panic. "Well, I reckon I did. Hell, he looked right at me. I could tell he recognized me."

"And you missed him," Bevo said in disgust. He had an idea that Chapel might not have even noticed Crown if his son hadn't flown off the handle and shot at him.

"I had to make a run for it," Crown said. "He was comin' after me, and I didn't have no time to reload my pistol, so I hightailed it outta there."

"You emptied your pistol at him and didn't hit him once?" Bevo charged. "I swear, I thought I taught you better'n that. You lost your damn head. You're lucky you only got hit in the arm."

"We better be ready when he shows up here," Corbett said as he walked up to join the conversation.

Bevo frowned. "Who said he's gonna show up here? You said you lost him last night. Are you sure about that?"

"Yes, sir, I'm sure," Crown answered. "That's why it took me so long to get back. I made sure he couldn't follow me." He could have told his father that he had gotten lost, and that was the real reason he didn't come straight back, but he saw no reason to subject himself to the ridicule of his brothers.

"Then he's probably not comin' here to this camp," Bevo said. "He don't know nothin' about this piece of land. Most likely he was just passin' through on some business for the law, and he didn't have no idea we was anywhere in the territory." He paused, then added, "Till you took a shot at him." For emphasis, he reached down and slapped Crown's hat off his head. "Damn it!" he roared. "When you pull a gun, kill somebody."

"Yes, sir, I'm sorry, Pa," Crown whined as he rescued his hat from the coals of the fire.

Bevo stood glaring down at his son for a long minute before speaking again. "But I reckon we'd best get
ready for the son of a bitch in case he does show up
here. And this time I'll make damn sure he's dead." He
had no idea whether or not the deputy actually knew it
was Crown who shot at him, so he might not be aware
that he had stumbled upon the gang that had left him
for dead. Being in Texas during those years, he had no
way of hearing that Chapel had survived. But he
wished to hell now that he had given him the mercy
killing he had denied him.

He was in no mood to put up with a vengeance-
seeking deputy marshal. He had enough problems
with the brother-in-law of the corpse that had disappeared from a grove of willows on the other side of the
river. He felt certain about what had happened to
the body. And the son of a bitch, a man by the name of
Anderson, filed claim on top of his for this land. Bevo
had no intention of giving up on his claim. It was the
perfect piece of ground for his plans to raise horses
and cattle that he planned to rustle in Texas and Mexico. He and his boys would eventually become legiti-
mate ranchers, and he would kill anybody who got in
the way of it. The first order of business was to take
care of this fellow, Anderson, and that would be done
if he ever showed up in the Outlet again. He hadn't for
some days now, and Bevo felt that it was a pretty good
bet he wouldn't, even though he did file on the land. *I
hope to hell he does*, he thought, *'cause if he's dead, he damn
sure won't cause any trouble.*

With thoughts returning to the work at hand, he
tossed the dregs of his coffee cup at the fire and ordered,

"All right, just in case we need the horses in a hurry, we'll saddle 'em up. Then let's get to work on that shack for your mama. It ain't gonna build itself." He could imagine that his wife was getting pretty testy, waiting down in Texas for him to come after her.

It was no more than half a day's ride for the two men on horses. Aided by the rough map that Sam had drawn, they agreed that the horseshoe bend in the Cimarron they were now looking at was no doubt the same that Sam had meticulously sketched on the scrap of brown wrapping paper. Close by the river, in a stand of tall cottonwoods, they saw a wagon, a tent, and the start of a cabin. Beyond, on the grassy bank, a few horses grazed. Chapel might have called the scene peaceful had the occupants of the camp been anyone other than Bevo Rooks and his offspring.

Leaving the horses below the back of the rise that swept gradually down to the river bluffs, Chapel and Tom climbed to the crest of the hill on foot and knelt to look the camp over more carefully. Chapel had no thoughts of capturing the four outlaws. The possibility of that was extremely remote, considering the reputation of the Rooks clan, so he wanted to be very sure that the four claim jumpers were, in fact, Bevo Rooks and his three sons. "We'll watch for a while to make sure," he told Tom. "I'll wait till dark before I move in on 'em."

"Don't go gettin' no ideas you're gonna do this all by your lonesome," Tom said. "You're gonna need some help, and I didn't ride over here just to watch the show."

Chapel turned to gaze upon the determined expression on the otherwise comical face. He was well aware that Tom could handle a rifle as well as any man, but he was concerned for his safety. As for himself, there had never been any thought of compromise. Rooks and his family had caused the territory enough grief to give cause for retribution of the deadliest kind. This was on his mind, but it was overpowered by the personal vengeance for the day they had left him for dead. Recalling that day even now caused an aching in his chest from the constant reminder there. He could not tell Tom that he had no concern for his own life. It made little difference to him if he lived or died, as long as he put a stop to Bevo Rooks. He had lived alone for as long as he could remember. There was no one he cared for, or cared for him, no family to return to, no friends to visit. And since being discharged from his duties as a deputy marshal for the Federal Court for the Western District of Arkansas, there had been no purpose for his life.

"'Pears like they're fixin' to homestead the place, don't it?" Tom broke into Chapel's thoughts. "Don't reckon they're figurin' on goin' straight, do ya?"

"I wouldn't think so," Chapel murmured.

"Look yonder!" Tom exclaimed, and pointed toward Crown Rooks, who appeared from behind the wagon, a white rag wrapped around his arm. "You musta hit that feller last night."

"Looks like," Chapel said as he continued to study the campsite, so as to remember it after dark. The thickness of the grove of cottonwoods was going to make things a bit more difficult to get clear shots at four targets, but the darkness would help a lone stalker. Where to put Tom was the question now. He didn't want to ask him to wade into the camp with guns blazing. As much of a nuisance as Tom seemed at times, he was the closest thing to a friend that he had ever had, and he might get him killed. He would feel bad about that. After he thought about it some more, he decided how he was going to attack.

"I'm gonna wait till dark, like I said," he began. "I think if I ride upriver a ways, I can come into the camp on the back side of that wagon, and get close enough to get off a couple of good shots before they know they've got company." Before Tom could interject, he answered his question for him. "I want you to cross over to the other side of the river and find you a place across from their camp. When I start shootin', that's gonna be the best chance of escape they're gonna have. And you'll be there to block that. Can you do that?"

"Well, I don't see why not," Tom replied. He hesitated for a moment, wondering if Chapel was primarily intent upon just getting him out of harm's way. But he decided it was a sensible thing to do, so he voiced it. "That seems sensible."

"All right, then," Chapel concluded. "Nothin' to do now but wait till dark."

As the shadows lengthened and the sun settled slowly into the western hills, the two stalkers prepared to leave the base of the rise and take their positions for the assault upon the camp. Chapel remained long enough to watch Tom lead his horse toward the river, until he could no longer see him for the screen of willows. With a feeling of grim satisfaction, he then stepped up in the saddle and turned his horse's head to the north, preparing to ride a wide circle around the camp to come upon it from the west.

Once he had completed the circle and reached the bank of the river, he tied the horse's reins to a serviceberry bush and proceeded on foot, making his way carefully to a gully in the bluffs where he paused to wait for darkness. From where he sat, he could see the horses, still saddled, tied in the scrubby bushes near the water. They were at a distance of perhaps one hundred yards. It was his thought that he might get a couple of clear shots at someone coming to unsaddle them.

The night seemed reluctant to descend upon the riverbank as he waited impatiently. It would have been his preference to walk into the camp with his rifle ready and announce his name and the reason for the attack— to let them know that they were finally being called to face up to their crimes. But he knew to do so would be suicidal. With luck, he might get two of them before being cut down by one of the others. That would leave it up to Tom to get the other two, and he wasn't sure he wanted to risk his friend. He checked his rifle again to make sure it was ready.

Finally the last pink rays of the sun disappeared and gentle night settled in, leaving only the light from the stars and the large campfire near the wagon. Still no one came to unsaddle the horses, so Chapel climbed out of the gully and made his way closer to a position behind a grass hummock. Now no more than fifty yards from the rear of the wagon, he had a clear shot at two of the men near the fire. He was about to move again to see if he could find a place that would put all four of the men in his sights when the rifle shot rang out. He immediately dropped to one knee, his rifle raised to his shoulder, ready to return fire. Then he realized that the shot had come not from the camp but from the opposite bank of the river—*Tom!*

The sudden shot caused pandemonium in the camp as the four around the fire dived out of the light of the flames. With his targets disappearing into the darkness, Chapel had opportunity for only one clear shot, and he cut one of them down as he ran for cover in the half-finished cabin. "Corbett!" Bevo Rooks roared in despair when he saw his middle son drop to the ground. Snatching his rifle from where it had been propped against a tree trunk, he began firing at the spot in the darkness where he now saw muzzle flashes from several different locations. "Crown! Cotton!" he yelled. "They got us surrounded! Grab everythin' you can carry and get to the horses before they cut us off!"

With pistols blazing away at the muzzle flashes near the hummock beyond the wagon, Crown and Cotton made their way to the horses. With their mounts secure, they led them back to the cover of the wagon while Bevo went to check on Corbett. In a few seconds, he was back, fuming mad. "He's gone. Corbett's gone," he wailed. With stray bullets chipping chunks of wood from the wagon, Bevo roared his defiance. "Is that you, Chapel? You killed my boy. You're a dead man!"

Moving as quickly as he could, Chapel continued to take a couple of shots at the wagon before moving several yards away and shooting again, then moving again in an effort to keep them from pinpointing his location. In the confusion of the gunfight in the dark, he was still puzzled by the first shot that spoiled the surprise. There had been no more shots from Tom as far as he could tell. His planned extermination had not occurred as he had hoped, but there was little choice now but to continue firing in hopes he might get lucky.

Behind the wagon, things were getting pretty hot. Crown was the first to express it. "We got to get the hell outta here, Pa. I can't tell how many of 'em there are, but they got us pinned down."

Bevo was furious, but he thought Crown was right. They couldn't fight someone they couldn't see. "All right," he said, "we'll make a run for it." He hesitated a moment to think of their best way out. Noticing the team of horses left in the open, he yelled, "Cotton, bring them horses here and hitch 'em to the wagon. Mind you don't get shot." Bevo and Crown laid down a blistering sheet of fire in the general direction of the shots coming at them while Cotton, on hands and knees, crawled over to fetch the horses and harness. When he was safely back, he and his brother hurriedly hitched the team while Bevo continued to return fire.

"All right, Pa, we're ready!" Cotton yelled. Mistaking his father's intentions, he asked, "You want us to go get Corbett?"

"No," Bevo answered. "Turn them horses toward that rise out yonder. Get all them cartridges outta there and get your horse. As soon as that wagon takes off, we're headin' the other way, toward the river. Realizing then what their father had in mind, the two brothers prepared to mount.

"Ain't we gonna take Corbett?" Crown asked.

"We ain't got time," Bevo shot back. "It don't matter now, anyway. There ain't nothin' we can do for him." He tossed the reins in front of the wagon seat and yelled, "Git!" At the same time, he smacked one of the horses on the behind, and for added encouragement he fired two pistol shots in the ground right behind them. It had the desired effect. The horses bolted, pulling the wagon out toward the open prairie, bumping wildly. Then, stepping up in the saddle, he yelled, "Let's go!" He took off in a gallop for the river, his sons in hot pursuit, all three bent low on their horses' necks.

"Damn!" Chapel swore. He hadn't counted on that. He would have bet any amount that if they ran, they'd run to the river. That was why he had posted Tom on the other side. He also would not have thought they'd take the wagon. There wasn't time to fret about it, so he ran back to get his horse, losing valuable time every second, he thought. In the saddle, he galloped off after the racing wagon.

Tom Turnipseed remained on the opposite bank of the river for as long as he could stand it with all the gunfire popping on the other side. He knew Chapel was going to be mad as hell at him for firing that shot, but he had only acted in response to what he saw as someone swimming toward him in the dark water. His shot had killed a large muskrat that was merely trying to cross unnoticed by the group of men around the fire. At last, his patience wore out, and he decided it was time for him to join the fight, so he got on his pony and urged him into the water. Suddenly the gunfire went silent. The next sound he heard was the splashing of hooves in the shallow water, and they were coming toward him. He reached for his pistol, but Cotton Rooks was faster with a handgun, and he knocked Tom from the saddle before Tom could raise his pistol to fire.

Galloping after the runaway wagon, Chapel heard the shot behind him, and the realization of what had happened hit him immediately. Although he was almost catching up with the crazed team pulling the wagon, he wheeled the buckskin around and hurried back toward the river, cursing himself for his stupidity. Taking no precautions against an ambush, he galloped straight through the camp, heading for the river, where he met Tom's horse climbing up the bank. He searched the dark water for some sign of Tom, but he could see no one. "Tom!" he called.

"Over here," Tom answered.

Chapel jerked his head to follow the sound and spotted Tom holding on to a log half submerged in the shallow water. "Are you hit?" Chapel asked, his eyes darting up and down the opposite bank as he made his way to him.

"They hightailed it," Tom gasped, "but they put a bullet in me first."

"How bad is it?"

"I ain't sure. It knocked me outta the saddle, though, and it hurts like hell, but I ain't spittin' up no blood or nothin'."

"Which way'd they go?" Chapel asked as he stepped down into the water. Torn between his desire to immediately get after the fleeing outlaws and taking care of Tom, he hesitated and peered in the direction Tom pointed. His conscience won out and he said, "Come on. I'll help you get back to that fire, and we'll see how bad you're hurt. Can you wade outta here if I help you?"

"I think so," he said, reaching up for Chapel's hand. A grunt of pain escaped his lips when Chapel pulled him up to his feet, but he said he was all right once he was standing. "I'm sorry about that shot before you was ready," he started. "I thought I saw one of 'em swimmin' right at me. It's so dark in this river, I couldn't tell."

"It wouldn't have made much difference," Chapel said. "It was pretty dark in that bunch of trees, too. Let's get a look at your wound. Looks like they hit you in the shoulder. Might not be too bad."

Now that the initial shock of being shot began to wear off, and he could take an honest assessment of his wound, Tom realized Chapel was right. It was not that bad. "Them fellers is gettin' away," he said. "You go on after 'em. I'll take care of my shoulder."

That was just what Chapel wanted to do, but he remembered how Tom had looked after him when he was riding back to Fort Smith, severely wounded. "I'll see for myself first," he insisted, and led Tom over by the fire. "Looks pretty clean," he decided after a quick examination. "Went into the muscle; didn't come out, though. You were pretty lucky."

"I was pretty dumb," Tom retorted. "I let 'em ride right up to me. If I'd stayed where you told me to, I'da been able to get at least two of 'em." He worked his arm back and forth a couple of times, testing the wound. "Hell, this ain't gonna slow me down a'tall. Tell you the truth, I'm more afraid I'm gonna freeze to death from these wet clothes. The worst thing that happened was I lost my hat. When he shot me, the damn thing drifted down the river somewhere." He shook his head sadly. "I thought a lot of that hat." He moved as close to the fire as he could without getting in it. "But, hell, I can go as soon as I dry off a little. Let's get after 'em."

Chapel was thinking fast at this point. He could readily see that Tom's wound wasn't serious unless he got it infected. "Have you got that bottle Sam bought you in your saddlebags?"

"Yes, sir," Tom said. "Good idea, we could use a little drink right now—might help warm us up."

"That ain't what I had in mind," Chapel said, then went over to the riverbank to retrieve the pinto. He pulled the bottle out and told Tom to lie down. Then he uncorked the bottle and poured a generous portion directly in the wound, causing Tom to emit a little yelp. "Maybe that'll clean it some. You really think you can ride?" When Tom answered that he surely could, Chapel said, "I want you to ride on back to Sam and get them started over here in the mornin'. You tell Sam that if he really wants to claim this land, he's gonna have to get on it and hold it before somebody else finds out about it. He's gonna need you to help him. I ain't so sure he's got the backbone to do it by himself. I'm gonna do my best to make sure they don't decide there ain't as many of us as they thought and come back to fight for their claim. Ask Martha to put a bandage on that hole in your shoulder." He paused to reconsider. "Maybe you'd be better off askin' Luella to do it. She won't faint at the sight of blood. Maybe she can dig that bullet outta there, too."

"I will," Tom said. "Let's take one little drink, though,

to help warm me up." He tipped the bottle back and drew a long slug of the fiery liquid. He offered it to Chapel, but he refused it. "What about that feller over there by the corner of the cabin?" Tom asked.

"Well, he ain't likely to go anywhere. Maybe you and Sam can drag him off in the woods somewhere so he won't scare the young'uns. Are you ready to ride?" Tom said he was, so Chapel caught the pinto's reins and led him over by the fire. "You and Sam hold this ground, and I'll be back when I'm done with the Rooks."

"Watch out for that one with the buffalo rifle," Tom warned.

"I will," Chapel replied. "I kinda hope he's the one lyin' over there by the cabin." He waited long enough to make sure Tom was on his way before he ran back to get his horse. In the dark he had nothing to go on except for the general direction Tom had pointed out to him. Made desperate by the thought that they might get away from him in the night, he crossed back over the river again and set out after them. He soon decided, however, that he was wasting his time and might even wind up riding into another ambush. Reluctantly, he turned the buckskin back to the camp, deciding that if nothing else, he could find a place to hide and keep an eye out in the event that the Rookses came back.

Pushing on through the night, following the Cimarron west, Bevo and his sons sought to distance themselves from the unknown number in the posse behind them. When their horses began to tire, they looked for some refuge along the wide, flat river. With the coming of daylight, the obvious tracks of the horses' hooves over the sandy expanse beside the river left a trail for anyone to follow, causing Bevo to curse their carelessness. They crossed over to the north bank at once, where the scrubby trees and brush grew in the raised bluffs. "We gotta rest these horses, or we'll be totin' them," Bevo said. "There's some taller trees up yonder a ways. We'll rest 'em there." When they walked the tired mounts into the trees, Bevo said, "Shinny up that tree, Cotton, and see if you can see anybody on our tail." Cotton did as his father said. By standing on his saddle, he was able to reach a sizable limb, and from it he was able to climb on up several more feet. "How far can you see?" Bevo asked.

"A pretty good ways back," Cotton replied. "I can see where we came across the river, but I don't see nobody comin' after us."

"You stay up there awhile longer and keep your eyes peeled," Bevo said. "Maybe we lost 'em; maybe we didn't. A posse of blind men could follow that trail we left." He turned to Crown then. "Take the horses down to water."

After about half an hour, Cotton began to complain. "I still don't see nobody, Pa. How much longer do I have to stay up in this damn tree?"

Bevo thought about it a moment longer before deciding. "I reckon you can come down now, but take a good look back before you do. We'da seen 'em by now if they was hot on our trail. I expect it was too dark for 'em to see our tracks where we came outta the river. The bank was grassed up pretty good there. They mighta had to wait for daylight—give us a chance to rest the horses up good."

"We just gonna keep runnin'?" Crown asked, watching his younger brother making his way down the tree. "We was the first ones on that piece of land, and I say we oughta go back and take it."

"That's what I say," Cotton said. "That claim belongs to us."

Bevo cast an impatient glance at first one and then the other before reprimanding them. "In the first place, *you* don't say; *I* say. Crown, you say you got a good look at the feller that shot you at that saloon." Crown nodded. "And you're sure it was that same deputy we left for dead?"

Again Crown nodded. "It was him, all right. Ain't no doubt about it."

"Well, if you had any sense at all, you'd know that he knows who we really are, else he'da not knowed to find us. He's a damn federal deputy marshal, and he's most likely got a posse with him, lookin' for us. And now they know our name ain't Brooks, so our claim ain't worth a damn, even if we weren't wanted in this territory. We ain't got no choice but to give it up and get the hell outta this part of the country."

"Ain't we gonna do nothin' about them killin' Corbett?" Cotton asked.

"Yeah," Crown spoke up, "what are we gonna tell Ma? She'll raise hell when we come back without him."

"I never said this thing was over," Bevo said. "I'm just sayin' we need to shake loose of this damn posse right now. Then I reckon we'll see about takin' care of Mr. Chapel." This seemed to satisfy his sons for the moment, although he was not really sure how he was going to accomplish the vengeance he promised. Crown was right—Pearl Mae was going to be fit to be tied when she found out that one of her boys was missing. The woman could work up a powerful wrath if she was of a mind to. On occasion in the past, he had seen cause to give her a licking when she had thrown a fit over something. But the last time he hit her, she had calmly told him that she was giving him that one, but if he ever hit her again, she was going to kill him. He knew she meant it. He also knew he could not go home unless he could tell her the man who shot Corbett was dead.

There were other things on his mind besides the death of Corbett. His plans to build a cattle ranch somewhere north of Texas had hit another snag. When he had heard about the opening up of the Oklahoma Outlet to settlers, he was sure it was his chance to claim a good piece of land on the Cimarron. His thinking was that in the wild rush of boomers racing to claim homesteads, there would be very little danger of the authorities' ability to determine who was legal and who wasn't. He cursed the luck that brought that one particular marshal to Guthrie on the very night Crown went into the saloon. *Chapel*—the name made his brain seethe with anger. The hated deputy and his posse had tracked him down. "Damn the luck!" He spat, causing both of his sons to look his way, wondering. Bevo glared back at them. "Cotton, get back up in that tree. Crown, build us a fire. I'm hungry. We might as well cook us up some of that side meat while the horses are restin'."

Cotton grunted in complaint but did as he was told. Crown said, "I'll build a fire, but we ain't got no side meat. It was in the wagon."

"Damn the luck!" Bevo roared again. "Why in hell didn't you get it outta the wagon? I swear, all you boys has got too much Crowder blood in you." Crowder was Pearl Mae's maiden name, and Bevo always blamed any show of ignorance on her family's influence on his offspring.

"You never said anythin' about the side meat," Crown replied in his defense. "All you said was to get the guns and cartridges outta the wagon."

"Well, did you think we was gonna give up eatin' while we was on the run?" Bevo demanded.

"I don't know," Crown answered. "We ain't got no coffee, either, and no coffeepot even if we did. They was all in the wagon."

"Crowder blood," Bevo muttered in disgust.

"I got some beef jerky in my saddlebag," Cotton called from his perch in the tree. "Ain't much of it, though."

"I got to have somethin'," Bevo growled. He was not a man to suffer hunger gracefully, so the finding of food moved high up on his priority list. He went over to search Cotton's saddlebags and found the small packet of jerked beef that Pearl Mae had given her youngest before they left to claim land. After taking a couple of strips of the tough meat for himself, he tossed the cloth packet to Crown. "Save some for your brother," Bevo said, and sat down to think over his situation. *Suppose there ain't no posse,* he thought. *Suppose the son of a bitch is by himself, and there was just one rifle jumping back and forth, doing all that shooting.* It was a possibility. *Nah, they wouldn't be dumb enough to send one deputy to get the four of us. Besides,* he remembered then, *what about that one on the other side of the river?* No, he decided, the deputy was not alone. After another few minutes of trying to decide the best thing to do, he made up his mind. He needed to get somewhere away from this river where he could replace the supplies and utensils he had lost—and where he could hunt something to eat without worrying about the posse hearing the shots. He knew just the place. He called Cotton out of the tree and told both boys to get the horses ready to ride. "We're goin' someplace where that posse will think twice before followin' us."

"Damn, Pa," Crown complained, "I was hopin' we'd take time for a little sleep. We rode all night long, and this arm is painin' me some."

"You can sleep later on," Bevo told him. "If we cut south from here, we oughta strike the North Canadian in about forty miles, maybe a mile or two more—a good hard day's ride. I ain't sure the horses are up to it after running off and on all night, so we'll make camp halfway there and get to Cheyenne Canyon tomorrow."

"Cheyenne Canyon?" Crown questioned.

"You oughta remember that canyon," Bevo said. "You was just a little feller when I took you there. Corbett and Cotton was still at home, hangin' on to their mama's skirt tail."

"That place where you shot that man in the mouth?" Crown asked, just then placing it. He remembered it—remembered being impressed by the assortment of outlaws hiding out there, confident that no lawman was likely to venture into that stronghold of danger-ous men. He had been proud of the respect those rough men had shown for his father.

"That's the place, all right," Bevo said. "We oughta

be able to find us some things there. That damn posse will play hell followin' us there." He didn't know if the rugged canyon had a name or not. The outlaws had just taken to calling it Cheyenne Canyon because some years earlier it had been a favorite winter camp for a band of Cheyenne before the government shipped them all off to the reservation.

Chapter II

The night passed with no sign of the return of the notorious clan, so Chapel crossed the river once more at first light and scouted the bank until he found the trail left by Rooks and his two boys on the grassy slope. It was slow going at first until he reached a point where the river was bordered by a wide sandy bank, and three sets of hoofprints told of the urgency of the Rookses' retreat. Chapel gave his horse a nudge with his heels, and the big buckskin picked up the pace. Remembering the last time he had tracked the murdering outlaw family, he scanned the terrain ahead of him constantly, watching for potential spots for ambush. When he came to the point where the Rookses had crossed over to the other side, he became even more cautious as his eyes traced the apparent path they had taken upon leaving the water. When he determined that the tracks were leading him into a stand of cottonwoods on the bluffs, he stepped down from the saddle and, using his horse for cover, walked toward the trees, his rifle barrel lying across the saddle, ready to fire at the first sign of movement.

As soon as he entered the trees, he dropped the buckskin's reins and made his way cautiously from tree to tree until he determined there was no one there. *But they were here*, he thought when he found the remains of a small fire that had burned only half of the dead branches before going out. Cold ashes and old horse droppings told him the men he was after had left this place some hours before, at least eight if he had to guess. The question to be answered at this point was, which way did they go from there? Leading his horse, he started out again in the same direction the Rookses had held to all along, searching for tracks as he walked. When he came to a clearing between the clumps of cottonwoods, it was obvious that they had not continued to follow the river west, so he returned to the clearing to try again. After a careful search, he found tracks leading back to the water's edge where they were mixed with many others. *This is where they were watering their horses while they were camped here*, he thought. He couldn't tell if there was one trail among the many tracks that could tell him if they had crossed over to the other side. Peering intently, he tried to see if there were any tracks on the wide sandy strip on the south side, but he couldn't tell. He stepped up in the saddle and urged his horse into the water. Sure enough, there were exit tracks on the other bank, but he was surprised to find that they no longer followed the Cimarron, instead continuing on a southerly course.

The trail never wavered from that direction throughout the day. The terrain changed somewhat from the flat prairie they had left behind, to a rolling land with more trees here and there, and gutted with narrow ravines. The trail was still fairly easy to follow, however. Judging from the hoofprints, the pace had been a good bit easier than the day preceding, indicating a sense of confidence on the part of the fleeing outlaws. *It's as though they're feeling almost safe,* he thought. Then it occurred to him that they were heading straight south to the North Canadian, and he remembered that Cheyenne Canyon was not far up the river if they continued on in this direction. The last time he had been to Cheyenne Canyon, he had been following a couple of cattle rustlers, and he had run into at least a dozen more fugitives, all hiding out in the rocky canyon. It was obvious now that Rooks was heading there, and Chapel could not help but hope he would be as successful in getting his man this time as he was the last time he was there. The canyon was a veritable fortress for the lawless with only one way in, and it had taken a cavalry patrol to clean them all out, his man in the bunch. It was one of the few times he had needed help to track down a fugitive.

It was early afternoon when Bevo and his two sons reached the bluffs overlooking a canyon thick with pines and towering cedars. The old trail he remembered down from the bluffs was still there, and as soon as he started down it, he felt a sense of safety. For here he was with his kind, and no lawman dared enter without a cavalry detachment. Following the trail, they descended through patches of buffalo grass and blue sage until reaching a small clearing at the foot of a waterfall. A few dozen yards distant, he saw the log cabin still standing, and he started for it, only to rein his horse to a stop when he heard a rifle being cocked and a man stepped out from behind a tree. "Looks like you fellers is lost," the man said, his rifle pointed straight at Bevo.

Bevo was startled, but for only a moment before retorting. "Hell no," he responded. "We ain't lost, and I'd thank you to get that gun outta my face before one of my boys puts some holes through that fancy vest you're wearin'."

"I don't think that would be too smart," another voice said, and a second man stepped out on the other side of the three riders, also with a rifle leveled at the uninvited guests.

"What the hell are you lookin' for down here?" Fancy Vest asked.

"A helluva lot better hospitality than what I'm gettin'," Bevo said.

"Who the hell are you, old man?"

"Bevo Rooks, by God," was Bevo's haughty reply, "and somebody who found this camp before you was born."

"Bevo Rooks!" Fancy Vest exclaimed. "Well, I'll be damned. You rode with my uncle, Luther Spears." He lowered his rifle at once.

"I did at that," Bevo replied, "or more like he rode with me. Yeah, I remember Luther—got hung over in Fort Smith as I recall."

"That's him," Fancy Vest responded proudly. "My name's Waylon Austin. That feller behind you over there is Pete Starke." He walked over beside Bevo's horse. "You ain't been around this territory in a while. Some folks thought you might be dead, or out of the business." He cocked his head in Crown's direction. "These your boys?"

"Two of 'em," Bevo said. "The other one's dead, killed just the other night when we had a run-in with a marshal's posse. That's Crown, and Cotton behind him."

"Oh," Austin said, "sorry to hear about your boy." Bevo's reply gave him immediate cause for worry. "A marshal's posse, you say? I hope to hell you didn't lead 'em here."

"Nah, probably not," Bevo said, although he was of a firm conviction that the posse was still dogging his trail. "Even if they did show up, it'd be more'n they could handle to take us here." Seeing the concern in Austin's face, he felt obliged to say, "Tell you the truth, we expected to find a lot of fellers still usin' this old camp, or we mighta led 'em someplace else. Are you two all that's here?"

"Afraid so," Austin replied. "That's kinda the reason me and Pete holed up here—figured the law thought this place was dead now." He glanced at his partner, and from Pete's expression, he figured he was still concerned about the possibility that the old man and his sons had led a federal posse to their camp.

"I was hopin' that old peddler with one eye that used to come through here to trade with the Injuns was still here," Bevo said. "We need some things. When that posse jumped us, we just got out by the skin of our teeth—left all our supplies behind." He paused to curse and shake his head. "That damn deputy, Chapel—I had a chance to shoot him once, and I didn't finish the job."

"I tried to tell him," Cotton started, but he was cut off immediately.

"Shut up, Cotton," Bevo snapped. "That son of a bitch was too ornery to die."

Austin and Starke exchanged puzzled glances. "Chapel, you say?" Bevo nodded. Then Austin went on. "You talkin' about Chapel, that deputy outta Fort Smith?" Again Bevo nodded. "Well, I'll be . . . You the feller that shot Chapel?"

Bevo started to answer in the affirmative, but upon catching a glimpse of Crown's expectant expression, he said, "My boy, Crown, did."

"Some folks said it mighta been you that done it," Austin said. "Chapel ain't a deputy no more. They kicked him out 'bout three years ago after he shot that half-breed, Billy Red Wolf, over in Atoka. You say he's ridin' with a marshal's posse?" When Bevo went stone silent for a long moment, Austin said, "You *have* been outta the territory for a spell, ain't you?"

Bevo still made no comment for a long time, causing the two outlaws standing beside his horse to wonder if he had suddenly had a stroke. The rage filling his veins was as devastating as a stroke, for he realized at that moment that he had been running from an imaginary marshal's posse. And the thought that he and his sons had been damn near driving their horses to death to escape one man was enough to almost drive him insane with anger. It was all coming back to haunt him, and he could no longer contain it. "He killed my boy. The son of a bitch killed my boy," he wailed. "I'll kill him. I swear to God I'll kill him, and this time I'll gut him like a hog and string his guts in a tree for the damn crows to eat."

Crown and Cotton were struck with the realization then. "There weren't no posse," Crown said. "There weren't but two of 'em, and we shot one of 'em when we crossed the river."

"*I* shot one of 'em," Cotton corrected quickly, unwilling to share the credit. "I was kinda thinkin' all them shots was just comin' from one rifle, but Pa said—"

Bevo cut him off, still fuming. "There wasn't no way to tell. It coulda been one or fifty."

"We coulda stayed right where we were," Crown couldn't resist stating, "and waited him out till mornin'. Then he'da been runnin' from us."

"And we wouldn'ta lost our grub and coffee," Cotton added. It had been a while now since they had anything solid to eat.

"Well, we can take care of that for you," Starke said. "Why don't you fellers step down and we'll go to the cabin. Me and Austin have been feeding offen a deer he shot day before yesterday."

"We're much obliged," Bevo said. The rage that had twisted his face seconds before began to slowly recede to a manageable level, although his burning desire for revenge would never leave him. The loss of a son had struck him mightily, but it was the humiliation of having fled from one man that stung him the most. He attempted to shake it off by promising himself that Chapel would pay. "How come you two fellers are holed up back here in this canyon?" he asked.

"We held up a stagecoach near Dodge City, up in

Kansas," Pete replied. "They got a posse after us, and
we had to get the hell outta Kansas."

"Let's get to that grub you was talkin' about," Bevo
said then. "My belly's been a-growlin' for two days."
They started toward the cabin. "I reckon if Chapel is
by hisself, he'll have better sense than to try to come in
here against five of us."

"I reckon," Austin agreed. However, another concerned glance at his partner confirmed that they both
were thinking along the same lines. Neither had had
any dealings with the notorious ex-lawman, but they
knew him by reputation as a cold and relentless hunter
of men, and there was no desire of either to know the
legend personally. Rooks, on the other hand, was feeling a lot easier about another confrontation with his
tracker, now that he was sure the odds were in his
favor.

Chapel stood beside a small stream while the buckskin
drank. A few yards away, the remains of a fire told him
that the trio he chased had stopped there to camp for
the night. As best he could guess, it was about a half
day's ride from here to the North Canadian River, so it
must have been late in the day for Rooks to decide to
stop here. That would mean they had been about eight
hours ahead of him. That time was cut considerably,
however, if they were headed to Cheyenne Canyon as
he figured, for he was confident he could get there
before dark without pushing his horse to do so. That
being his belief, he let the buckskin take his time at the
stream. When the sun was about halfway between
high noon and sundown, he called the grazing horse

and stepped up in the saddle, then started out again toward the mountains in the distance. Again recalling the last time he had tracked Rooks and his three sons, and his encounter with the Sharps buffalo rifle, he was not eager to repeat his mistake, so he intended to approach them after dark.

It had been a few years since he had ridden into the canyon where the Cheyenne used to camp, but he was confident he could find it again. Some of the original outlaws, who came in after the Indians left, had built a log cabin at the bottom of the canyon close by a waterfall. It had served as a hotel for fugitives, so his concern would have to be how many guns might be waiting for him now—and with that in mind, how close he could get to Rooks before he was stopped. One thing he knew for sure was that the way the cabin had been situated, anyone riding down the narrow trail could be seen for more than a hundred yards as he descended into the valley. His best chance, he decided, was to hide his horse in the trees on the slopes and make his assault on foot, and at night. These were the thoughts on his mind when he approached the range of hills that rose up out of the prairie to form a series of ridges and narrow canyons. It was time to be extra alert until he could reach their protective cover, and he didn't feel completely safe until he had reached a shallow ravine that led up to a low ridge thick with oak and sweet gum. Pausing then to figure out where he was in relation to Cheyenne Canyon, he decided it was west of where he now stood, and closer to the river. With that in mind, he began to work his way across a series of hills with many large open spaces of grass on their crests, bordered by thick belts of oaks. As he progressed, gradually the lay of the land came back to him, so that he began to remember cuts and draws, streams and ravines. He had hunted here before. When he came to the bottom of the steep hill that formed one side of the canyon he sought, he dismounted and led his horse across a small stream to a stand of red oak trees. Here he made his camp.

Once he was satisfied that his horse was well hidden, he started up through the trees on the side of the hill. If he remembered correctly, the trail into the cabin could be seen from the top of the hill. It was as he remembered. Upon gaining the top of the ridge, he could see most of the trail that led down to the waterfall, but to see the cabin itself, he would have to work his way farther down the slope. So he started down the steep slope until he reached an outcropping of rock, crowned by one huge boulder. Using the boulder as cover, he was afforded an unrestricted view of the cabin and the corral behind it.

There were six horses in the corral and smoke coming from the stone chimney, so he figured there were two or three others besides Rooks and his two sons, depending upon whether or not one of the horses was a packhorse. He glanced up at the sky. The sun was already sitting atop the mountains west of him. In a short time it would be dark, so he speculated that however many were using the cabin as a hideout were most likely in for the night and his fight would be against five or six men—if the others chose to participate in Rooks' fight. It was not entirely to his liking. He had no idea who else was using the cabin. He had no fight with them. They might not be outlaws at all, so he made up his mind to try to restrict his war against Rooks and his two sons only—unless the others chose to fight.

As he knelt there, watching the cabin below him, someone walked out the back door to attend to nature's call. From his rocky perch, he could not be sure if it was one of the men he sought or not, so he knew he was going to have to work his way farther down the slope to identify his targets. Even then, he was not certain he could tell Rooks' sons from the strangers they were sharing the cabin with. It was rapidly growing darker at the moment, anyway, so whatever his plan, he was going to have to initiate it tomorrow. Now he was concerned about getting back to his camp on the other side of the hill before total darkness set in.

Back at his camp, he pulled the saddle off his horse and led him out of the trees to let him graze on the grassy bank of the stream. Since it was almost a hard dark in the tiny gorge, he decided it would be safe to build a fire, knowing it was unlikely the smoke could be seen down in the canyon, even if someone took a notion to look for it. When he climbed into his blanket to sleep that night, it was with the fatalistic feeling that tomorrow would begin his day of reckoning with Bevo Rooks and his evil litter. Sleep did not come easily, however, for he found it hard to drift off now that he was so close to his prey. To add to his problem, stray thoughts of Luella Cochran stole into his mind, and he wondered why the woman bothered him. After a few fitful lapses into a state of unconsciousness, he gave it up and decided to scout the slope above the cabin for no other reason than to keep an eye on it. The ascension of a three-quarter moon helped in finding his way along the steep hillside.

Waylon Austin walked over to the corner of the corral to talk to his partner, Pete Starke, while Bevo and his boys were sitting around the table inside the cabin, finishing the pot of coffee Pete had made. Keeping his voice down, taking no chance of being overheard, he shared a concern that had been bothering him ever since the Rookses had ridden into the canyon. "I don't know about you, but damned if I ain't a mite uneasy knowin' that feller Chapel might be snoopin' around here anytime now."

"I've been thinkin' the same thing," Pete admitted. "Rooks mighta brung a world of trouble down here for me and you."

Waylon nodded thoughtfully. "He did a lot of crowin' about there bein' just Chapel by hisself against the five of us, but damned if I don't believe I'd rather have a sheriff's posse after me than that son of a bitch." He took a quick glance back at the cabin to make sure they were still alone. "I'm thinkin' this ain't our fight. Chapel ain't no deputy no more. He ain't got no reason to be lookin' for me and you. This trouble is between Rooks and him, and I say let them work it out."

"Ol' Bevo ain't gonna be too happy if we run out on him, if that's what you're sayin'."

"What I'm sayin' is we oughta saddle up and get the hell outta here before Chapel shows up—and not say nothin' about it till we're ready to ride out," Waylon said.

"When?" Pete asked.

"Hell, tonight," Waylon replied. "Why wait around till that devil starts shootin' at us?"

Pete didn't answer right away while he weighed the proposal in his mind. He would admit to himself that he was hesitant to ignite Bevo Rooks' wrath, but compared to having Chapel on his trail, he decided that Waylon was probably right—they should get the hell out of there, given the chance. "All right," he said, "I say let's do it, but how are we gonna get our possibles together, saddle our horses, and get away without Bevo or one of his boys catchin' on to what we're doin'?"

"Well, now, that's a good one," Waylon said. "I don't know." He thought about it for a while before continuing. "I reckon we can just try to sneak a little out at a time." Then he had an idea. "I've got a couple of bottles of rye whiskey left in my war bag. Why don't I bring 'em out and we'll have us a party tonight. Maybe if we get 'em drunk enough, they won't pay no mind to what we're doin'."

"That might work at that," Pete said. "I hate to waste a couple of bottles of good whiskey, but I can't think of nothin' better."

The plan was set then, so they ambled back into the cabin where Bevo and his two sons were still sitting at the kitchen table. "What we need around here is a little somethin' to liven things up," Waylon announced when he and Pete came in the back door.

"Ha," Crown blurted. "That'ud take some doin'."

"I just might have a little somethin'," Waylon volunteered. He picked up his saddlebags and pretended to be looking for something in them. "I know where it is—out in that lean-to with my saddle." He turned and went out the back door again, relieved when no one seemed to notice that he carried the saddlebags with him. If Bevo or either of his sons was curious, none of them showed it, content instead to sit there and let the venison digest. Encouraged by their lack of interest in his movements, he took a few minutes to load the packsaddle on their spare horse. Then, hurrying back inside, he brandished both bottles of whiskey, setting them down in the middle of the table. "I reckon this oughta rub some of the dust offen your throat," he exclaimed to Bevo.

Bevo's eyes lit up. "It might at that," he said, and reached for one of the bottles. The appearance of the whiskey served to arouse Crown and Cotton. Both reached for the other bottle at the same time, but Crown was a shade quicker. He laughed at Cotton as he went after the cork with his teeth. The party went better than Waylon and Pete had expected, and none of their houseguests noticed that they were barely sipping away at their glasses while Bevo worked steadily at one bottle he kept all to himself. Crown and Cotton were soon competing to see which one could outdrink the other. Before much time had passed, Bevo got sleepy and laid his head down on the table. In a few minutes, he was out. It took a while longer for the younger men, but by midnight both of them were dozing in front of the fireplace, oblivious to the stealthy activities of Starke and Austin.

Moving as quickly and as quietly as possible, they moved all of their belongings out of the cabin, including the frying pan and coffeepot. When their horses were saddled and the packhorse loaded, Waylon took one last look inside the door to make sure no one was stirring. "Dead to the world," he whispered to Pete, so they led their horses out of the corral, closed the gate, and climbed aboard. Holding their mounts to a walk, they headed toward the trail that led up and out of the canyon.

Once they reached the top of the high bluffs that surrounded the canyon, they paused to look back toward the cabin. "I don't see no sign of anybody," Pete said. "I think we got away with it."

"Maybe."

Both riders jerked upright, startled by the deep voice that suddenly came from the trees beside the trail. Before there was time for them to react, he stepped out of the shadows, his rifle trained on them. Like a ghostly form that had suddenly materialized in the moonlight, he stood before them in fatal judgment.

"Chapel!" Waylon blurted fearfully. He had never laid eyes on the notorious ex-lawman before, but there was no doubt in his mind who he was. Fearing for his life, Waylon considered drawing his weapon, but the muzzle of the Winchester looking at him seemed to dare him to try it.

Pete, equally horrified, but able to loosen his tongue, pleaded, "We ain't lookin' to cause you no trouble, Mr. Chapel, honest to God. We're just tryin' to clear outta here for good."

Chapel searched their faces intently, making sure they were not any of the Rooks clan. "Who's down in that cabin?" he asked, just to confirm what he already knew.

"Bevo Rooks and his two sons," Waylon was quick to answer. "There ain't nobody else, and we ain't got nothin' to do with 'em. That's why we was leavin'. Me and Pete, here, are peaceable folks."

Chapel figured the two were probably outlaws running from the law from some part of the territory. Otherwise, why would they be hiding out in Cheyenne Canyon? He had no interest in them, however, unless they had chosen to stand with Bevo Rooks, so he stepped away from the trail and waved them on. "If I see you back here, I'll figure you changed your mind and I'll shoot on sight," he warned as they filed past. It was not said to frighten them; he was just stating a simple fact.

"Yes, sir," Waylon stammered gratefully. "You don't have to worry about seein' us again." He refrained from informing the grim figure that the men he had come for were in a near-helpless condition, having finished two bottles of rye whiskey. It would be a simple matter to walk in that cabin and kill the three of them. There was, however, an outlaw code, so he kept his tongue. He would brag about it to Pete after they had beaten their retreat.

Waylon's assessment of the situation in the cabin was not entirely as he thought, for Cotton Rooks was roused from his stupor by the sudden need to empty his stomach of the evil contents taken in excess. He stumbled out the front door of the cabin to answer the urgent call in time to see the two riders slowly fading into the darkness of the trail out of the canyon. He was helpless to stem the disgusting wave deep inside his stomach already threatening to crest, so he had no choice but to endure the unpleasant process. Once it was finished, and the rush of the cold night air helped to sober him to a degree, he was able to figure out what he had just seen—Waylon and Pete were running out on the three of them. In Cotton's mind, this was a cowardly and traitorous act, and a prime opportunity to shoot someone. He determined to take care of the situation himself, then gloat about having done it while his father and older brother were sleeping off a drunk.

With no time to lose, he ran back inside to retrieve his rifle, glancing hurriedly at the two slumped in sleep as he went back out the door. On a dead run, he headed up the trail after the slow-walking horses. His step was not as steady as it could have been. The effects of the whiskey were gradually wearing off, but there was still enough alcohol in his system to give him confidence in what he was doing. When he had advanced halfway up the trail, he was able to see them when the moon came from behind a cloud—they had stopped at the head of the trail for some reason. Afraid he might not get another chance when they abruptly decided to ride, he raised his rifle and fired.

Up at the head of the trail, the sudden snap of the bullet between them, followed almost immediately by the report of the rifle, caused the two outlaws to bolt for the trees and safety. Equally startled, but quick to react, Chapel turned to drop on one knee while Cotton continued to fire. He could see the youngest Rooks standing squarely in the middle of the trail, so he took his time to take careful aim before squeezing off one round

that found the middle of Cotton's chest. Cotton took
three steps backward before dropping to the ground,
dead. Kneeling, Chapel remained there, watching the
trail below him and searching for the others.

The abrupt uproar of rifle fire shook Bevo and Crown
from their slumber to scramble for their weapons. "See
what it is!" Bevo directed when he saw Crown hurry to
a window. Then, looking around him, he exclaimed,
"Where the hell is everybody? Where's Cotton?"

"Them two fellers is gone!" Crown blurted, looking
toward the corral, now bathed in moonlight. "Their
horses ain't in the corral!"

"What the hell?" Bevo demanded, still totally confused, for he had been confident that no one would
attack them in Cheyenne Canyon without a sizable
posse. "Cotton!" he yelled, but there was no answer.
"Come on, Crown—out the back door!"

Outside the cabin, Bevo gulped the cold night air in
an effort to clear the cobwebs from his cluttered mind.
He saw right away that Crown had been right when he
said that Austin and Starke had left in the middle of
the night, but he could make no sense of the reason.
His first thought had been to make sure they had not
run off with the horses, but their three horses were still
in the corral. The thing that worried him now was
what had happened to Cotton—and where had the
shots come from? The answer had to be Chapel—that
devil had found them.

"Pa, look," Crown said, and pointed toward an object halfway up the trail that looked as if it might be a
body.

At once, a feeling of dread came over the old man.

Could it be Cotton? The question caused him to flush with anger even before he knew for sure it was his son. Without pausing to think of the possible consequences, he ran toward the body, with Crown close behind. Before they could reach Cotton's body, they were forced back by a series of rifle shots that kicked up the dust next to the corpse. "Up there!" Crown yelled, seeing the muzzle flash from Chapel's rifle. They both threw a series of shots at the last sighting. "Keep firin'," Crown said. "Cover me while I get Cotton." While his father did so, Crown sprinted to the body lying in the middle of the trail and dragged it to a sizable tree out of the line of fire.

"Let's get him back to the house," Bevo said. "We can't take care of him out here."

Crown, who was bent over his brother's body, looked up at his father and gave him the bad news. "We can't do nothin' for him, Pa. He's dead."

"No!" Bevo roared out his rage at having lost two sons to the nightmare that had come to haunt him. Furious, he stepped out from behind the tree and emptied the magazine of his rifle into the darkness at the top of the ridge. When the hammer finally fell on an empty chamber, his fire was returned by a bullet that kicked up dirt between his feet. It was enough to restore his common sense, and he jumped back behind the tree. The close call only served to increase his anger. "We need to get up that ridge and get that bastard," he blurted.

"That's what he wants us to do," Crown argued. "He wants us to try to come after him, 'cause we'd have to get out in the open to go up that trail."

Still infuriated, Bevo nevertheless saw the wisdom in his son's argument. "You're right," he conceded as he looked to each side of the canyon and the steep cliffs that made it almost impossible to climb the bluffs in any way except the narrow trail up the center. "We'll be better off holin' up in the cabin and makin' him come to us. Help me carry Cotton. I ain't gonna leave him out here." Being careful to keep the trees between them and the top of the trail, they carried Cotton's body back inside the house and laid it on the floor. "You watch that trail in front. I'll set by the back door in case he figures some way to get around behind us." He had heard some talk years before from one of the outlaws who had hidden out in the canyon that there was a back way out of there. But there had never been any need for one, so no one bothered to try to find it. If there was one, it was certainly not obvious, and that bunch that the soldiers killed a few years back sure as hell didn't know about it. But he couldn't afford to take any chances that Chapel might have knowledge of one and try to come in behind them.

There was no more rifle fire from the cliffs above the cabin throughout the rest of the night, a night that seemed excruciatingly long to Bevo and Crown. As the first rays of the sun found their way down between the bluffs, both men continued to stare, bleary-eyed with aching heads, at the rear and front approaches to the cabin. There was a sense of security, however, with the onset of sunlight, enough to allow Bevo's defiant attitude to return. His bold confidence had slipped somewhat during the long dark hours, with nagging stories he had heard about the notorious hunter of men.

"Let him come down that trail if he wants us so bad. I'll fill him full of lead." He got up from his seat on the floor by the back door and took a few seconds to stretch his legs and arms in an attempt to ease some of the tension that had set in. "Let's make us some coffee," he said. "He ain't likely to show his face while it's daylight."

"I'll make it, Pa," Crown volunteered before Bevo had a chance to tell him to do it. When Crown vacated his post by the front window, Bevo moved up to take his place. After freshening the fire in the fireplace, Crown soon discovered there was no coffeepot. It dawned on him then. "They took the coffeepot when they left last night," he informed Bevo.

"We might have a little settlin' up with those two saddle tramps when we finish with Chapel," Bevo said, his positive mood already ambushed. "Find a pot or pan to warm some water. I need some coffee."

"I got one," Crown said a few moments later. He took the pot and filled it with a handful of coffee beans. Using the handle of his revolver as a hammer, he smashed the beans in the bottom of the iron pot. Then he blew into the pot to blow out some of the odd pieces of husk. When he went to the water bucket near the fireplace, he found it empty. No one had filled it the night before, and he was faced with a decision he hadn't counted on. If they were going to have coffee, someone was going to have to walk over to the creek and fill the bucket. "There ain't no water," he announced, then waited to see what his father would say to that.

"Damn!" Bevo swore. He considered the risk involved in moving across the backyard to the creek for a moment before insisting. "I need some coffee bad.

My head's about to split open." Still Crown did not volunteer to fetch the water. "Use the corner of the house for cover, and take a good look back toward that trail before you run across there to the crick," Bevo told him. "It'd be a helluva shot from up in them bluffs. I'd go get it, but you can move a helluva lot faster than I can."

"Hell," Crown replied, "it was a helluva shot that got Cotton last night. I don't wanna stick my ass out there for that bastard to shoot at."

"I'm tellin' you it's too long a shot from up where he is, and you'll have the cabin between you and him for most of the way," Bevo said. "Cotton was standing out in the middle of the trail, halfway up the hill. Anybody coulda made that shot. I'll cover you. I wasn't gonna let you run out there without me watchin' for you. Now grab ahold of that bucket and get goin'. We need some coffee."

Crown was not convinced that the risk was as small as his father suggested. He had come to believe that this demon who hunted them would not be stopped until he had killed all of them, but he could not bring himself to buck the old man. Reluctantly, he walked over, picked up the bucket, and stood by the back door for a long minute before easing it open to peer out. Everything was quiet, with only the hunting cry of a hawk high above the canyon wall to break the silence, so he opened the door just wide enough to allow him to slip through with the bucket. Standing pressed against the wall of the cabin, he searched the bluffs above him, then swept the cliff above the waterfall before inching his way to the corner of the building. *If he was behind us,* he told himself, *he would have already taken a shot at me.* Encouraged to a small degree, he took a few tentative steps away from the protection of the cabin, then a few steps more with still nothing from the bluffs. Thinking to take advantage of Chapel's evident lack of attention, he hurried over to the creek and swiped the bucket in the cold bubbling water. With his bucket over half-full, he walked quickly back toward the cabin. He was almost back behind the corner when he heard the dull thud of the bullet as it hit the wooden bucket. The next slug caught him in the hip, spinning him around and dropping him to the ground. "Pa! I'm shot!" he cried out as the bucket rolled over and over on its side, spilling the contents in the dirt.

Inside, Bevo jumped when he heard the shots fired. Standing at the side of the window, he strained to see from where they had come, but he was not quick enough to spot the source. Hearing Crown cry out in pain, he ran to the back door in time to see his son lying fifteen or twenty feet from the corner of the cabin. "Crown!" Bevo cried out in agony when he saw that his one remaining son was seriously wounded. As he stood there trying to decide what to do, two more shots rang out, kicking up dirt near Crown, and he saw from the angle that Chapel was opposite the front of the cabin. He was reasonably sure then that the building would still offer protection from the shots, so he went out the door and inched his way along the back wall to the corner of the cabin.

"Pa, help me," Crown pleaded as rifle slugs continued to kick up dirt and chip hunks from the log wall.

Nearing a state of panic then, Bevo was reluctant to

leave the cover of the cabin wall for fear Chapel would change his position to one with a better angle to shoot from. "Crawl back to the cabin, Son," he finally cried.

"I don't think I can," Crown replied fearfully "My hip."

"You've got to try," Bevo cried. "I can't come get you—can't take a chance on both of us gettin' shot."

"I can't, Pa."

"You've got to before he gets the range and puts another'n in you."

Realizing then that his father was not going to risk getting shot to help him, Crown rolled over on his belly and forced himself to drag his body toward the corner of the cabin. Inch by painful inch, he clawed the hard-packed ground and pulled himself slowly to the safety of the wall where his father stood waiting anxiously. When almost there, he cried out once again as a bullet struck his lower leg. Still Bevo would not risk exposing himself to the rifle fire from the cliff. To avoid being shot to pieces, Crown called on every ounce of determination he possessed and dragged himself to the corner of the cabin where his father could take his wrists and roughly pull him to cover. Once he was safe, Bevo pulled him back to the door and into the cabin, leaving a bloody trail behind him.

"You're bleedin' like hell," Bevo said as he looked at the wound in Crown's hip. It showed no signs of slowing down. Exhausted from his efforts to save himself, Crown could only lie on the kitchen floor holding his hand over the hole, trying to stop the flow of blood that had now soaked most of his trousers. With his thoughts darting rapidly back and forth between his wounded son and the death-dealing maniac up on the bluff above them, Bevo was striving to keep his wits about him. Any thoughts he had possessed about meeting the danger head-on were rapidly turning to a panic to escape the devil chasing him.

Doing the best he could to stay conscious, Crown was dismayed by his father's inability to take charge of the situation. He knew the time would be short before Chapel decided it was the moment to approach the cabin. "He'll be comin', Pa," he gasped. "We've got to be ready." Even as he uttered the words, he began to feel dizzy from the blood loss, but he fought to remain alert.

"I know, I know," Bevo replied nervously. "You're right—we've got to be ready." His mind was not on preparing a defense, however, for he was thinking only of escape, and hauling his wounded son would be a major problem. How long would Chapel be content to remain up on the bluffs, watching for an open target? That was the question that burned in Bevo's brain. His thoughts turned then to the report of a secret escape trail out behind the waterfall. Was there really one? And could he find it? The fellow who had told him about it was sure there was a trail that climbed up the canyon wall, although he had confessed that he had never seen it. His thoughts were interrupted then by his son.

"We've got to keep an eye out," Crown uttered with great effort, puzzled by his father's apparent indecision. "Help me over by the front window where I can watch the front."

"Right," Bevo replied. "You need to be up front there with your eyes open." Crown could not bear to stand, so Bevo dragged him to the front window and let him lean against the wall, then handed him his rifle. "Don't go to sleep on me, now. When he decides he's had enough fun up in them bluffs, he'll come down. And that's when we'll get him. He's got to come in the front or the back." When he was satisfied that Crown was alert enough to stay awake for a while, he left him and went to check the one window on the side of the cabin. As he passed in front of the window, he was startled by a rifle slug that barely missed him and ripped a furrow in the window frame. "He's moved around to this side!" Bevo yelled, his heart in his throat after the close miss.

Bevo Rooks was scared. He had been scared a couple of times before, but this time was not like any time in his life. This man Chapel had been as close to death as any man could be when he and his three sons had left him on the prairie to be eaten by the buzzards, but he refused to die. And one by one he was relentless in killing the members of his family, his sons, until there was no one left but him and Crown, and Crown could surely not last out the day. What sense would it make for him to wait around for Chapel to come down from those cliffs to settle with him? None, he decided, so he started thinking fast. The last shot had come through the side window. To have made it, Chapel would have had to be on the east bluffs. That should put the cabin between the east wall of the canyon and the corral. Bevo's only chance to escape was to use the cover of the cabin to run out the back, and trust that Chapel would be unable to see him. There might not be a back trail out of this trap he was in, but he was afraid to wait for the executioner with Crown. There were also thoughts of being trapped inside the cabin with the possibility that Chapel might try to set it on fire and force him out in the open. He didn't like the image that created, so he made up his mind to try to sneak out the back. If he couldn't find a trail out, then a hole to hide in where Chapel would have to come to him would be better than the cabin.

There was just a hint of conscience when he thought about the abandonment of his last son, his oldest boy, whom he had decided to name Crown because it sounded like royalty. It was going to be difficult to explain to Pearl Mae what had become of her sons. She might be angry with him for leaving Crown alone now, but she wasn't here to understand the circumstances. Crown wasn't going to make it, and what better way to honor his father than to hold the demon off long enough for Bevo to escape? *She's just going to have to take my word for it,* he thought. *I'm wasting time.*

He hurried back to the front of the cabin to find Crown still leaning against the wall beside the window. The young man was still bleeding profusely, but his eyes were open and on the trail that led out of the canyon. "You gotta hold on there, boy," Bevo told him. He was alarmed at the sight of so much blood, and immediately concerned that Crown might die too soon. He needed him to delay Chapel as long as possible. "Here," he said, grabbing one of Cotton's shirts. "Hold this tight against that wound to slow that bleedin' down some."

"I don't think I'm gonna make it, Pa," Crown moaned.

"Sure you are, Son. As soon as we take care of this son of a bitch, I'll fix you up good as new—take you home where your mama can take good care of you. Just make sure you're ready to use that rifle when the time comes. I'm gonna go outside now to take a look around, and I'll be right back."

"Don't be gone long," Crown pleaded. "I'm hurtin' awful bad, and I don't wanna be alone in here." The sight of his younger brother's body lying near the front door was a grim reminder of what his fate might be.

"You won't be alone long," Bevo assured him. "I'll be right back to take care of you. Ain't I always took care of you?"

"I reckon," Crown replied weakly.

"All right, then," Bevo said in as cheery a voice as he could manage in the midst of the fear that was eating away like a great caterpillar in his insides. "I'll be right back." With that one final lie to his son, he hurried through the cabin to the back door, picking up his saddlebags on the way.

Outside, he once again hugged the rear wall of the cabin, wondering if he was making a mistake after all. The open space between the cabin and the shed in the corral looked like a distance of one hundred yards, instead of the actual twenty-yard expanse. He turned to look back at the threatening cliffs above him; he knew there was death lingering there, with his name on its lips. Calling on all the courage he could muster, he ran for the corral.

Almost stumbling in his efforts to hurry across the open ground, he reached the cover of the corral shed, gasping for breath, his heart in his throat. He took a moment to catch his breath, encouraged by having made it without being shot at. Then, moving as quickly as he could, he led his horse up to the shed and saddled it. He took another moment to decide whether or not to take the other horses with him. Then, to satisfy his conscience for deserting his son, he decided to leave Crown's horse in case his son was able to stop the deadly hunter. It might be too much trouble to bother with leading two horses, anyway, so he decided to take Cotton's horse. That way he could swap off during his run, sparing them.

Ready to ride, after saddling Cotton's horse, he found his nerve endings were tingling all over his body. He was afraid that this close to escape, something would happen to prevent it. Still there was no rifle shot from the bluffs on the other side of the cabin. As a further precaution, he pulled out a couple of poles from the corral so he could ride out the back instead of going out the gate. Leading the horses and using them for cover, he walked along the creek until he reached the cover of the trees near the waterfall. Here he stopped and tied his reins to a tree limb while he made his way in behind the cascading water crashing down from seventy feet above. Crestfallen, he found no secret passage behind the water, only a solid rock cliff. The discovery was devastating, and it left him in desperate indecision. He was afraid to go back to the cabin, feeling he had already pushed his luck in managing to get as far as he had without being seen. Going back to his horses, he looked beyond the waterfall at the end of the box canyon, no more than seventy-five yards away. He was trapped!

He thought again of his wounded son, leaning against the wall, and hoped, even prayed, that Crown would stop the relentless hunter. *I can't stay here*, he thought, but knew he was not going back to stay with Crown. His best bet to find a hole to make a stand was in the trees between the waterfall and the back of the box canyon. *Maybe I can hide back in those trees. Maybe Crown can hold on long enough to get him*. That appealed to him much more than going back to face Chapel. *I'll find me a place to hole up and wait to pick him off if he gets by Crown and comes looking for me*. That was as good a plan as any in his desperate situation, so he grabbed his horse's reins and started back through the trees, hugging the steep rock wall.

When he reached the corner of the canyon wall, he quickly considered where he was going to hole up and wait for Chapel. Seeing a bent-over pine next to the wall, he decided it was his best option. He could climb in behind the tree, leave his horses tied to the tree for extra cover, and hope for the best. So he wasted no time in scrambling into the bushes fronting the tree. Once he got behind the branches of the pine, he found himself looking at a hollowed-out chamber in the solid rock wall. Immediately his heart started racing with excitement and hope. He made his way into the dark hollow, following it for about twenty-five yards until, finally, it opened up to a narrow defile that formed a passage wide enough for a horse. He had found it! The tale was true; he had discovered the secret back door to the canyon. With the joyful realization that he had been spared the confrontation with the notorious ex-lawman, he ran back to get his horses. Once again, his feeling of bravado returned to buoy his confidence, with never a regret or sense of shame for sacrificing his only remaining son to cover his escape. He was struck once more with the unpleasant task of telling Pearl Mae that he was coming home without any of her sons. She would no doubt raise hell about it, but he told himself he'd whip hell out of her if she made too much fuss. He was unaware that there would be no one waiting for him this time when he returned home. Pearl Mae had packed up her shabby possessions and gone home to Kansas. She had thought about leaving a warning note for him, that if he tried to come after her, she would shoot him on sight. But she didn't leave it, because Bevo couldn't read.

Chapter 12

It was early afternoon when Sam, Martha, Luella, and the children saw their chosen piece of land on the Cimarron. They had been surprised to encounter a team of horses pulling an almost-empty wagon some two miles short of their destination. Tom was able to solve the mystery for them, remembering that Rooks had tried to use the wagon as a decoy. "It's one helluva coincidence," he said. "Them horses coulda pulled that wagon to Kansas or somewhere. But I reckon you've just got yourself another wagon and team." Luella and Sammy climbed on the wagon and followed Sam the rest of the way. Over the next few days, they were to gain a couple more horses that the notorious clan had left in their haste to escape. One of them brought tearful memories to the women when they discovered Loafer, Link's bay gelding, near the river.

Remembering what Chapel had asked him to do, Tom didn't wait for Sam's help. Instead, he rode on ahead of the wagons to remove Corbett Rooks' body from the clearing. The wound in his shoulder was tender to the touch, but it did not unduly restrict the movement of his arm. To make the job easier, he looped a rope around the corpse and let his horse do the work of dragging it away from the campsite. He wasn't prepared to dig a hole in the prairie at the time, so he dragged the body a considerable distance, planning to take care of the burial later. He noticed a couple of buzzards following along over him, so he thought it a good possibility they would take care of most of the work, and he'd just have the bones to bury. There were more important things on his mind now, and they had to do with Chapel and Bevo Rooks. He had assured his stoic friend that he would help Sam get settled on his claim, and that was what he intended to do, but he had in mind getting it done a great deal quicker than Chapel meant.

He returned to the clearing in time to see Sam and his family descending the rise that swept down toward the river. He could see Martha with little Jenny standing behind the wagon seat, both straining to see the site of their future home. Luella was driving the extra wagon with Sammy. *I hope to hell this place turns out to be the home they were searching for,* he thought. He rode forward to meet them then.

Sam pulled the wagon to a stop in the center of the clearing and gave Martha a hand down while Jenny jumped from the back and scampered off toward the river with Sammy, eager to explore the new land. "This is a little closer than the last time we were here," Sam remarked, as he stood looking at the initial logs of the cabin Rooks had started.

"I don't know what you've got in mind," Tom said, "but it looks like you've got a start on a cabin there."

"Well, it's not in the right place," Martha said before Sam could reply. "The house needs to be closer to the river, near those trees on the bank." Tom looked at Sam, and they both grinned.

"You heard the boss," Sam said. He started unhitching the horses. "I reckon I'll just hobble 'em and let 'em graze. It'll be a while yet before I'll be able to start on a house. I've got some plans drawn up for the house we want, but for now I'll get a tent set up, and that's gonna be our home for a spell."

"I expect I'll want my own cabin," Luella remarked, surprising them all. There had never been a word from her before that she planned to live apart.

"There'll be plenty of room for you in our house, Lou," Martha assured her. "Why would you want to live in a place by yourself? You need family."

"I didn't say I wanted to live away from you," Luella insisted, "just in a cabin all my own."

Martha looked at Sam as if seeking an explanation for her sister's change of heart. He merely shrugged. It made no difference to him, just more work. "I expect we'd better build our house first, so we'll have somethin' to live in while we're building the other one," Sam said.

"Come on," Tom said. "We'd best get started."

There was an urgency in his manner that seemed a little unusual to Sam, so he felt it necessary to comment. "I can set up our camp by myself, Luella can do a man's work, and Sammy's a fair help, so if you're anxious to go after Chapel, don't stay here on my account. This is our land, fair and square, and I intend to keep it—fight for it if I have to." He paused to grin. "Besides, you can't do much more than get in the way with that bad shoulder."

"Well, there is some unfinished business that needs to be took care of," Tom admitted, "and I need to be doin' part of it."

"If it's Chapel you're worried about," Martha commented, "I shouldn't think you'd have to. He seems highly capable of taking care of himself."

"Maybe," Tom allowed, "but there's three of 'em, and they ain't an easy bunch to get along with. If you folks are sure you'll be all right, I'll help you get your camp set up, and then I'll go see if Chapel needs some help."

"That's fair enough," Sam said. Then he looked at Martha, who gave him a confirming nod.

So they spent the rest of the day setting up the tent that would be their home while the house was being built. Martha and Luella fixed a big supper for them, and the next morning Tom rode out to track Chapel down, promising that they both would be back to help with the house.

The trail he picked up on the other side of the river was not a hard one to follow, for the three outlaws were in too great a hurry to worry about their tracks. Chapel had no need to disguise his, so the net result was a trail that young Sammy could have followed. Tom's biggest concern was to catch up to Chapel before it was too late. Bevo Rooks and his two sons were a dangerous trio to tangle with.

The object of Tom's concern lowered himself on a rope from the edge of the east wall of Cheyenne Canyon. He had waited until dark before descending the steep face of the cliff, knowing that he would be hanging help-lessly for a brief time, exposed to anyone who might chance to look his way. His rope was only long enough to get him to a point still about ten feet above the can-yon floor, so he dropped to the ground, rolling as he did to absorb the shock of his heavy body's landing. Still crouching, he untied the rawhide cord that held his rifle and pulled it off his shoulder, brushing the dirt from the weapon. Since there had been no gunfire to greet his arrival from above, he remained there for a few moments, listening. There were no sounds to indi-cate movement of any kind inside the cabin.

Rising to his feet, he made his way around the back of the cabin, with still no sign of anyone. He looked to-ward the corral and discovered it was empty of horses. His first thought was that they had somehow managed to escape, possibly getting by him while he was setting up to descend the east wall. But then a movement in the shadows near the front of the cabin caught his eye. He whipped around, ready to fire, to find it was a horse casually walking across the front yard. Glancing back at the corral, he could see that the gate was closed. It was enough to make him even more cautious. He moved up close beside a rear window and tried to look inside, but there was no light inside, so he could see very little. Something was not right, he decided, wary of a trap, but he continued working his way around the cabin.

Moving carefully around the front corner of the building, he stopped suddenly when he saw the barrel of a rifle protruding a few inches from the corner of the front window. It was trained on the trail that led down into the canyon. They were waiting in ambush for him. He dropped to his hands and knees and crawled under the window so he could shoot from the opposite corner. The rifle did not move, so he eased himself up and pulled his handgun, thinking it easier to use in a confined space. With one hand ready to grab the rifle barrel, he whipped his pistol up to fire, but he did not pull the trigger, for the man did not move. Chapel stared at the still body for a few moments. It was leaning against the wall and looked to have been dead for quite a while. In the dim light he could tell that it was another one of the sons. Looking in the window then, he saw Cotton's body lying near the door. This was the one he had shot in the middle of the trail. Where was the old man?

He went to the door and pushed it open, shoving Cotton's body aside in the process. There was little doubt that Bevo had fled. The cabin was empty of living persons. What Chapel could not understand was how he had slipped by him. The only time he did not have the top of the entrance trail in view had been the few minutes he was lowering himself down the cliff on the rope, and it would have been one hell of a coincidence if Bevo had chosen that time to make his escape. No, he decided, the man must still be down there in the canyon, but he began a search of the corral and the shed first, alert every second to the possibility of walking into a trap. It was then that he noticed the poles missing at the back of the corral and knew at once that Bevo must have ridden out that way. He had not gone up the trail in front at all. The question to be answered now was whether or not the craven killer was still hiding somewhere, or was there a back way out of the canyon? The problem facing him at this point was that it was too dark to find tracks leading away from the corral. If he tried to make some sort of torch to light the tracks, he would be inviting Bevo to take a shot at him, if in fact he was hiding somewhere in the canyon. It was still a long time before daybreak. He had no choice but to wait.

While he waited for daylight, he returned to the top of the cliff, walking up the common path in front, knowing he was inviting a shot in the back if Bevo Rooks was hiding in the canyon somewhere. He didn't think that likely, however, because his gut feeling that Bevo was no longer there was growing stronger and stronger. It just didn't make sense that, at some point while he was moving all around the cabin and corral, the outlaw didn't take a shot at him. Still able to watch the trail out of the canyon, he retrieved his rope. Afterward, he paused to think about it for a few seconds before deciding to go down the other side of the ridge to get his horse, convinced now that Bevo was gone. There had to be a back door to Cheyenne Canyon.

The remaining hours of darkness gave him plenty of time to think, and many thoughts came to his mind of the long road he had traveled to this point, sitting at the top of the trail leading down to the outlaw cabin. One man was left of the murderous clan that had left him for dead, and he would track him into hell itself, if necessary. His biggest regret was his failure to deliver justice to the two outlaws he had been unable to track down after the murders of his mother and father. He would never give up hope that he would one day find the two, but he was realistic enough to know that too many years had passed, and the odds were not in his favor. There were other things that came to mind: his time with Long Walker and the Chickasaws; his many years as a deputy marshal—and there was Luella. This was the most perplexing of his thoughts, for he could not explain why he thought of her at all. There were certainly no feelings for her, as a man would think about a woman. Searching his past life, he realized he had never had feelings along those lines. His life had been a constant death hunt, with no room in his mind for anything beyond tracking and capturing, or killing his prey. It was too late for him to think about a woman, he decided with a grunt to punctuate the end of his reverie.

Slowly, the faint light of predawn crept toward the deep canyon, and he prepared to step up in the saddle. Convinced there was no one left alive in the canyon, he nevertheless waited and watched, for he could never forget a time once before when he had ridden blindly into an ambush that resulted in his near death. Rapidly now, the early rays of the sun probed the still canyon, and soon the floor was bathed in sunlight that dissolved the dark shadows and danced across the sparkling waterfall. He stepped up and settled himself in the saddle. The buckskin turned his head to question, and Chapel answered with a slight nudge of his heels. The big horse stepped smartly down the narrow path with Chapel sitting tall in the saddle, certain that Rooks had once again fled, rather than settle the issue face-to-face.

He checked the cabin again, where the bodies of

two of Bevo's sons lay undisturbed. Taking their weapons and what ammunition he could find, he left the cabin and checked the corral, where he found the remaining horse standing and waiting. He saddled the horse with a saddle he found in the shed, tied the extra weapons and saddlebags on, then tied it on behind the buckskin. There was no sense of haste in his movements, but no waste of time, either, for he was confident that he would find Bevo's trail and he would follow it to an end that was certain in his mind. With light enough to see now, he easily followed the tracks from the back of the corral that led to the waterfall. Based on the circle of prints, it appeared that Rooks had walked behind the fall, but the hoofprints continued on toward the box end of the canyon. As a precaution, he looked behind the waterfall, and, like Rooks, found nothing but a stone wall. It was obvious that Bevo was not sure if there was a door, but he had evidently found it. A few minutes later, the passage out of the canyon was obvious to see, for Rooks had left a wide trail of broken branches through the brush that fronted the leaning pine guarding the entrance.

Leading his horses, he walked through the twenty-five-foot natural tunnel to reach a narrow trail that wound around a granite outcropping, then along a narrow chasm, barely wide enough for a horse and saddle to pass through. He looked straight up at the blue sky between walls nearly sixty feet high. The thought occurred to him that, had Rooks lain in ambush atop one of those walls, it would have been the solution to his problem. Still leading his horses, he began to climb as the rocky trail continued upward, snaking its way toward the top of the mountain. After a distance of perhaps a quarter of a mile, the trail emerged from its narrow confines to arrive in the open fir forest that covered the top of the ridge. Here, he would have to become more careful, he thought, but Rooks had made no effort to disguise his trail, having made his way down the mountain as quickly as possible.

Once clear of the mountains, Rooks had set out to the south. Chapel picked up his tracks on the south bank of the North Canadian River. They were heading straight south, and judging by the length of the stride, Rooks was not sparing the horses. Holding his own horses to a more sustainable pace, Chapel rode doggedly after him, unaware that he was being tracked as well. Tom Turnipseed was no more than half a day behind him.

It was early in the afternoon when Chapel reached the banks of the Canadian River, following tracks that now showed the weary condition of Bevo's horses, for the hoofprints were uneven and extended in some places, indicative of a horse too tired to keep from dragging its hooves. *He's going to have to rest them, or kill them*, he thought as the tracks led down into the water. There were no signs of letup where the outlaw climbed out of the water on the other side, the trail continuing on, always straight south. It appeared that Rooks was running to Texas just as fast as he could get there.

Less than an hour later, he saw the horse, standing idle near a trickle of a stream, its head hanging down, and he knew immediately that what he had expected had happened. The horse had been ridden nearly to death, and Rooks had to leave it because it could no longer keep up with the other horse. Rooks had not even taken the time to pull the saddle off the exhausted animal. It was a fair guess that Bevo's remaining horse was likely not in much better shape than this one, and Chapel figured he was probably rapidly catching up with the outlaw now. The weary horse stood still when Chapel rode up beside it and stopped. He dismounted and pulled the saddle and bridle off and discarded them by the stream before getting back in the saddle and pushing on, following a single set of tracks now.

Right at dusk, Chapel approached a group of hills that looked out of place in this part of the territory, with heavily wooded gulches and ridges, and a spring-fed creek flowing through a canyon with red sandstone cliffs and gulches. He had been there once before. It had once been a stop for wagons traveling the California Road to the west, and a favorite camp for Indians seeking protection from the cold winters. He cautioned himself to be alert as he neared the hills, because the tracks he followed told him that Rooks was going to be forced to stop. His horse had begun to stumble at this point. Though far from the state of exhaustion that Rooks' mounts had shown, Chapel's two horses were in need of rest as well. He pushed them on at a slow walk, following a ravine that led to the creek where he dismounted and made his camp. As he had done at Cheyenne Canyon, he planned to leave his horses there and scout the canyons on foot, for he felt reasonably sure that Rooks was camped in the hills also, forced to rest his horses.

Standing atop a high sandstone bluff above the creek, he looked out over the expanse of crags and cuts before him, with heavily wooded ravines and coulees, any of which could be hiding Bevo Rooks. His concentration was on a notch between two red sandstone cliffs approximately a quarter of a mile south of him. This was where Rooks' tracks had pointed and where Chapel would follow after the sun went down. He was almost certain the man he had trailed was not far away from the bluff he now stood upon. His horse would not take him much farther. Chapel could feel the nearness of the murderous miscreant in his gut, but there was no sense of anxiety or excitement in the anticipation of a final showdown with the man responsible for so many murders and robberies. Instead, he was filled with a grim determination to finally rid the world of the last of the evil Rooks clan, leaving him with only one lingering failure to haunt his mind.

He remained on the bluff until the sun finally dropped behind the hills to the west and darkness settled down upon the canyon. Making his way back down to the creek and his horses, he prepared to end his death hunt. After pulling the saddle off his extra horse, he left it there and climbed aboard the buckskin once more. "If things go like I plan," he told the patient horse, as he checked his rifle, "I'll let you rest up good after I'm done." Then with a nudge of his heels, he headed toward the notch between the cliffs.

As the darkness deepened, the stars began to appear overhead, but there was no moon to light his way, a condition he preferred. When he reached the mouth of the notch, he found that it led back toward the creek, and at the end, it seemed to form a pocket of pines and fir trees—and in a small clearing in the middle, he spotted a brightly burning campfire. Rooks had evidently thought he had far outdistanced any pursuer. He had made no effort to hide his fire. Chapel stepped down from the buckskin and looped the reins over the limbs of a bush. Drawing his Winchester from the saddle sling, he proceeded cautiously on foot.

Alone now, with all of his sons dead and with no gang members to rely on, Bevo Rooks had almost run his horses to death in his attempt to escape back home to Texas. One of the horses had to be discarded because it was slowing him up. He was running solely on fear, so much so that he would risk no chance of being taken by surprise. *Surely,* he thought, *I must be too far ahead for him to catch up.* But he was afraid to go to sleep, knowing the grim hunter was back there on his trail somewhere. So now, backed up against a sandstone cliff, he sat, shivering in the chilly evening air while a warm fire burned lustily some thirty or forty yards away.

His shivering stopped abruptly when, off to his left, he caught site of something, or someone, moving in the trees near his campfire. His heart leaped immediately into his throat as he realized that his fears had been realized. Almost paralyzed with fear, he raised his rifle up to defend himself. Then he realized that the figure was not coming toward him but continued to move toward the fire. *He doesn't see me!* The thought caused the blood to flow in his veins again when it was apparent that the fire he had made as a precautionary decoy had worked. His dread of a few moments before having been swept away by the knowledge that he now had the upper hand, he moved slowly away from the wall and maneuvered to a position from which to fire. Making his way as close as he dared, he propped his rifle against a tree to steady his aim, for he was trembling. This time it was not from fear or the cold night air. It was with the excitement he could barely contain on being presented with the broad back of his tormentor. *This time, you son of a bitch, you'll stay dead.*

Chapel paused to look carefully ahead of him. He could see what appeared to be a rolled-up blanket on the other side of the fire. It struck him then that something wasn't right about the camp. The fire was much larger than was needed for a one-man camp, and he suddenly sensed a trap. He started to turn and withdraw, but it was too late, for the .44 rifle slug slammed his right shoulder, causing him to drop his rifle and stumble into a clump of bushes.

"Damn!" Rooks cursed when Chapel had turned just as he pulled the trigger, saving him from the shot that was aimed squarely between his shoulder blades. Seeing the big ex-deputy drop his rifle, however, he hurried to finish him off before he had a chance to retrieve it. Crashing through the underbrush as he ran, eager to put a bullet into the brain of the demon hunter, he hesitated to pull the trigger when he found Chapel apparently helpless to defend himself. With his rifle pointed at Chapel's head, he took time to gloat over his victory. "Well, now ain't this somethin'? The big, bad Chapel. You was wantin' to catch me, was you? Well, here I am. You caught me. Whaddaya gonna do about it?" He stood glaring down his rifle barrel at the helpless man, enjoying his advantage. "You know, I could finish you off real quick, but you killed my boys, and you're gonna have to pay for that. And this time, I'm gonna stay here and watch you die before I leave you." He took a couple of steps over to the side and reached down to pick up Chapel's rifle. "That's a fine-lookin' rifle. That's a '73 Winchester, ain't it? Maybe if you ask me real politelike, I'll kill you with it." When Chapel refused to respond with anything but a deadpan expression, Rooks said, "You ain't sayin' nothin', but I know you're 'bout shittin' your britches." His elation was at such a high level that he was having trouble containing himself, eager to kill his victim but not wanting the scene to end too soon to enjoy it fully.

Chapel endured the taunting as he faced almost every situation, with a stoic silence that made most people uncomfortable. His arm was numb and seemed to be useless to him, but he was resolved to make a fight of it. He could not come this close to seeking vengeance and not make an attempt to take Rooks with him. He wasn't sure he could make a quick lunge for Rooks before he took another bullet, but he was going to try. He had let himself get careless in getting ambushed. It was stupid on his part, and he couldn't argue that he probably deserved to get shot for the second time he had blundered into an ambush by the wily outlaw. His only hope was to get the chance he needed to attack, and by holding his silence, he felt he was buying time until Rooks got careless.

"Get up from there," Rooks ordered.

"Go to hell," Chapel responded.

"Damn it, I said get up from there!" Rooks roared.

"What for?" Chapel demanded. "You're gonna shoot me whether I'm up or not."

"Damn you. I'll shoot you where you sit!" He raised his rifle and aimed it at Chapel's head.

"I wouldn't if I was you." Both men were startled by the voice that came from the woods behind them. Rooks, his rifle hip-high, spun around, seeking a target. The voice, now a few steps to the side, came again. "Take it easy, Bevo. You're liable to hurt somebody with that thing."

Rooks was in a state of panic, looking right and left for the mysterious voice that came out of nowhere. Then the owner of the voice stepped out of the shadows near the fire, causing Rooks to stare in disbelief. "Well, I'll be damned—Tom Turnipseed. Where in the hell . . . ? I ain't seen you since we split up back on the Clear Boggy. What the hell are you doin' here?"

"Followin' him and lookin' for you," Tom said. "You look like you put on a few years since I saw you last."

"You got a helluva lot of room to talk," Bevo replied, his tone almost jovial upon recognizing one of his old gang members. "You're sproutin' a lot of gray hair yourself." He chuckled at his remark. "So you was followin' him, was you? Well, you got here just in time to see me kill him. This son of a bitch killed my three sons."

"That a fact?" Tom replied. "Well, that kinda seems fair to me, seeing as how you killed his mother and daddy."

Puzzled, Bevo asked, "What are you talkin' about?"

That day back there in '65, on the Red River, that was his ma and pa that you and Webb and Little Bit shot down, and that was his ma that you raped before you burned the house down."

Stunned, Bevo turned to stare down at the man who had hunted him for so long, scarcely able to believe his ears. When he turned back to face Tom, it was to find a rifle aimed at his gut. He screamed in horror when the slug tore through his belly, followed by a second in his chest. Dropping his rifle, he fell to his knees, clutching his stomach and staring wide-eyed at his executioner.

"I told you then I didn't want no part in such doin's," Tom said. He stood over the dying man until Bevo finally gasped his last painful breath. Then he turned his attention to Chapel, who was still stunned by what he had just heard. "How bad are you shot? I'm sorry I didn't get here sooner, but damn it, I never figured on you being surprised by that snake." He looked at the wound when Chapel still did not respond vocally. "Maybe it ain't so bad—looks like he put your right arm outta work for a spell, though. Here, lemme get-cha up outta that bush, and over by the fire, so I can see better."

Finally Chapel found his voice. "What the hell were you talkin' about? What you said about my ma and pa—you were there?"

"Yeah, I'm sorry to say. I was there. I didn't take no part in it, any of it, but I saw it all, and I didn't do nothin' to try to stop it, and it like to made me sick. I wasn't strong enough to do anythin' about it. There was too many of 'em against me. I ain't ever forgave myself for not splittin' with 'em right then and there, but I was in on that bank job at Sherman, and I was afraid they'd kill me if I tried to quit 'em. So I stayed with 'em when we rode up to Atoka, but when I saw they was fixin' to do the same thing to those folks on that farm, I made up my mind I was gonna stop 'em. Then you showed up with that Remington buffalo gun, and I didn't have no choice but to run. As soon as I got the chance, I split off with Bevo there"—he nodded toward the body at his feet—"and left him on Clear Boggy." He gazed into Chapel's eyes, his usual comical features twisted into a painful mask of regret. "So I'm the only one left of the seven that killed your folks and burned your home. You finally found us all, and I reckon it's up to you what you're gonna do about it." He picked up Chapel's Winchester and handed it to him.

The whirlpool in Chapel's brain was still spinning with the sudden flood of startling facts, and he could only stare in disbelief at the repentant soul standing contritely before him as if awaiting sentencing for his crimes. Chapel did not miss the significance of the act of handing him his rifle. He was convinced that Tom was facing up to his guilt and willing to accept whatever punishment he saw fit. One by one, the seven had been executed, except for the remorseful Tom Turnipseed. This day, this moment was what Chapel had lived almost his entire life to reach, twenty-seven years when death was the hunter—and now the final judgment was his. He continued to stare at Tom for a long moment more, not realizing he was in the process of experiencing something that had never been a part of his hunt for vengeance—*compassion*. Finally he spoke. "How about takin' another look at my shoulder and see if you can get that bullet outta me? Then we can get on back to the Cimarron to see if we can help those folks."

Relief swept over Tom's face, like the waters of a

flood, carrying away the angst that had been there before. "You mean it? You believe I didn't want to hurt your folks?"

"Yeah, I reckon," Chapel replied, "although I know what a damn liar you are. Besides, I guess if you hadn't showed up when you did, I'd likely be with the rest of your gang in hell."

Chapter 13

It was early in the evening when the two riders forded the Cimarron River and rode into the camp. There was already evidence of work starting to build a home. The logs that had already been in place in Bevo Rooks' cabin had been snaked down to a location closer to the river, and Sam had obviously been busy felling trees along the riverbank. Sammy was the first to see the returning riders, and he gave a yell to announce them. Close to the riverbank, Luella, notching logs with an axe, paused in her work to watch them when she heard Sammy's call. Seeing Chapel's arm in the sling that Tom had fashioned, she shook her head, exasperated, but then conceded that it was better than seeing him come home lying across his saddle. She made no move to run to meet them, as the others had, but continued to gaze in their direction, much as she would have when considering whether or not to buy a horse or a cow.

She had given Chapel a lot of thought while he was

away on his quest for vengeance. She hoped he was done with the hunt. From the looks of the wounded arm, it was apparent that he had found Rooks. Maybe he was satisfied, and maybe she and Martha could be satisfied that Link's death had been avenged. In her thinking about Chapel, she had admitted that he more nearly fit her choice for a mate. Sam was right for Martha, but Luella needed someone as strong as she, someone who was bigger than the wild country they were seeking to tame. It might be a successful partnership, she decided, but he needed a hell of a lot of work before he was housebroken. "All right, then," she sighed, dropped her axe, and walked over to greet them.

"It's all done with," Martha called out to Luella when she walked up to the gathering. "There won't be any need to worry about Brooks, or Rooks, trying to take our land. It's ours."

"Glad to hear it," Luella said. "Looks like it wasn't done without a cost," she remarked, nodding toward the wounded Chapel. "Just look at them," she said, pretending to be exasperated. "Two men with only two good arms between them. Let's see how bad you're hurt," she said to Chapel, then pulled the sling aside and looked at the crude bandage Tom had applied.

"It's all right," Chapel said. "Tom got the bullet out. I'll be able to help with the work to get you folks set up." He fidgeted nervously as Luella examined the wound.

"You'll be lucky if you don't get blood poisoning," Luella commented. "Let's get rid of this rag and clean it up a little better." She threw the bloody bandage into the fire. She fixed him with a stern look, and added, "It wouldn't hurt you to get a bath all over." He answered her with a look of utter astonishment. Martha, an interested observer, cast a disapproving glance at her sister, but Luella refused to meet it. Smiling at Tom then, she said, "You two are probably hungry, so why don't you get something to eat now, and I'll finish cleaning up that wound afterward."

"That suits me," Tom responded eagerly.

"Are you just going to leave that wound uncovered like that while we eat?" Martha asked, her nose squinched up in disgust.

"It won't hurt it," Luella replied. "If it bothers you, don't look at it."

With only the two women aware of the campaign taking place for a possible union, the family and friends sat down to eat the meal Martha had finished preparing just before the two men returned. Tom smacked his lips and said, "A man could get used to this, couldn't he, Chapel?" Both women looked at once toward the somber man to see his reaction.

"I suppose so," Chapel said.

After supper was finished and the dishes cleaned up, Sam sat down by the fire with Tom to enjoy a pipe, while questioning him on the events that led up to Chapel's wounded shoulder. Chapel sat off by himself, as was his custom, until Luella came from the wagon with a bottle of whiskey she had hidden away for emergencies, and some spare cloth for bandages. "Come on," she said. "We'll go over by the water and clean up that wound." He could think of no reason not to, so he dutifully got to his feet and followed her.

With no conversation while she first cleaned his

wound with water, then splashed it generously with whiskey, she finished the job quickly. When he thanked her and started to get up to leave, she put her hand on his shoulder to bid him stay. "I've got something to say, something I want you to think about." Puzzled, he sat back. She continued. "We're aiming to build a good working farm here, and to build it the way we want to, we'd do better with a strong man to work with Sam and me." She let that soak in for a moment to see if he would follow her logic, but he exhibited no emotion beyond puzzlement. "What I'm suggesting is that you're probably going to keep drifting when you leave here with nothing much else in your future. And that doesn't make a whole lot of sense, because you're not getting any younger—and I'm not, either." There was a dim spark of understanding in his eye, but he was not ready to believe she might be implying what it appeared. *Damn,* she thought, *am I going to have to hit him over the head with a hammer?* But she continued. "I'm a strong woman, and I've seen a helluva lot of women homelier than me, but you know, you're not the handsomest man I've ever seen, either. So what I'm saying is that we could both do worse for a mate."

At last the full force of her proposition hit him with an impact similar to that of the .44 slug that had struck his shoulder. "You mean get married?" he blurted, hardly able to believe his ears.

"Well, yes," she replied.

Amazed by the incredible proposal, words failed him. Never in his life had he ever entertained thoughts of marriage, primarily because he was busy with a life of hunting men, either for vengeance, or as a deputy marshal. But another major impediment in thoughts of this nature was the simple fact that he was aware of his grim countenance that more often than not frightened people. She stared at him, questioning the confused look in his eye, waiting for some response. Finally it came. "Are you sayin' you love me?" he stammered.

"Love you? Hell no, I don't love you!" Her reaction was automatic, without thinking. "I'm sure as hell a match for you, though." At once he looked bewildered, so she was quick to assure him, lest he walk away in anger. "I just mean that I don't even know you, but I think we'd make a good team. Between the two of us, there wouldn't be anything that could whip us. As far as love, well, we'd just have to see. If it comes along, then that would be even better." She watched his reaction then, a bit bewildered herself, now that she had offered the idea. "Just think it over and let me know what you think about it. If it doesn't appeal to you, then no harm done."

"I don't have to think it over," he replied at once. "I ain't likely to get another offer."

"Don't try so hard to sell yourself," she said. "I might have to reconsider." He didn't realize she was being facetious. "All right, then, we've got a deal," she said, and extended her hand. He shook it. "Now I'm damn sure you're gonna have to take a bath."

The reaction to their news was predictable. Sam was delighted to hear that Chapel was going to be there permanently, while Martha rolled her eyes to the heavens in despair, convinced that Luella had made a contract with the devil himself and that eventually, on some dark stormy night, he would decide to murder them all. Tom Turnipseed might have been the happiest of them all, convinced that he had been privileged to witness the evolution of a man returned from the dead to wreak havoc on evildoers, and to even forgive him of his earlier offenses against him. His happiness was complete when Sam suggested that the foundation for the cabin Rooks had started was still intact and that he should complete it and join them in building a farm.

"I expect you'll want a separate cabin built off by itself," Chapel said to Luella, since he had not been present when she had previously announced that requirement to the others.

She turned to look at him in amazement. "Of course I want a separate house. It's gonna be a job getting you saddle-broke. I'm gonna need some room and plenty of privacy."

"You sure 'nough are," Tom Turnipseed said with a delighted chuckle, still trying to get used to the idea of the unlikely union.

Chapel shifted his stoic gaze from Luella to Tom, then back to Luella, wondering himself about the prospects of a successful relation with the strong-willed woman. He knew very little about creating a strong relationship with a woman, and he was still somewhat baffled that Luella was in favor of it. *I ain't sure,* he thought, *but I guess it's better than living alone. Maybe it'll work.* The more thought he gave it, the more he decided it might work at that. Very slowly his lips twitched, and the corners of his mouth began to rise ever so slightly. No one but Tom noticed, and only he could understand the significance of it. His face broke out with a wide, satisfied grin, for he was witness to a phenomenon that might be greater than seeing a man return from the dead—he had seen the grim hunter smile.

Read on for an excerpt from
the next exciting historical novel
from Charles G. West,

A MAN CALLED SUNDAY

Available from Signet in June 2012.

Chief scout Ben Clarke looked over the group of Crow Indians who had volunteered to act as scouts for General George Crook's winter campaign against the hostile Sioux. Principal among the hostile leaders, Sitting Bull and Crazy Horse had refused to obey orders from Washington to report to the reservation, and it was now up to the army to punish them. Scanning the line of warriors standing before him now at Fort Laramie, Clarke's gaze was captured by one among them, and he paused to study the lean features of a lone white man. Dressed in buckskin from head to toe, the man would have passed for an Indian had it not been for the shock of sandy hair, tied in a single strand between his shoulder blades. A closer look revealed deep-set gray eyes that locked, unblinking, on Clarke's. "You're Luke Sunday, ain't you?" Clarke asked, certain the man could be no other. He received a single nod in response.

Ben Clarke was as informed as any white man in

the territory, but this was the first time he had come face-to-face with Luke Sunday. He knew him only by tales he had heard from others who had chanced upon the man the Crows called Dead Man. He would have dismissed the rare sightings as nothing more than tales the Indians had created had it not been for verification by John Collins, the sutler at Fort Laramie. Collins said there was such a man named Luke Sunday who had come into his store a couple of times to buy .44 cartridges. He said the man was short on conversation and never lingered once his purchases were made. He didn't know where Sunday got his money to pay for the ammunition for the Henry rifle he carried, but he supposed it came from the trading of furs. Ben couldn't help but be fascinated by the chance encounter with an Indian legend, so while the Crows were being issued ammunition and weapons, he called Sunday aside. "You speak English?" Clarke asked, not sure whether the man had been raised from childhood by Indians, as some folks believed.

Again, Luke nodded, then spoke. "I do," he said, somewhat surprised that Clarke had to ask.

It was Clarke's turn to nod thoughtfully. "Well, I wasn't sure since you came in with the Crows," he said. "I've hired on close to thirty white scouts for this campaign, some of 'em the best in the business. All of 'em claim to know the Powder River country like the back of their hands. What about you? You know the country between here and the Yellowstone?"

"About as well as the next man," Luke answered.

"I reckon there'll be plenty of opportunity to find out," Clarke said. "I've been runnin' scout details for the army for a helluva long time. How come I ain't ever run into you before?"

"I wasn't this low on money for cartridges till now," Luke stated frankly.

Ben took another few moments to study the man's face before deciding. "I reckon I'll take a chance on you even though I've already got more scouts than I'll probably need."

Although Luke's shrug in response may have seemed indifferent, he was genuinely grateful for the employment. It had been a hard winter so far, and what little money he had managed to accumulate was rapidly running out. He had no real quarrel with the Oglala Lakota. It was a Hunkpapa Lakota war party that had killed his parents. Now the Sioux were at war with the United States, so he felt no qualms about scouting for the army against them. He did find it odd, however, that Clarke said he was going to take a chance on him, as if he was going to interview each of the Crow scouts who volunteered. It didn't occur to him that Clarke meant to measure him against his proven senior scouts.

"I'm gonna send you out with Bill Bogart," Clarke continued. "He's worked for me before. Sometimes he's hard to get along with, but if you just do what he says, you'll be all right, I reckon." He turned and pointed to a large man with a full beard the color of pine straw. "He'll be scoutin' for Colonel Reynolds most of the time. You might wanna go on over and tell him I said you'll be ridin' with him and his partner."

Luke nodded, but hesitated for a moment. "All right if I collect my cartridges first?" he asked. Judging by the arming of the Crow scouts, he was concerned that the soldiers might run out of cartridges before he got his.

"I reckon," Clarke answered. Then, out of curiosity, he motioned toward the ash bow strapped on Luke's back. "You any good with that thing?"

"I get by," Luke replied.

"Ben Clarke told me that I'll be ridin' with you," Luke announced as he approached the large man standing by one of the campfires, talking to a smaller, dark-complexioned man.

"Is that so?" Bogart replied, not particularly impressed by the sandy-haired man clad in buckskins. "What might your name be?"

"Luke Sunday," Luke replied.

"Luke Sunday," Bogart repeated, trying to recall. He turned to his friend and asked, "You ever hear of Luke Sunday?" His partner shook his head. Bogart turned back to the stranger. "This here's Sonny Pickens. Me and him has scouted for the army for the last five years. How come we ain't never run into you before? I expect I know, or know of, every scout hired for this campaign, but I ain't never heard of you. Where the hell have you been scoutin'?"

"Round about," Luke answered without emotion.

"Round about," Bogart repeated, obviously amused; then he glanced at Pickens and smiled. "Looks like we got us a greenhorn to break in, Sonny." Turning back to Luke, he said, "I'll let you ride with us, but the best thing you can do is keep your eyes open and do what I tell you, and maybe you'll learn somethin'." Luke shrugged in response. He wasn't out to impress the man or his partner. He had simply signed on for the pay and the supplies. Bogart continued: "We're fixin' to get goin' here as soon as the colonel gets his soldier boys in the saddle, so, Sunday, you can get started by saddlin' them two horses yonder." He pointed to a gray and a sorrel tied by the stream.

Luke figured that was about as far as he intended to be buffaloed. "How about if I shine up your boots before we go, too?" His deep-set gray eyes locked with Bogart's, so that his next statement would not be misunderstood. "I signed on as a scout. The sooner you learn that, the easier it'll be for us to get along."

A brief silence followed before Bogart responded. He was accustomed to throwing his weight around, especially with new hires, but this one had a lethal look about him that warned of potential trouble—much like the sensation of cornering a bobcat. He was bigger by half than the rangy stranger, but he wasn't sure the contest would be worth the pain. After thinking about it, he forced a wide smile and, with an exaggerated wink for Pickens, said, "Damn, Sonny, he ain't as green as I thought. I expect we'd best get saddled up. We're 'bout to pull outta here, headin' to Fort Fetterman." Bogart let it pass as a harmless incident, but he still smoldered inside. He wasn't accustomed to anyone showing that much backbone when he stared them down. *I'll be teaching you a hard lesson before we're done,* he promised silently.

Designated the Big Horn Expedition, General Crook's troops marched two days to arrive at Fort Fetterman. The fort was known as a hard-luck post by the troops stationed there due to its desolate location. The fort was situated on a high bluff on the south side of the North Platte River, above the valleys and LaPrele Creek, where it was subjected to heavy snows and freezing winds during the long winters. Water had to be carried up the bluffs from the river, and the soil was unsuitable for growing fresh vegetables. So all supplies had to be brought in from Fort Laramie or Medicine Bow Station on the Union Pacific Railroad. Desertions were common.

Upon arriving at Fetterman, Crook was informed that Sitting Bull and Crazy Horse had been reported to be in camp somewhere near the headwaters of the Powder and the Tongue rivers. Anxious to catch the Lakotas in their winter camp, General Crook left Fort Fetterman on the first of March and headed north. Luke Sunday found that he was little more than a forward scout for the column, along with Bill Bogart, Sonny Pickens, and a few other scouts. His excellent knowledge of the country was not really needed since the column followed an oft-used government road through eastern Wyoming.

Five more days found the expedition at the ruins of Fort Reno, where Crook established his supply depot. Pushing on from Reno, the troops continued their march through the freezing country until the scouts came upon frequent travois trails left by many Indians, and all of them heading toward the Powder River. Convinced that he had found Sitting Bull's camp, the general divided his command and ordered Colonel Joseph J. Reynolds on a night march with three hundred men and rations for one day. Out in front of the column by about two miles, Luke and the other scouts searched for the hostile camp.

It was shortly before dawn when the scouts found a large Indian village on the west bank of the Powder River. From their position, high on a plateau that stood about five hundred feet or more above the village, it was difficult to see clearly through the fog that had settled upon the river. Bill Bogart had seen all he needed to see, however. "We'd best get right on back to tell Colonel Reynolds we found them Sioux he's been lookin' for," he said, his breath forming a white cloud as it struck the frozen air.

Luke Sunday wasn't ready to assume as much. From where the small party of scouts now stood, and it not yet daylight, he couldn't be sure whose village it was without a closer look. When the others immediately started to act upon Bogart's opinion and turned their horses back the way they had just come, Luke felt it was his duty to speak. "Hard to say who that is down there on the other side of the river, with it being so foggy. Might be old Two Moons' village—he's Cheyenne—and he ain't at war with anybody."

"Horseshit!" Bogart responded. "I don't need to get no closer to know that's a Lakota village. Hell, I can smell 'em. We already know Sittin' Bull's camp is on the Powder, him and Crazy Horse, and that's sure as hell a big village down there. Couldn't be nobody else, so let's get ridin' and tell the colonel we found 'em, so he can hit 'em before they wake up good." He glared impatiently at Luke, halfway expecting his disagreement since he didn't know how far the newly hired scout would push the issue.

No one he had talked to really knew much about Luke Sunday, and this bothered Bogart. Sunday had not volunteered any information about his past, and he was the kind of man a person would hesitate to question. Had he been inclined to ask, Bogart would have found that no one in General Crooks' column knew much about the man—and only a few outside his command had rumored knowledge. There were a couple of different stories—both hearsay that came from the sutler's store at Fort Laramie—about his prior life before he arrived that day at the fort and signed on as an Indian scout. One story had it that he was kidnapped by a band of Cheyenne warriors when he was a baby. Others were certain that he was born to a Crow mother and father. That version failed to explain why, up close, he didn't look like an Indian, especially when you considered his light, sandy hair.

He had spent some time with the Cheyenne as well as the Crows. That much was obvious, because he spoke both languages well—when he spoke at all. A tall, rangy man of few words, Luke made no effort to fit in with the other thirty-odd white scouts hired by General Crook at Fort Laramie that February. With the exceptions of chief scout Ben Clarke, Louis Richaud, Frank Grouard, and a few others, most of the white scouts were little more than cutthroat drifters, cattle rustlers, bank robbers, and probably murderers. Luke had little in common with any of them, and seemed to be more comfortable with the Crow scouts, who called him Dead Man because of his seemingly lifeless gray eyes that looked at a man as if seeing right through his skull and reading his thoughts. That lifeless gaze was fixed now on the likes of Bill Bogart as the lumbering bully insisted to Luke and the other two scouts that they had found the combined camps of Sitting Bull and Crazy Horse.

"I reckon I'll move in closer to get a better look at that camp," Luke said after he thought the situation over. It made no sense to him to attack a village before you were certain about who you were attacking.

"You're a hardheaded cuss, ain't you?" Bogart retorted. When Luke made no reply, Bogart said, "Suit yourself, but we're ridin' back to get Colonel Reynolds. You go nosin' around close to that village and get yourself caught, and the colonel will most likely have your hide for givin' away his surprise—if the Sioux ain't already scalped you. And after he's through with you, I might decide to give you a good ass-kickin' myself." He hesitated for a few moments to see if Luke wanted to challenge the threat. When he did not, and just remained sitting passively on his horse, Bogart turned to the other scouts and said, "Come on, boys. Let's get goin'. Let this jackass go see if he can get hisself scalped."

No other series packs this much heat!

THE TRAILSMAN

#340: HANNIBAL RISING
#341: SIERRA SIX-GUNS
#342: ROCKY MOUNTAIN REVENGE
#343: TEXAS HELLIONS
#344: SIX-GUN GALLOWS
#345: SOUTH PASS SNAKE PIT
#346: ARKANSAS AMBUSH
#347: DAKOTA DEATH TRAP
#348: BACKWOODS BRAWL
#349: NEW MEXICO GUN-DOWN
#350: HIGH COUNTRY HORROR
#351: TERROR TOWN
352: TEXAS TANGLE
#353: BITTERROOT BULLETS
#354: NEVADA NIGHT RIDERS
#355: TEXAS GUNRUNNERS
#356: GRIZZLY FURY
#357: STAGECOACH SIDEWINDERS
#358: SIX-GUN VENDETTA
#359: PLATTE RIVER GAUNTLET
#360: TEXAS LEAD SLINGERS
#361: UTAH DEADLY DOUBLE
#362: RANGE WAR
#363: DEATH DEVIL

**Follow the trail of Penguin's Action Westerns at
penguin.com/actionwesterns**

Charles G. West

Outlaw Pass

When impetuous Jake Blaine doesn't return home
from a prospecting trip in the gold-rich gulches of
Montana, his staid older brother Adam sets out to
find him. But his investigation draws unwanted
attention from some very dangerous men—who are
more than happy to bury Adam to keep their secrets.

Also Available
Left Hand of the Law
Thunder Over Lolo Pass
Ride the High Range
War Cry
Storm in Paradise Valley
Shoot-out at Broken Bow
The Blackfoot Trail
Lawless Prairie

**Available wherever books are sold or at
penguin.com**

S805

"A writer in the tradition of Louis L'Amour and
Zane Grey!" —*Huntsville Times*

National Bestselling Author

RALPH COMPTON

DEADWOOD GULCH
A WOLF IN THE FOLD
TRAIL TO COTTONWOOD FALLS
BLUFF CITY
THE BLOODY TRAIL
SHADOW OF THE GUN
DEATH OF A BAD MAN
RIDE THE HARD TRAIL
BLOOD ON THE GALLOWS
BULLET FOR A BAD MAN
THE CONVICT TRAIL
RAWHIDE FLAT
OUTLAW'S RECKONING
THE BORDER EMPIRE
THE MAN FROM NOWHERE
SIXGUNS AND DOUBLE EAGLES
BOUNTY HUNTER
FATAL JUSTICE
STRYKER'S REVENGE
DEATH OF A HANGMAN
NORTH TO THE SALT FORK
DEATH RIDES A CHESTNUT MARE
RUSTED TIN
THE BURNING RANGE
WHISKEY RIVER
THE LAST MANHUNT
THE AMARILLO TRAIL
SKELETON LODE
STRANGER FROM ABILENE
THE SHADOW OF A NOOSE
THE GHOST OF APACHE CREEK
RIDERS OF JUDGMENT
SLAUGHTER CANYON

**Available wherever books are sold or at
penguin.com**

S543